ROSEMARY SUTCLIFF

The Lantern Bearers

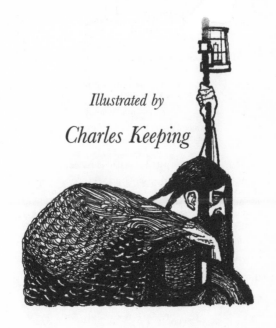

Illustrated by

Charles Keeping

OXFORD
UNIVERSITY PRESS

7·99

OXFORD
UNIVERSITY PRESS

Great Clarendon Street, Oxford OX2 6DP

Oxford University Press is a department of the University of Oxford.
It furthers the University's objective of excellence in research, scholarship,
and education by publishing worldwide in

Oxford New York

Auckland Cape Town Dar es Salaam Hong Kong Karachi
Kuala Lumpur Madrid Melbourne Mexico City Nairobi
New Delhi Shanghai Taipei Toronto

With offices in

Argentina Austria Brazil Chile Czech Republic France Greece
Guatemala Hungary Italy Japan Poland Portugal Singapore
South Korea Switzerland Thailand Turkey Ukraine Vietnam

Oxford is a registered trade mark of Oxford University Press
in the UK and in certain other countries

Published in the United States
by Oxford University Press Inc., New York

First published 1959
First published in this edition 2007

British Library Cataloguing in Publication Data

Data available

Printed in Great Britain

ISBN 978-0-19-275506-3

7 9 10 8 6

Paper used in the production of this book is a natural,
recyclable product made from wood grown in sustainable forests.
The manufacturing process conforms to the environmental
regulations of the country of origin.

Britain at the time of this story . . .

Contents

The Terrace Steps

AQUILA halted on the edge of the hanging woods, looking down. Below him he could see the farmstead under the great, bare swell of the downs: the russet-roofed huddle of buildings, the orchard behind, making a darker pattern on the paleness of the open turf, the barley just beginning to show its first tinge of harvest gold, the stream that rose under the orchard wall and wandered down the valley to turn the creaking wheel of the water-mill that ground their corn.

Almost a year had gone by since the last time that he had stood here and looked down, for it was only last night that he had come home on leave from Rutupiae, where he commanded a troop of Rhenus Horse—Auxiliary Cavalry; there had been no regular legions in Britain for forty years now—and every detail of the scene gave him a sharp-edged pleasure. It was good to be home. And really, the place didn't look so bad. It was not what it had been in the good old days, of course. Kuno, who was the oldest man on the farm, could remember when there had been

vine terraces on the south slope; you could see the traces of
them still, just below the woods here, like the traces of the
old fields and the old sheep-runs that had had to be let go
back to the wild. It was the Pict War that had done the
mischief, so long ago that even Kuno couldn't remember,
though he swore that he could, and, when he had drunk
enough heather beer, used to tell everybody how he had
seen the great Theodosius himself, when he came to drive
out the Saxons and the Painted People. But though
Theodosius had swept Britain clear, the damage had been
done and the countryside had never been the same again.
The great houses had been burned, the slaves had revolted
against their masters, and the big estates had been ruined.
It hadn't been so bad for the small estates and farms,
especially those that were not worked with slave labour.
Kuno was very fond of telling—and the hearing of it
always made Aquila feel humble, though he was sure that
it should make him proud—how in the bad time, the
Killing Time, when the slaves revolted, the free men of his
own farm had kept faith with his great-grandfather.

Because he was seeing his home again for the first time
in almost a year, he was piercingly aware of it, and the
things it stood for, and aware also how easily it might
be lost. Old Tiberius's farm, not many miles farther
seaward, had been burned by the Saxon raiders last year.
When you thought about it, you realized that you were
living in a world that might fall to pieces at any moment:
but Aquila seldom thought about it much. He had lived in
that world all his life, and so had at least three generations
of his kind before him, and it hadn't fallen to pieces yet,
and it didn't seem likely that it would do so on this rich
and ripening day with the powdery whiteness of July lying
over the countryside.

There was the sound of flying feet behind him, and a

brushing through the undergrowth and Flavia his sister was beside him, demanding breathlessly, 'Why didn't you wait for me?'

Aquila turned his head to look at her. 'I got tired of propping up the wall of Sabra's cot, being stared out of countenance by that yellow-eyed cat of hers, while you chittered inside.'

'You could have stayed inside and chittered too.'

'I didn't want to, thank you. Besides, I wanted to get back here and make sure the farm hadn't run away since breakfast.' It was an odd thing to say, born of his sudden, unusual awareness, and they looked at each other quickly.

'It is queer how one feels like that sometimes,' the girl said, grave for the moment. And then the shadow passed, and she was sparkling again. 'But it hasn't run away—and oh! it is so lovely that you are home again, Aquila! And look, here's honeysuckle with crimson tips; and here's clover, and blue scabious, as blue as a butterfly. I shall make a wreath for myself for dinner as though it were a banquet; just for myself, and not for you or father at all, because men look silly in banquet wreaths, especially if they have galley-prow noses like yours!' And while she spoke, she was down on her knees, searching among the leaves for the tough, slender scabious stems.

Aquila leaned against a tree and watched her, making a discovery. 'You have grown up while I have been away.'

She looked up, the flowers in her hands. 'I was grown up before you went away. More than fifteen. And now I'm more than sixteen—quite old.'

Aquila wagged his head sadly. 'That's what I say. I don't suppose you can even run now.'

She sprang up, her face alight with laughter. 'What will you wager me that I do not reach the terrace steps ahead of you?'

'A new pair of crimson slippers against a silver buckle for my sword-belt.' Aquila pushed himself from the tree-trunk as she swooped up the skirt of her yellow tunic with the flowers in its lap.

'Done! Are you ready?'

'Yes. *Now!*'

They sprang away side by side over the short downland turf, by the level-and-drop of the old vine terraces, by the waste strip at the head of the cornland where the plough team turned, skirting the steading yard on flying feet. Flavia was half a spear's length ahead of him as they reached the steps of the terrace before the house and whirled about under the old spreading damson tree that grew there. 'Well? Can I still run? I can run faster than you can now, and I'm a girl!'

Aquila caught her by the wrist. 'You have sharp, hollow bones like a bird, and it is not fair.' They flung themselves down on the step, panting and laughing, and he turned to look at her. He loved being with Flavia again, he always had loved being with her, even when they were small. She was two years younger than he was, but Demetrius, their Greek tutor, declared that they had been meant to be twins and something had gone wrong with their stars to bring about the two years that one must wait for the other. Flavia's hair had come down and was flying about her shoulders; hair as black and harsh as a stallion's mane, and so full of life that she could comb sparks out of it when she combed it in the dark. He reached out and gave it a small, brotherly tug.

'Brute!' Flavia said happily. She drew up her knees and clasped her arms round them, tipping up her head to the sunshine that rimmed the damson leaves with gold and made the little dark damsons seem almost transparent. 'I do love being alive! I love the way things look and feel and smell! I love the dustiness of July, and the dry singing the wind makes through the grass, and the way the stones are warm to sit on, and the way the honeysuckle smells!'

There was something almost fierce under her laughter; but that was always the way with Flavia: the fierceness and the laughter and the sparks flying out of her hair. She turned to him with a swift flash of movement. All her movements were swift and flashing. 'Show me the dolphin again.'

With an air of long-suffering, Aquila pulled up the loose sleeve of his tunic and showed her, as he had showed her yesterday evening, the dolphin badge of their family rather inexpertly tattooed on the brown skin of his shoulder. One of the Decurions at Rutupiae had learned the trick from a Pictish hostage, and during the bad weather, when there was not much else to do, several of them had let him try his skill on them.

Flavia ran a finger-tip over the blue lines. 'I'm not sure that I like it. You're not a Pict.'

'If I had been, I'd have had stripes and spirals all over me, not a nice neat little dolphin . . . It might come in very useful. If I were away from home for a long, long time, and when I came back nobody knew me again, like Odysseus, I could take you quietly aside and say, "Look, I've got a dolphin on my shoulder. I'm your long-lost brother". And then you'd know me again, like the old slave when she found the scar of the boar's tusk on Odysseus's thigh.'

'Maybe I'd say, "Oh stranger, anyone may get a dolphin tattooed on his shoulder". I'd be more likely to recognize you by your nose, however long that had been away.' She turned to the tangle of honeysuckle and small, downland flowers in her lap, and began to arrange them for her garland. 'Are you as glad to be home as we are to have you, even though it is only one year and not twenty, like Odysseus?'

Aquila nodded, glancing about him at the familiar scene. From close quarters one could see more clearly that the farm had known better days: the out-houses that needed re-roofing, the wing of the house that had once been lived in and was now a grain-store, the general air of a place run without quite enough money, without quite enough men. But the pigeons were paddling in the sunlight below the terrace steps, and a flicker of brilliant blue showed where Gwyna was coming up with a milk-pail; and he was home again, sitting on the sun-warmed steps where they had sat as children, talking nonsense with Flavia.

Something moved in the farmyard, and Flavian their father came out from the stable, talking with Demetrius. Demetrius, who never smiled himself, said something at which their father laughed, flinging up his head like a boy; then he turned and came striding up towards the terrace, with Margarita his old wolf-hound at his heels.

Aquila half-rose as he drew near. 'We're sitting on the terrace steps; come and join us, sir.'

And their father came and sat down on the top step, with Margarita between his knees.

'Aquila owes me a pair of crimson slippers,' Flavia said, reaching up to lay an arm across his knee. 'He said I was grown up and couldn't run any more.'

Their father smiled. 'And you aren't, and you can. I heard the two of you skirling like curlews all the way down from the top woods. Mind you keep him up to paying his wager!'

He was fondling Margarita's ears, drawing them again and again through his fingers, and the freckled sunlight under the leaves made small, shifting sparks of green fire in the flawed emerald of his great signet ring with its engraved dolphin.

Aquila twisted on his lower step to look up at him. It was hard to realize that Father was blind. There was nothing to show for it but the small scar that the Saxon arrow had made in his temple; and he came and went about the farm with that quick, sure stride, never seeming at a loss to know where he was or in what direction he wanted to go. Now he turned to his son and asked, 'How does the farm look to you, after a year away?'

'The farm looks good to me,' Aquila said, and added with perhaps a little too much vehemence, 'It looks so sure—as though it had been here as long as the downs have been here, and must last as long as the downs remain.'

'I wonder,' their father said, suddenly grave. 'I wonder how long it will last—just how long any of this life that we know will last.'

Aquila shifted abruptly. 'Oh, I know . . . But the worst never seems to happen.' Yet the worst happened to Tiberius, last year, said something in his mind, and he hurried on, as much to silence it as anything else: 'When Vortigern called in that Saxon war band and settled them in the old Iceni territory to hold off the Picts, five—no, six years ago, everyone wagged their heads and said it was the end of Britain. They said it was calling the wolf in over the threshold; but Hengest and his crew haven't done so badly. Settled quite peacefully, seemingly; and they *have* held off the Picts, and left us free to concentrate what Auxiliaries we still have along the Saxon shore to hold off their pirate brothers. Maybe Vortigern wasn't such a fool after all.'

'Do you really think that?' his father said very quietly, and his fingers checked on Margarita's ears.

'It is what quite a lot of the others at Rutupiae think.'

'The temper of the Eagles has changed since my day. Do *you* think it?'

There was a moment's silence and then Aquila said, 'No, I suppose not, really. But it is more comfortable to think that way.'

'Rome has done too much of thinking what is comfortable,' his father said.

But Aquila was not for the moment listening. He was looking away down the valley to where a small figure had just come into sight on the wagon-way that led up from the ford and the ancient track under the downs. 'Sa ha,' he said softly, 'someone coming.'

'Who is it?' said his father.

'No one I know. A little bent man—looks as though he's carrying a basket on his back.'

He thought that both his father and Flavia were suddenly alert in a way that he did not understand. He thought that there was a feeling of waiting about them. A few moments went by, and then his father asked, 'Can you see yet what it is that he carries?'

'Yes. It is a basket. And something else—a lantern on a pole. I believe he is one of those wandering bird-catchers.'

'So. Stand up and signal to him to come to me here.'

Aquila glanced at his father in puzzled surprise, then stood up and waved his arm above his head until the small, trudging figure saw the signal and flung up an arm in reply. 'He is coming,' he said, and sat down again.

A short while later a small, earth-coloured man with a sharply pointed face like a water-rat's came round the corner of the out-buildings and stood before the terrace steps, swinging the great reed basket from his shoulders almost before he had come to a halt. 'I greet my lord. My lord would like some fine fat quails, only caught this morning?'

'Take them up to the kitchen,' Flavian said. 'It is a long time since you were here last.'

'I have had a long walk since I was here last,' the man returned, and something in his rather hurried voice suggested that the reply was a thing arranged beforehand. 'It is all of two hundred miles from Venta to the Mountains.'

As he spoke the words, he glanced aside out of doubtful dark eyes at Aquila, and Flavian, seeming to sense the swift, uneasy glance, said, 'Nay, there is nothing that need make you ill at ease, friend. My son is quite to be trusted.' He took a slim wax tablet from the breast of his tunic. 'The quails up to the kitchen. My steward will pay you. And this to the usual place.'

The man took the tablet without looking at it, and stowed it in the ragged breast of his own tunic. 'As my lord bids me,' he said. He made a wide gesture of farewell that took in all three of them, and shouldering his basket again, turned and trudged off round the corner of the house towards the kitchen quarters.

Aquila watched him go, then turned back to his father. 'And what did that mean, sir?' He thought Flavia knew.

Flavian gave a final pull to the old hound's ear, and released her with a pat. 'It means a message up to Dynas Ffaraon in the Arfon mountains.'

'So?' Aquila said. 'What message is that?'

There was a little silence, but he knew that his father was going to tell him.

'I am going back into ancient history,' Flavian said at last. 'Much of it you will know, but bear with me none the less, it is better to have the whole thing . . .

'When Theodosius came to drive out the Picts that old Kuno so dearly loves to talk about, his lieutenant was one Magnus Maximus, a Spaniard. And when Theodosius went south again, he left Maximus in command behind him. Maximus married a British princess, daughter of the line that had ruled in the mountains of Northern Cymru since before we Romans came to Britain; and owing in part to his wife's blood, years later the British troops proclaimed him Emperor in opposition to Gratian. He marched to meet his fate, taking with him most of the Legions and Auxiliaries from the province; and his fate was death. That you know. But he left behind him a young son in Arfon—Constantine.'

Aquila moved abruptly, the tale suddenly laying hold of him. 'Constantine, who saved us after the last of the Legions were withdrawn.'

'Aye. When Rome could do no more for us, and was herself a smoking ruin—though she has recovered in some sort since—we turned to Constantine of Arfon; and he came down from the mountains with his tribesmen behind him, and led us and them to victory and a sweeping back of the Sea Wolves such as there had not been for twenty years before. For upwards of thirty more, with Constantine holding the reins from Venta, things went well for Britain, and the Saxons were driven back again and again from our shores. But in the end Constantine was murdered in his own hall. A Pictish plot, but there have always been many of us believed that Vortigern, who came out of the West as a mere Clan Chieftain of the Ordovices to follow him in his later days and married his sister Severa, was at the root of it. Maybe he thought that if a wife's lineage could raise her husband to the Purple once, it might do so again. Save that it wasn't the Purple he wanted, but power of another kind. Always he has been the spearhead of the hothead party which sees Rome as the Tribes saw her four hundred years ago, which has learned nothing in the years since, which is blinded by its dreams and sees the danger of the Saxon hordes as a lesser evil than the rule of Rome. So

Constantine died, and Vortigern contrived to seize the chief power in the land, though never the full power. But there were still Utha and Ambrosius, Constantine's sons in his old age.'

'Yes,' Aquila said, 'I remember. It caught my imagination because they were not much older than I was, and I must have been about eight when it all happened and they disappeared.'

'They were snatched away by a few of their father's household, back to Arfon, to the safety of the mountains; and for ten years Vortigern has held virtually all power in the province—if power it can be called, when he must rest his weight on a Saxon war band to hold off the Picts, *and* on the hated Auxiliaries of Rome to hold off the Saxons . . . ' He moved a little, putting out a hand to feel for the rough edge of the step beside him. 'Utha died a year or so since, but Ambrosius is now come to manhood.'

Aquila looked at him quickly, realizing the significance of that; that the wild Cymric princeling newly come to manhood among the mountains, to an age to bear his shield, was by right of birth the natural leader of those who held to the ways of Rome. 'And so——?' he said.

'And so—seeing that it was so, seeing also that the General Aetius, he who was Consul two years ago, was campaigning in Gaul, we sent to him, reminding him that we still held ourselves to be of the Empire, and begging him to bring us the help and reinforcements that we need, to rid the province both of Vortigern and the Saxon hordes, and resume it for Rome. That was last autumn.'

Aquila caught his breath. 'And that was the reply?'

'No,' his father said. 'As yet there has come no reply.'

'Then—what was the message that you sent?'

'Merely a short agreed passage from Xenophon, copied

out for me by Flavia. About the middle of each month the message goes through, by the hand of our friend the bird-catcher, or one of several others, to make sure that the signal route is still open.'

' "It is all of two hundred miles from Venta to the Mountains",' Aquila quoted. 'That is how you know that it is the right person to give it to.'

His father nodded. 'I wondered whether you would pick on the password.'

'But it was last autumn that the word went out to Aetius, you say? And it is high summer now. Surely there should have come some reply long before this?'

'If it is coming at all, it must surely come soon,' his father said with a sudden weariness in his voice. 'If it does not come very soon, it may well be too late to come at all. Every day adds to the danger that Vortigern the Red Fox will smell what is in the wind.'

The sunlight faded while they sat silent after that, and the twilight came lapping up the valley like a quiet tide, and the sky above the long wave-lift of the downs was translucent and colourless as crystal. The scent of the honeysuckle in Flavia's garland seemed to grow stronger as the light faded, and a bat hovered and darted by, pricking the dusk with its needle-thin hunting cry. Old Gwyna came across the atrium behind them to light the candles, scuffing her feet along the floor just as she had done for as long as Aquila could remember.

Everything just as it always had been at the time of the 'tween lights; but he knew now that under the quiet surface the home that he loved was part of the struggle for Britain, menaced by other dangers than the chance raids of Saxon pirates.

Suddenly he felt the passing moment as something that was flowering and would not flower again. 'Though I sit here on ten thousand other evenings,' he thought, 'this evening will not come again.' And he made an unconscious movement as though to cup it in his hands, and so keep it safe for a little longer.

But he could not keep it. Their father drew his long legs under him and got up. 'I hear Gwyna with the lights, and it is time to change for dinner.'

Even as Aquila sprang up also and caught Flavia's hand to pull her to her feet, he heard the beat of horses' hooves coming up the valley. They checked, listening, and Margarita pricked her ears.

'More comers. It seems that we are the hub of the world this evening,' Aquila said.

Their father nodded, his head at the alert, listening angle that was so much a part of him. 'Whoever it is, he has been riding hard and his horse is weary.'

Something held them there on the terrace, waiting, while the rider came nearer, disappeared behind the out-buildings and reined in. In a little, they heard voices, and the tramp of feet, and Gwyna came along the terrace with a man in the leather tunic of an Auxiliary behind her. 'Someone for the young master,' she said.

The man stepped forward, saluting. 'A message for the Decurion Aquila, sir.'

Aquila nodded. 'So—give it here.' He took the tablet that the man held out, broke the sealing thread, and stepping into the light of the atrium doorway, opened the two wooden leaves and glanced hastily over the few words on the wax inside, then looked up. 'Here's an end to my two weeks' leave, then. I'm recalled to duty.' He swung round on the waiting Auxiliary. If it had been one of his own troop he might have asked unofficial questions, but the man was scarcely known to him. 'Is your horse being seen to? Go and get a meal while I make ready to ride.

Gwyna, feed him and bid Vran to have Lightfoot and the bay gelding ready to start in the half of an hour.'

'Now I wonder, I wonder, what this may mean,' his father said, very quietly, as the man tramped off after Gwyna.

No one answered as they moved into the atrium. The yellow radiance of the candles seemed very bright, harshly bright after the soft owl-light of the terrace outside. Aquila looked at Flavia, at his father, and knew that the same thought was in all three of them . . . Could it be that this was anything to do with the appeal to Aetius in Gaul? And if so, was its meaning good—or bad?

'Need you go tonight?' Flavia said. 'Oh, need you go tonight, Aquila? You will get back no sooner in riding in the dark.' She was still holding her almost completed banquet wreath, crushed and broken in her hand. It would never now be finished.

'I can be at the next posting station before midnight,' Aquila said, 'ten miles on my way. Maybe I'll get my leave again soon and be back for our banquet. Put me up some bread and cheese, while I collect my gear.' He flung an arm round her thin, braced shoulders, and kissed her hurriedly, touched his silent father on the hand, and strode out towards the sleeping cell to collect his gear.

For Aquila, though he could not know it, the world had begun its falling to pieces.

2

Rutupiae Light

TWO evenings later, Aquila and the Auxiliary were heading up the last mile of the Londinium road towards the grey fortress of Rutupiae that rose massive and menacing above the tawny levels, with all the lonely flatness of Tanatus Island spread beyond it: Rutupiae, fortress of the Saxon Shore, that had seen so much happen, that had known the last legion in Britain. And what now?

They clattered over the timber bridge that carried the road in through the dark, double-gate arch, answering the sentry's challenge that rang hollow under the archway, and in the broad space below the stable rows Aquila handed over the army post-horse that he rode to his companion, and set out to report to the Commandant.

When he first reported at Rutupiae to join his troop, the great fortress, that had been built to house half a legion, and where now only a few companies of Marines and three troops of Auxiliary Horse rattled like dried peas in the emptiness, had seemed to him horribly desolate. But the hunting and wild-fowling were good, and he was a cheerful and easy-going lad who made friends easily with his own kind. And in the business of learning his job, and his growing pride in his troop, he had very soon ceased to notice the emptiness. But he was once again sharply conscious of it this evening as he threaded his way through the square-set alleys of the great fort, heading for the Praetorium. Perhaps it really was emptier than usual at this hour—though indeed there were sounds of something going on very urgently, down towards the Watergate and the harbour. A troop of horse trotted past him on their way up from stables; but otherwise he saw scarcely a living soul, until he came to the Praetorium buildings, passed the sentry at the head of the Commandant's stairs, and stood before Titus Fulvius Callistus as he sat at his big writing-table, filling in the duty rotas for the day. At least that was just as usual, Aquila thought; but as he cast a passing glance at the papyrus sheets on the table, he realized that they weren't the usual duty rotas at all, but lists and papers of some other kind.

'Reporting back for duty, sir,' Aquila said, with the informal salute demanded by the fact that he was still in civilian dress.

Callistus ticked something on his list, and looked up. He was a leathery little man with a piercing eye. 'Ah, I hoped that you would be back tonight,' he said, and ticked off three more items on his list. 'Any idea why I recalled you?'

'No, sir. Your messenger didn't seem to know anything, and he wasn't one of my men—didn't care to ask him much.'

Callistus nodded towards the window. 'Go and look out there.'

Aquila looked at him an instant, questioningly, then crossed to the high windows and stood looking out. From this room high in the Praetorium there was a clear view of the Watergate, and, between the jutting bastions of the Curtain Wall, a glimpse of the inner harbour and the roadstead beyond. One of the three-bank galleys—he thought it was the *Clytemnestra*—was made fast alongside the jetty, taking on board supplies; he could see the small, dark figures on the gangways. There was a swarming of men about the Watergate, stores and fodder and war supplies being brought down under the watchful eye of a Centurion of Marines. Felix, his particular friend, who commanded another troop of horse, was down there struggling to disentangle a mishap of some kind. He saw him waving his arms in his efforts, as though he were drowning. He heard a trumpet call, and beyond in the roadstead the other galleys lay at anchor, quiet above their broken reflections, yet clearly waiting to be away.

'Looks like making ready for embarkation,' he said.

'Looks like what it is.' Callistus laid down his pen and got up, and came across to join him in the window. 'We are being withdrawn from Britain.'

For a moment Aquila could not make the words mean anything. They were so unbelievable that they were only sounds. And then their meaning came home to him, and he turned his head slowly, frowning, to look at the Commandant. 'Did you say "withdrawn from Britain", sir?'

'Yes,' Callistus said, 'I did.'

'But in Our Lord's name, why?'

'Question not the orders of the High Command. Possibly it is considered that our few companies and crews will die more serviceably under the walls of Rome the next time the barbarians choose to sack the city, than here in the mists of this forgotten province in the North.'

Forgotten province; yes, they were that all right, Aquila thought. They had their answer to that desperate appeal to Aetius, all the answer that they would ever have. He heard himself asking, 'Is it a clean sweep? All the remaining garrisons?'

'I imagine so, yes. Rome is scraping the lees from the bottom of the cask. We have been here four hundred years, and in three days we shall be gone.'

'In three days,' Aquila said. He felt that he was repeating things stupidly, but he felt stupid, dazed.

'We sail on the third evening tide from now.' Callistus turned back to his littered table. 'And since that leaves little time for standing idle, go and get into uniform and take over your troop, Decurion.'

Still dazed, Aquila saluted and left the room, hurried down the stairway and across the parade-ground below the Pharos. The vast plinth, long as an eighty-oared galley and three times the height of a man, rose like an island in the empty space, and from it the great central tower sprang up, crested with its iron beacon brazier against the sky. A few shreds of marble facings, a few cracked marble columns upholding the roof of the covered ways for the fuel-carts, remained of the proud days, the days when it had stood shining in wrought bronze and worked marble here at the gateway to Britain, for a triumphal memorial to Rome's conquest of the province. But they had used most of the broken marble for rubble when they built the great walls to keep the Saxons out. The tower rose up bare and starkly grey as a rock, with the seagulls rising and falling about it, the evening light on their wings. The light was beginning to fade; soon the beacon would be lit, and the night after it would be lit, and the night after that, and then there would be no more Rutupiae Light.

Aquila hurried on, across the parade-ground and up to his sleeping cell in the officers' block. He changed into uniform, obscurely comforted by the familiar feel of leather tunic and iron cap and the weight of his long cavalry sword against his thigh, and went to take over command of his troop again.

Later, much later that night, he scratched a few hasty lines of farewell to his father. He knew that among the men in the great fort who must sail in three days' time, many would be making frantic efforts to arrange for wives and children to follow them, for all men must know that now Britain was doomed. One or two of his own troop had already come to him for help and counsel; a young, worried trooper wanting to get his parents out to Gaul, an old one in tears for a wife who must be left behind. . . . He had done what he could, but he felt so helpless. It was no good trying to do anything about his own family. Nothing, he knew, would shift his father from a post of duty, even though it was duty to a lost cause; and even if that had not been so, he would never have abandoned the farm and the farm-folk. And Flavia would remain with their father whatever came. So he wrote his letter, sending them his dear love, and promising Flavia her crimson slippers one day. He gave it to an orderly for dispatch, knowing that there would be no time for any farewell message to reach him in return, and lay down to catch a few hours' sleep before he turned out at cockcrow to early Stables.

During the days that followed, Aquila seemed to be two people: one getting on with the business of making his troop ready for embarkation, the other all the while fighting a battle of divided loyalties within himself. It began after the letter to his father had gone, while he lay wakeful in the darkness with the sea sounding in his ears. One didn't hear the sea much in the daytime, save when there was a storm, but at night it was always there, even in a flat calm, a faint, persistent wash of sound like the sea in a shell. It seemed to be out of that faint sea-wash in the silence that the knowledge came to him that he belonged to Britain. He had always belonged to Britain, but he hadn't known it before, because he had never had to question it before. He knew it now.

It was not only because of Flavia and his father. Lying in the darkness with his arm over his eyes, he tried quite deliberately to thrust them from his mind, pretend that they did not exist. It made no difference; even without them, he still belonged to Britain. 'How odd!' he thought. 'We of the Outposts, we speak of ourselves as Roman; we think of ourselves as Roman—with the surface of our minds—and underneath, it is like this.' And they were sailing in three days' time, less than three days, now.

And presently the three days had dwindled down to a few hours.

He longed to talk about it to Felix, good old Felix with whom he had so often gone wild-fowling on Tanatus Marshes. But he knew that Felix, who was also native born, though his roots were not struck so deeply in the province as Aquila's were, would be having trouble enough of his own. Besides, something in him knew that this was one of those things that must be faced alone.

Only there seemed so little time to think, to be sure. And now the last feverish hours of getting the horses into the transports were over, and the men had been marched aboard while the brazen orders of the trumpets rang above the ordered tumult; and there was scarcely anything more to do. A flamed and feathered sunset was fading behind the Great Forest, and the tide was almost at the flood, running far up the creeks and inlets and winding waterways; and amid the last ordered coming and going, Aquila stood on the lifting deck of the *Clytemnestra*. The stern and mast-head lanterns were alight already, as the daylight dimmed, and any moment now the great fire-beacon on the crest of the Pharos should have sprung to life. But there would be no Rutupiae light tonight to guide the fleets of the Empire. The last of the Eagles were flying from Britain. Any moment now the trumpets would sound as the Commandant came down from the Watergate and stepped on board, and the landing-bridge would be raised, and the Hortator's hammer would begin the steady, remorseless clack-clack-clack that beat out the time for the slaves on the rowing benches.

Aquila suddenly saw himself going to the Commandant in that last moment, laying his drawn sword at his feet, saying, 'Sir, everything is in order. Now let me go.' Would Callistus think that he was mad or hysterical? No, oddly enough—for there had never been a word between them save in the way of duty—he knew that Callistus would understand; but he knew also that Callistus would have no choice but to refuse. The choice was his. Quite clearly and coldly, in the still moment after the three days' turmoil, he knew that he must make it alone.

He turned to his old, grey-whiskered optio beside him, who had taught him all that he knew of soldiering, all that he knew of the handling of a troop—he had been so proud of his troop—and gripped his leather-clad shoulder an instant.

'God keep you, Aemilius. I'll be back.'

He turned to the head of the landing-bridge and crossed over, quickly and openly as though in obedience to some last-moment order. No chance to bid good-bye to Felix, none to take leave of Nestor, his horse. He strode by the last remaining figures on the jetty, the native dockyard hands, no one particularly noticing him in the fading light, back through the Watergate into the desolate fort.

Everything in him felt bruised and bleeding. He had

been bred a soldier, coming of a line of soldiers, and he was breaking faith with all the gods of his kind. Going 'wilful missing'. The very words had the sorry sound of disgrace. He was failing the men of his own troop, which seemed to him in that moment a worse thing than all else. Yet he did not turn back again to the waiting galleys. He knew that what he was doing was a thing that you couldn't judge for other people, only for yourself; and for himself, he did not know if it was the right thing, but he knew that it was the only thing.

He was scarcely aware of his direction, until he found himself at the foot of the Pharos. The ramp for the fuel-carts led steeply upward to the vast plinth, and at the head of it the mouth of the covered way gaped dark and empty in the gathering dusk. He mounted the ramp quickly and strode forward into the darkness. He was in the square hollowness of the tower foot where the fuel-carts were housed. The carts were there now, ranged side by side, mere blots of darkness in the lesser darkness. The dry, musty smell of baled straw was in his nostrils, and the sharp tang of pitch that had soaked into the stones of the walls. He turned to the narrow stairway that wound up the wall like the spiral twist of a snail shell, and began to climb.

He was only half-way up when he heard, faintly through the thick walls from the world outside, the trumpets sounding the Commandant on board. Any moment now he would be missed. Well, they would have little time for searching. They would not miss the tide for one junior officer gone wilful missing. He climbed on, up and up, stumbling a little, through chamber after chamber, with the sense of height increasing on him, past the deserted quarters where the men on beacon duty had lived like peregrine falcons high above the world. The grey dusk seeping through the small windows showed the dark shapes of the debris they had left behind them—rough wooden furniture and cast-off gear, like the stranded flotsam on the shore left when the tide flows out, as Rome's tide was flowing out. Up and up until the stairway ran out into open air, and he ducked at last through a little low-set doorway into complete darkness, into the 'Immediate Use' fuel store just below the signal platform. Feeling with outstretched hands, he found the ranged barrels of pitch, the straw and brushwood and stacked logs. A gap opened to his questing hand between the brushwood and the wall, and he crawled into it and crouched there, pulling the brushwood over again behind him.

It wasn't a good hiding-place, but the tide would be already on the turn.

For what seemed a very long time he crouched there, his heart beating in slow, uneven drubs. From far, far below him, in another world, he thought he heard the tramp of mailed sandals, and voices that shouted his name. He wondered what he should do if they came up here and found him, skulking like a cornered rat under a garbage pile; but the time passed, and the footsteps and the calling voices came and went, hurrying, but never mounted the stairs of the forsaken tower. And presently the trumpets sounded again, recalling the searchers lest they lose the tide. Too late now to change his mind.

More time passed, and he knew that the galleys would be slipping down the broad river-way between the marshes. And then once more he heard the trumpets. No, only one. The call was faint, faint as the echo of a seabird's cry; but Aquila's ear caught the sad, familiar notes of the call. In one of those galleys slipping seaward, somebody, in savage comment on what had happened, or merely in farewell, was sounding 'Lights Out'.

And now that it was all over, now that the choice was made, and one faith kept and one faith broken, Aquila drove his face down on to his forearm against the whippy roughness of the brushwood bundles, and cried as he had never cried before and would never cry again.

A long while later he turned himself about in his hiding-place, and ducked out on to the narrow stairway, spent and empty as though he had cried his heart away. Dusk had long since deepened into the dark, and the cold moonlight came down the steps from the beacon platform, plashing silvery from step to step. And as he checked there, leaning against the wall, the silence of the great fortress came up to him, a silence of desolation and complete emptiness. On a sudden impulse he turned upward towards the moonlight instead of down into the blackness that swallowed the descending stairway, and stumbled up the last few steps, emerging on the beacon platform.

The moon was riding high in a sky pearled and feathered with high wind-cloud, and a little wind sighed across the breast-high parapet with a faint aeolian hum through the iron-work of the beacon tripod. The brazier was made up ready for lighting, with fuel stacked beside it, as it had been stacked every night. Aquila crossed to the parapet and stood looking down. There were lights in the little ragged town that huddled against the fortress walls, but the great fort below him was empty and still in the moonlight as a ruin that had been hearth-cold for a hundred years. Presently, in the daylight, men would come and strip the place of whatever was useful to them, but probably after dark they would leave it forsaken and empty to its ghosts. Would they be the ghosts of the men who had sailed on this tide? Or of the men who had left their names on the leaning gravestones above the wash of the tide? A Cohort Centurion with a Syrian name, dying after thirty years' service, a boy trumpeter of the Second Legion, dying after two . . .

Aquila's gaze lengthened out across the marshes in the wake of the galleys, and far out to sea he thought that he could still make out a spark of light. The stern lantern of a transport; the last of Rome-in-Britain. And beside him the beacon stack rose dark and waiting. . . . On a sudden wild impulse he flung open the bronze-sheathed chest in which the fire-lighting gear was kept, and pulled out flint and steel and tinderbox, and tearing his fingers on the steel in his frantic haste, as though he were fighting against time, he struck out fire and kindled the waiting tinder, and set about waking the beacon. Rutupiae Light should burn for this one more night. Maybe Felix or his old optio would know who had kindled it, but that was not what mattered. The pitch-soaked brushwood caught, and the flames ran crackling up, spreading into a great golden burst of

fire; and the still, moonlit world below faded into a blue nothingness as the fierce glare flooded the beacon platform. The wind caught the crest of the blaze and bent it over in a wave; and Aquila's shadow streamed out from him across the parapet and into the night like a ragged cloak. He flung water from the tank in the corner on to the blackened bull's-hide fire-shield, and crouched holding it before him by the brazier, feeding the blaze to its greatest strength. The heart of it was glowing now, a blasting, blinding core of heat and brightness under the flames; even from the shores of Gaul they would see the blaze, and say, 'Ah, there is Rutupiae's Light.' It was his farewell to so many things; to the whole world that he had been bred to. But it was something more: a defiance against the dark.

He vaguely, half expected them to come up from the town to see who had lit the beacon, but no one came. Perhaps they thought it was the ghosts. Presently he stoked it up so that it would last for a while, and turned to the stairhead and went clattering down. The beacon would sink low, but he did not think it would go out much before dawn.

He reached the ground level; the moonlight hung like a silver curtain before the doorway, and he walked out into it and across the deserted fortress, and out through a postern gate that stood open, and away. He had the sudden thought that for the sake of the fitness of things he should have broken his sword across his knee and left the pieces beside Rutupiae Light, but he was like to need it in the time that lay ahead.

3

The Wolves of the Sea

THE posting-stations were still in existence, but to
use them without a military permit cost money,
and Aquila had never been one to save his pay, so
it was upward of a week later when he came at last up
the track from the ford, on an evening of soft mizzle rain.
He saw the light in the atrium window and made for it,
brushing the chill, spattering drops from the low branches
of the damson tree as he mounted the terrace steps. He
crossed the terrace and opened the atrium door, and stood
leaning against the doorpost, feeling like a very weary
ghost.

Margarita, who would have been baying her head off
at a stranger's footfall before he was half-way up the valley,
had risen, stretching and yawning her pleasure, and came
padding across the tiled floor to greet him, with her tail
swinging behind her. For an instant he saw the familiar
scene caught into perfect stillness in the candle light as
though it were caught in amber: his father and Demetrius
with the chess board between them—they often played
chess in the evenings, on a board with faint ridges between

the ivory and ebony squares; Flavia sitting on the wolfskin rug before the low fire, burnishing the old cavalry sword that she had taken down, as she often did, from its place above the hearth. Only the look on their faces, turned towards the door, was not familiar; the blank, startled, incredulous look, as though he were indeed a ghost that had come back to them mired with the white chalky mud of his journeying.

Then his father said, frowning, 'Is that you, Aquila?'

'Yes, Father.'

'I thought that the last of the Eagles had flown from Britain.'

There was a little silence. Then Aquila said, 'I have deserted the Eagles.'

He pushed off from the doorpost, and came in, closing the door behind him against the rain that was dark on the shoulders of his leather tunic. Old Margarita was rubbing her head against his thigh, and he put down a hand to fondle her, without being aware that he did so. He was standing before his silent father now. Demetrius would not judge him, he knew: Demetrius judged no man but himself; and Flavia would care for nothing but that he had come home. But with his father it would be another matter. 'I belong to Britain,' he heard himself saying; not trying to defend himself, simply telling his father what had happened. 'More and more, all those three days, I found that I belonged to Britain. And in the end—I let the galleys sail without me.'

For a long moment his father still sat silent, with the chess-piece he had been holding when Aquila entered still in his hand. His face, turned full on Aquila, was stern and uncompromising. 'Not an easy choice,' he said at last.

'Not an easy choice,' Aquila agreed, and his voice sounded hoarse in his own ears.

His father set down the chess-piece with careful precision.

'Nothing, *nothing*, Aquila, excuses deserting the Eagles. But since it seems to me very probable that in your place I should have done the same as you have done, I can scarcely pass judgement on you.'

'No, sir,' Aquila said, staring straight before him. 'Thank you, sir.'

Old Demetrius smiled a little under his long upper lip, and shifted his own piece on the board.

And Flavia, who had sat ever since he appeared in the doorway, as though caught in some witch's spell of stillness, flung aside the naked sword and sprang up, and came running to set her hands on his shoulders. 'Oh, Aquila, I'm so glad, glad, *glad* that you did let them sail without you! I thought I should have died when your letter came . . . Does Gwyna know you are here?'

'Not yet,' Aquila said.

'I'll go and tell her, and we'll bring you some food—much, much food. You look so hungry. You look——' She broke off, her eyes searching his face. 'Oh, my dear, you said that I had grown up in a year, but you have grown up in twelve days.'

She put her arms round his neck, and held him fiercely close, her cheek pressed against his; then ran from the room calling, 'Gwyna! Gwyna! Aquila's home again! He has come back to us after all, and we must feed him!'

Behind her, Aquila crossed to the fire that burned British fashion on a raised hearth, at the end of the room, and held his hands to it, for he was cold with the rain. Standing there, he said to his father, only half in question, 'No word out of Gaul?'

'I imagine the withdrawal of our last troops is all the word out of Gaul that we shall ever receive,' his father said. He turned in his chair to follow the direction of Aquila's voice. 'Rome has cut her losses, where the province of Britain is concerned, and what the future holds for the province, or for any of us, God knows. Whatever it is, I am glad that you will be sharing it with us, Aquila.'

Two evenings after Aquila's homecoming, they had a fire again, not so much for warmth as to fight the cheerlessness of the summer gale beating against the walls; and with dinner over and the candles lit—you couldn't get oil for the lamps any more—the atrium had taken on its winter aspect, the sense of safety and shelter within firelit walls, and the storm shut out, that belongs to winter time. Aquila had drawn a stool to the side of the hearth, and Flavia had settled herself on the rug beside him, leaning against his knee while she combed and combed her hair. The chessboard had not been brought out tonight, and instead Demetrius, with a scroll spread before him on the table, where the candlelight fell brightest, was reading to their father from *The Odyssey*.

' "For two days and two nights we lay there, making no way and eating our hearts out with despair and the unceasing labour. But on the third morning bright-haired Dawn gave us clear daylight; wherefore up went our masts and white shining sails . . . Indeed that time I all but came unscathed to my Fatherland, only for the swell and the sea currents and a north wind which united against me as I worked round Cape Maleia and drove me wide to Cythera." '

Aquila heard the familiar sentences above the beating of the wind, and realized for the first time that Demetrius had a beautiful voice. His gaze wandered about the room that he had known all his life, brushing over the small household shrine with the sign of the Fish painted on the wall above it, the couches with their coverings of deer-skins and gay native rugs, his father's sword hanging above the hearth, the pretty tumble of women's gear—Flavia had never in her life put anything away. His gaze lingered on his father's face, alert and listening in the firelight, his hand with the great dolphin ring fondling Margarita's head on his knee; on Demetrius's grey and gentle features bent over his scroll. Demetrius had been a slave until their father had bought him to be their tutor, and given him his freedom; and when he was no longer needed as a tutor, he had stayed to be Flavian's steward and his eyes. Demetrius was a stoic, a man to whom life was a discipline to be endured with dignity and death a darkness to be met without flinching. Maybe that was what he had taught himself in his slave days, to make them bearable. It came to Aquila suddenly how terrible it must be to be a stoic: but he did not believe that Demetrius was really like that; he loved ideas and people too much. His gaze dropped to Flavia, combing her hair in the firelight that made a glow all round her. She was looking up at him through the dark, flying strands as she flung it this way and that, sweeping the comb through it. And as she combed, she was humming, so softly that the sound would not reach her father or Demetrius at all; a dark, thin, sweet humming that Aquila could barely catch above the voices of the summer storm.

He bent down towards her, his arm across his knee. 'What are you nooning?'

She glimmered with laughter. 'Perhaps I make a singing magic. What would you say if I told you that I combed my hair—just like this—and made a singing magic, on the evening that the galleys sailed, to call you home again?'

He looked at her with unexpected soberness. 'I don't

know. But I do not think that I should ever feel quite the same about you again.'

Flavia stopped combing. 'No,' she said, 'I knew that you would not. That is why I did not do it, though I longed to—you can't know how I longed to—because I knew that if I did, and it worked, I should have to tell you. I don't know why, but I should have to tell you, and I couldn't bear that you should not feel the same about me again.'

'Do you know,' Aquila said, 'I don't think I could, either.'

A few weeks ago he would not have dreamed of saying that to Flavia; he would scarcely have thought it to himself. But now it was different; now, when the present moment mattered so much, because there mightn't be anything to come after.

The wind that was roaring up the valley fell away into a long trough of quiet, and in the hush, faint and far off and infinitely sad, rose the hunting cry of a wolf. Aquila cocked up his head, listening. It wasn't often that you heard the wolves in the summer, they were a winter sound; and hearing the long-drawn howl between gust and gust of the storm, he grew freshly aware of the warmth and shelter of the firelit atrium.

Demetrius checked in his reading, to listen also; and Margarita bristled, growling deep in her throat without raising her head from her lord's knee.

'The Forest Wolves call to their brothers of the Sea,' Flavian said, grimly.

Aquila looked at him quickly, knowing that in the past few days there had been several raids on farms nearer the coast. He had seen the distant glare of one such burning farmstead as he followed the downs homeward. It was for that reason that the farm-hands all slept in the house now.

The wind swooped back. Demetrius took up his reading once more at the place where he had broken off, and the group around the fire settled again. But Margarita continued growling, her ears pricked forward, her coat rising a little. She prowled to the door and back, turned round three times after her own tail, and collapsed at her lord's feet, but almost at once she was up again, still growling.

'Hush now. Have you never heard the wolf kind before?' her lord said, and she licked his thumb and sat down again, but still with raised, uneasy head. A few moments later, Bran the sheep-dog barked from the farm-hands' quarters, and she sprang up, baying, was silent a moment to listen, then broke out baying again.

'I wonder if it *is* the Wolves,' Aquila said, half-rising as he spoke, his hand going to his sword.

And almost in the same instant a wild cry broke through the storm, and a babble of shouting rose in the night outside.

'Name of Light! What is that?'

Aquila didn't know which of them had asked it, but the answer was in all their minds. They were all on their feet now, Demetrius rolling up his precious scroll as the door burst open, letting in a great swoop of wind to drive the smoke billowing from the hearth and set the candle-flames streaming, and Finn the shepherd appeared on the wings of the storm, wild-eyed and panting.

'It is the Saxons! They are all about us! I blundered into them when I went to see to the sheep.' The others were crowding in after him, old Kuno and the farm-hands, all with their weapons, for in these days men were never far from their weapons; little, shrivelled, valiant Gwyna with a long knife from the kitchen, the other women all with what they had been able to catch up. At least there were no children, Aquila thought, only Regan's baby, that was so young it would know nothing . . .

Flavian was quickly and surely issuing his orders; he must have been prepared so long for this to happen, known so exactly what it would be like when it did. The dogs had ceased their baying, and crouched snarling with laid-back ears. Aquila had crossed in two strides to the open doorway. No point in closing it; better to die fighting than be burned in a trap. He called back over his shoulder as red fire sprang up in the farmyard below and he glimpsed the flanged helmets against the uprush of flame.

'They're questing through the out-houses, firing them as they close in. They're driving off the cattle. Lord God! There must be two score of them at least!'

'So. At all events we have a space to breathe until they finish with the byres,' his father said.

Despite the wind, despite the shouting and lowing outside and the red glare that was beginning to beat up from below the terrace, there was a sense of quietness in the long atrium, where the farm-hands with their hastily-snatched-up weapons stood to their appointed places. Aquila supposed that it was the knowing without any doubt that one was going to die, but he thought also it was something that flowed from his father standing in their midst, a kind of strength that was like confidence. Demetrius carefully returned his scroll to the open scroll chest, closed the lid, and, reaching up, took down a long, slender dagger from among the beautiful weapons on the wall. In the leaping, storm-driven light his face was as grey and gentle as ever.

'I think I expressed to you my gratitude for my freedom at the time,' he said to Flavian, testing the blade. 'I have never spoken of it again. I should like now to thank you

for the years that I have been a free man, and—I find on
reflection—an extremely happy one.'

'Nay, man, there is no debt that you have not paid; and
no time for thanks, on either side, between you and me.
Will somebody bring me my sword?'

Aquila, who had turned away from the door, leapt
to take it down. He drew it from the worn sheath, and
casting the sheath aside, set the weapon naked in his
father's outstretched hand.

'There it is, sir.'

His father's strong fingers closed round the grip, and
there was a faint smile on his mouth. 'So—it is a long
time, but the feel is still familiar . . . They will not know
that I am blind. It doesn't show, Aquila?'

'No, sir,' Aquila said, looking for what he knew was
the last time into his father's thin, scarred face. 'It doesn't
show.'

The shouting was drawing nearer, sounding from all
round them now. Flavian crossed with a sure step to the
shrine at the far end of the atrium, and laid his naked
sword for an instant before the little shielded light that
burned quite steadily in the flower-shaped altar lamp.

'Lord, receive us into Thy Kingdom,' he said, and took
up his sword again, and turned towards the open door.

Aquila also was standing with drawn sword, his arm
round Flavia. She felt light and hard and braced in the
curve of it. 'Try not to be afraid,' he said.

'I don't think I am,' she returned. 'Not really afraid.
It—doesn't seem real, does it?'

No, it didn't seem real. It didn't seem real even when
the shouting and the tumult burst upward into a new
savagery and the first Saxon came leaping up the terrace
steps to meet the resolute figure of the master of the
house, standing with drawn sword in the doorway.

After that, for a while, Aquila knew only a red chaos; a great splurge of shouting in his ears and the snarling of the hounds and the ring and clash of weapons; and Flavia with a high, fierce cry snatching the dagger from his belt as he sprang into the doorway beside his father. The flare of fire-brands was in his eyes, and the flash of the fire on leaping saex blades. There seemed flame everywhere, ragged, wind-blown flame, and the bull's-horned and boar-crested warriors thrusting in on them out of the rolling smoke. The rafters were alight now over their head, the flames running along them in bright waves before the wind, and the atrium was full of smoke that tore at the defenders' lungs, choking and blinding them. But there were fewer defenders now; only seven where there had been nine, only six—old Kuno was down, Finn too, and Demetrius. A blazing shutter gave way, and a Saxon sprang in yelling through the high window-hole; and now they were beset from behind as well as before. A man in a great flanged helmet, with the golden torc of a chieftain about his neck, made for Flavian with war-axe up-swung for a blow that there could have been no turning even if the man at whom it was aimed had been able to see it coming. Aquila saw his father fall, and with Flavia fighting like a young fury beside him, hurled himself forward against the leaping saex blades to make a last rallying point of his body.

'To me! To me! Close up!'

Through the red haze that beat before his eyes he saw a snarling face with eyes that seemed all blue fire, and wild yellow hair streaming from beneath the great flanged helmet; he drove the point of his sword in over the golden torc, and saw the man drop his axe in mid-swing and stagger back, clutching at his throat with blood spurting between his fingers; and laughed, knowing that at least his father was avenged.

He did not feel the blow that fell glancing on his own temple and brought him down like a poled ox. He only knew that he had leapt forward in time—how much time he didn't know—and everything seemed to be over, and he was still alive, which bothered him because the two things didn't fit. He was being dragged to his feet, which seemed odd too, for he did not remember being on the ground, dazed and half blind with the blood running into his eyes. And then he heard Flavia shrieking his name, 'Aquila! *Aquila!*' and wrenched round in his captors' grasp to see her carried past, struggling like a wild cat, over the shoulder of a laughing, fair-haired giant. He tried to spring towards her, dragging his captors with him, but they were all about him, his arms were wrenched behind his back, and he was flung to his knees, struggling until his heart seemed like to burst and blood pounded like a hammer in his temples. For a moment the world darkened and swam in a red haze about him; Flavia's shrieks died as though somebody had stifled them with a hand over her mouth.

Somehow, fighting still, he found himself thrust to a halt with his arms twisted at his back, before a huge man who stood at the head of the familiar terrace steps under the scorched and shrivelled skeleton of the damson tree. The glare of the wind-driven fire that seemed all about them played on his helmet and yellow hair and beard, and made shifting fish-scale jinks of light on the byrnie he wore. And his face, Aquila saw, was the face of the man he had killed for his father's death. But there was no gold torc round this man's neck, and no red hole above it, and therefore it could not be the same.

He stood with arms folded on his breast, staring at Aquila under down-drawn golden brows. Something sparkled green on one great hand, and Aquila, ceasing to struggle now, gasping and spent, knew that it was his father's ring.

'Aye,' the huge Saxon said after a long scrutiny, 'it is the man who slew my brother.'

Through the beating in his head, Aquila understood the meaning of the guttural words, for he had not served a year with Lower Rhenus troops without learning something of the Saxon tongue. He dragged up his head, trying to shake the blood out of his eyes. 'Your brother, who slew my father on the threshold of his own house!'

'So! And he speaks our tongue,' the huge Saxon said, and he smiled, as a wolf smiles. 'Vengeance for a kinsman is sweet. I also, Wiermund of the White Horse, I find it sweet,' and with a slow deliberateness he drew the stained saex from his belt, fondling it, dandling it in his big hands . . .

Aquila waited, his eyes on the Saxon's face. He heard the roar of the flames, and the cattle lowing as they were rounded up, and under it the quietness, the dreadful quietness, full of only the wind. And even the wind was dying now. He was aware of the bodies that lay crumpled and grotesque in the red glare of the fire, bodies of his own folk and of the Sea Wolves; his father and the Saxon Chieftain lying together in the doorway; even Margarita lying dead at her lord's feet, where she must have crawled to him in her last moment. He did not feel very much about them, because he knew that in a few moments he would have joined them. Flavia was the only one he felt anything about—Flavia.

Wiermund of the White Horse had already raised his saex for the death-blow when, far off, above the hoarse moaning of the gale-torn woods, rose a cry that Aquila had heard once already that night: the cry of a hunting wolf, answered by another from away over towards the flank of the downs.

Wiermund checked, listening. Then he lowered his blade, and the smile broadened and broadened on his face until it was a snarl. 'Aiee, the wolf kind smell blood,' he said. 'Soon they will come following their noses.' He seemed to consider a moment, still fingering his saex blade. Then, abruptly, he drove it back into the sheath. 'Take him out to the wood-shore and bind him to a tree.'

The warriors about him looked quickly at each other, and then uncertainly at their leader.

'Alive?' someone said.

'Alive until the wolf kind come,' said the dead Chieftain's brother simply; and a growl of agreement, a grim breath of laughter ran from one to another of the war band. 'Aye, leave him to the wolves! He slew Wiergyls our Chieftain!— They call the wolves our brothers, let the wolves avenge their kin!'

They half thrust, half dragged him down the terrace steps skirting the blazing farm-yard, and away up to the tongue of the woods above the old vine terraces, where he had stood with Flavia looking down on their home so short a time ago. At the last moment he began to struggle again, wildly, desperately. It was one thing to brace oneself for the quick dispatch of the saex blade, but quite another to stand unresisting to be tied to a tree for living wolf-bait. His body revolted at the prospect and went on struggling without anything to do with his will. But all his strength seemed to have gone from him, and he was powerless in their hands as a half-drowned pup. They stripped him naked; someone brought a partly charred wagon-rope from the blazing shed, and with the sound part of it they lashed his hands behind his back and bound him to the trunk of a young beech tree. Then they drew off and stood about him, very merry.

He forced up his head against the intolerable weight that seemed to bear it down, and saw their shapes dark against the glare of the blazing farmstead.

'So, bide there with a good fire to warm you until the wolf kind come,' said the man who had been the Chieftain's brother, and he called off his warriors like a hunter calling off his hounds. Aquila did not see them go, only he realized suddenly, through the swimming confusion in his head, that he was alone.

Only the wind swept up the valley, and below the wind he heard the silence. The fires below were sinking; and there would be no more fires in the valley where the hearth fire had burned for so many generations of men; and the silence and the desolation washed up to Aquila like the waves of a dark sea, engulfing him. Swirling nightmare pictures washed to and fro on the darkness of it, so that he saw over and over again the last stand in the atrium doorway, and his father's death, so that he saw over and over again the hideous vision of Flavia struggling in the hands of the barbarians that set him writhing and tearing at his bonds like a mad thing until the blood ran where the ropes bit into him.

He must have lost consciousness at last, because suddenly the grey dawn was all about him, and the gale quite died away. The wolf kind had not come. Maybe there were too many of their human brothers hunting these hills; for he heard the mutter of voices, and the first thing he saw when his eyes opened on a swimming world were a pair of feet in clumsy raw-hide shoes, and the lower rim of a Saxon buckler. Men were standing round him again, but he realized dimly that though they were Saxons, they were not last night's band, but a new raiding party that had come questing out of the woods to find that others had been before them.

'Nay then, why should you meddle with another man's kill?' someone was protesting in a deep growl of exasperation.

And somebody else was hacking at his bonds with a saex blade, saying through shut teeth, 'Because I have a mind to him, that's why.'

The last strands parted, and Aquila swayed forward. He struggled to keep upright before these new tormentors, but his numbed legs gave under him and he crumpled to the ground, his wrists still bound behind him. The man who had cut him from the tree straddled over him hacking at his remaining bonds, and as the last strands of those also parted, he rolled over and saw, frowning upward through the throbbing in his head, that it was a lad younger than himself, a mere stripling in ring-mail byrnie, with a skin that was clear red and white like a girl's under the golden fuzz of his beard.

'Get some water from the stream,' said the stripling to the world in general; and it seemed that somebody must have brought it in his helmet, for suddenly the iron rim was jolting against Aquila's shut teeth. Someone dashed the cold water into his face, and as he gasped, a wave of it went down his throat, making him choke and splutter, yet dragging him back to life whether he would or no. As his head cleared, he realized that there were about a score of men standing round him, with laden ponies in their midst. Clearly they had had better luck with their raiding in other places than they had in this one.

'What Thormod the son of Thrand should want with another's leavings is a thing beyond my understanding,' said the voice that he had heard before; and Aquila saw now that it belonged to a bull-necked individual with red hair sprouting out of his nose and ears. 'If you would carry home a slave at the summer's end, let it be one of your own taking.'

The boy he had called Thormod stood over Aquila still, the red of his face spreading over the white from the gold collar he wore to the roots of his yellow hair, though he was yet half-laughing. 'Ran the Mother of Storms fly away with you, Cynegils! Must you be for ever telling me what I should do and what I should not do? He has a dolphin on his shoulder, and often Bruni my grandsire has told me how in his seafaring days he knew always when he saw a dolphin that his luck would be good, wherefore he took the dolphin for his lucky sign. And therefore I've a mind to take this other man's leavings for a gift to my grandsire that I reckon will catch at his fancy more than a jewelled cup or a little silver god.'

'As for the dolphin, it is but painted on and will surely wash off,' somebody said, bending to peer more closely at Aquila as he half-lay in their midst.

'Nay, it is pricked in after the manner of the patterns that the Painted People wear. I have seen their envoys.' The boy Thormod spat on his hand and rubbed it to and fro over the tattooing on Aquila's shoulder, then held up his hand triumphantly. 'See, it does *not* wash off!'

Somebody laughed. 'Let the boy take his findings; it is his first raiding summer.'

'Also I am Sister's Son to Hunfirth the Chieftain,' said the boy.

A tall man with eyes that were very blue in a square, brown face reached out an arm heavy with bracelets of copper wire and shining blue glass, and caught him a lazy buffet on the side of the head. 'Not so loud, my young cockerel. No man's word counts more than another's in my ship, saving only my own. Nevertheless, we've room for another rower since Ulf was killed, and you shall take him—and be responsible for him—if you've a mind to.'

And so, still half dazed, Aquila was jerked to his feet, and his hands twisted again behind his back and strapped there. And when the little band of Saxon raiders turned seaward, climbing the long slope of the downs, they carried Aquila stumbling in their midst.

Behind him the valley was left to its silence, and nothing moved save the last faint smoke that still curled up from the blackened ruins of his home.

4

Ullasfjord

SINCE noon the two longships had been nosing
their way between the shoals and sandbanks of a
wide firth; and now the sun was westering and the
shadows of the fierce dragon prows reached forward, jade
and milky across the bright water, as though the vessels
smelled their own familiar landing-beach and were eager
to be home.

The striped sails were down, and the crews had taken to
the oars. The *Sea-Snake* followed in the wake of the
Chieftain's great *Storm-Wind*, and beyond the high, graceful
sweep of the stern, Aquila, pulling with the rest, saw only
the tumbled brightness of the sunset spreading up the sky.
Against the blaze of it, Wulfnoth the Captain stood braced
and watchful at the steer-oar, his voice coming down to
them giving the rowing time to which it seemed that rowers
and vessel answered as though they were one living thing.

'Lift her! Lift her!'

To Aquila, used to the slave-rowed Roman galleys, it
seemed very strange, this rowing by free seamen, among
whom he alone was a slave. He had not resisted when he
was pressed into rowing. It would have been useless and
pointless to resist. Besides, better have something to do;
less time for thinking.

But the trouble was that one could row and think at the same time. He had found that out all too soon. And now, his body swinging to the rhythm of the oars, his mind went dragging and straining back over the long trail; back to that hideous forced march over the downs—there had been harebells up on the high downs; odd that he remembered that now—and down over the seaward marshes to the little dark, deadly longship lying in the hidden creek of Regnum Harbour. Out beyond Vectis they had met the *Storm-Wind*, and together put in to replenish supplies. He remembered the fires inland and the screaming, and the cattle driven down for slaughter on the beach, more cattle than they could eat or carry away, wantonly slaughtered and left on the tide line when the *Storm-Wind* and the *Sea-Snake* spread their wings once more. It was like a waking nightmare in his mind. But it was not so terrible as the nightmares that came to him when he slept; the terrible dreams in which he heard Flavia shrieking his name in unutterable fear and agony, saw her carried by, stretching her arms to him, on the shoulders of a golden horror, half man, half beast, and fought to go to her against the stranglehold of a great tree that wrapped its branches about him with thick, throaty laughter and held him fast.

He never dreamed of his father or the others. Maybe that was because for them the horror was over. For Flavia, too, it was most likely over, long before this, but he could not be sure, and the thought of her alive in the hands of the barbarians was at once his greatest torment and the thing that made him go on living himself.

He was aware now, as the firth turned more northerly, of a sudden quickening excitement among the crew. Men began snatching glances over their shoulders, and as the longships rounded a low headland, a triumphant shout went up. Aquila, glancing over his shoulder also as he swung to his oar, made out a distant huddle of turf roofs crowding under the shelter of a great dyke, as ponies huddle under a hedge when a storm blows over, and the low, long spines of boat-sheds above the oyster paleness of the beach. As they swept nearer, he could see that the landing-beach was speckled with people. Clearly they had been seen from afar, and the whole settlement had come crowding down to welcome the longships home from their summer's raiding.

Now the Captain's voice rose into swifter chant. *'Lift her! Lift her!'* And the *Sea-Snake* leapt forward like a mare that smells her own stable, coming round in a great swooping curve in the white wake of the Chieftain's keel. Now she was heading straight for the shore through the broken water of the shallows; and Wolfnoth's voice rang out: 'In oars! Out rollers! Now—run her in, brothers!'

The oars were unshipped and swung in-board, the long rollers caught up from their places beneath the thwarts, and with a shout the Sea-Wolves were out over the gunwales, thigh deep in the cold, white water. Shouting and cheering, they ran her up through the shallows in the wake of the *Storm-Wind*, splashing a yeasty turmoil of surf all about them. The people of the settlement came plunging down to meet them, to set their shoulders to the galley's light sides and man the rollers and run them far up the sloping beach out of reach of the tide, churning the pale sand and shingle as they had churned the bright water of the shallows.

And now, in a score, a hundred places at once, it seemed to Aquila, men were greeting their women-folk and bairns, these men whose name beyond the Great Water was written in terror and fire and sword, loudly kissing their yellow-haired women and tossing up squealing children and thumping younger brothers on the back. Under the watchful eye of Hunfirth the Chieftain where he stood in the bows of the *Storm-Wind* with the flame of the sunset all about him, the booty was being got out from below decks, tumbled overboard on to the shingle, and carried up past the boat-sheds. Aquila, standing beside the *Sea-Snake*, soaked to the waist like all the rest, and with the wet, grey shingle heaving under him with the long North Sea swell, watched the harvest of a whole summer's raiding tumbled in heaps along the tide-line: fine weapons and lengths of rich stuffs, bowls and cups of precious metals, the worked ivory cross from a church, lying among the brown and amber sea-wrack.

Thormod was whistling for him; Thormod, standing straddle-legged and proud from his first season's raiding. Aquila stiffened, making for the moment no move to obey the summons. But rebellion would be merely stupid; and his stomach revolted at the idea of big barbarian hands on him, of being dragged up the shingle and flung down like a shock of oats at the feet of this red-and-white-and-golden stripling to whom it seemed that he belonged as though he were a dog.

He shut his teeth and threw up his head, and walked forward, trying not to sway to the swaying of the shingle under him. Naked save for a twist of cloth about his loins, he was all disdainful Rome in the hands of the Barbarians, as he halted before Thormod.

At Thormod's side a very tall man stood leaning on a staff; an old, bent giant with hair and beard as fiercely white as a swan's feathers, and eyes that were mere glints of blue ice almost hidden under the crumpled folds of his lids. 'See, here he is,' the boy said. 'I give him to you, Bruni my Grandfather. I brought him home for you because of the thing on his shoulder.'

'So—that is most curious.' The old man stretched out a huge, gaunt hand and ran a finger with obvious pleasure over the blue tattoo-marks as Aquila stood rigidly before him. 'Aye, I ever counted the dolphin a lucky beast.' The bright, hooded eyes studied Aquila from head to heel and back again. 'He has been wounded. Is that the mark of your saex, Grandson, there on his temple?'

Thormod flushed, as Aquila had seen him flush before.

'Na,' he said unwillingly. 'That was another man's work. I found him bound to a tree close by a house that was gutted by some that came before us. And I saw the sign on his shoulder, and it seemed to me that he had been set there that I might bring him to you.'

'So.' The old man nodded. 'It is good to have a dutiful grandson. Yet nevertheless, when *I* followed the seamew's road for the first time, we took our own captives and booty, and not that which was left by other men.'

'Can I help it if another was before me?' Young Thormod flung up his head in retort. 'If I had come upon him first, I would have taken him just the same. With my naked hands I would have taken him, if need be!'

Bruni looked from his angry grandson to the captive standing before him in the harsh, windy, sunset light, taking in the frowning gaze and the set of his mouth, as Aquila gave him back stare for stare; and for an instant there was a glint of harsh humour in his eyes under their many-folded lids. 'With your naked hands? I doubt it. Nevertheless, it is in my mind that you would have tried, young fool that you are . . . Sa, I thank you for the gift of the dolphin. He shall be thrall to me in place of Gunda, who was slain by the bear last winter.'

And so Aquila, who had been Decurion of a Roman Cavalry troop, became Dolphin, thrall to old Bruni, a thing of less account than a good hunting-dog. Nobody troubled to ask his own name, nor even to think that perhaps he had one, nor did he trouble to tell it. It belonged to another life, not to this life on the tide-swept, gale-torn shores of Western Juteland. Juteland; the land of the Jutes; for though, like the rest of his kind, he had thought of all the raiders from across the North Sea as Saxons, the men into whose hands he had fallen were Jutes.

The settlement of Ullasfjord clustered about the painted Hall of Hunfirth the Chieftain, whose antler-crested gables caught the first light that slid over the moors at the day's beginning, and the last sunlight up the firth from the open sea at the day's end; each farm-house in its own garth with its outbuildings and bee skeps and few wind-torn apple trees. Beyond them was the corn-land and the rough pasture, and beyond again was the wild. The farmstead of Bruni, like most of the rest, was a long, barn-like building, warm under deep turf thatch that was held down against the spring and autumn gales by ropes of twisted heather as thick as Aquila's wrist. From the door at one end an aisle led between stalls for the horses and oxen to the house-place at the far end, where the fire burned on a hearth of cobbles in samelled clay, and the family lived and ate and slept: old Bruni himself, and Aude, who was Thormod's mother, and Thorkel the younger boy, and sometimes Thormod, though for the most part he slept in the Chieftain's hall among the other young warriors. There were hay-lofts above the stalls, and there Aquila slept with the two farm-thralls, smelling their unwashed bodies and the warm breath of the kine, as the autumn darkened into the winter.

Among Thormod's share of the booty from the summer's raiding was a bronze box beautifully and curiously enriched with blue and green enamels. By and by it would be traded with one of the merchant kind who appeared from time to time, but for the present it was stowed in the great kist carved with writhing dragon-twists under the high window. Neither Thormod nor his kin had taken much interest in what was inside it, since it did not seem to be anything of value. But on an evening wild with an autumn gale and the firth roaring like an open sea, Aquila came into the house-place carrying driftwood for the fire, and found Bruni and his grandsons bending together over something that the old man held, the bronze box open beside the hearth, while Aude the mother tended the evening meal of oatmeal porridge, broiled cod and beans.

As Aquila checked an instant between the last of the stalls, Bruni was saying disgustedly, 'Nay, I can make neither stem nor stern of this thing. Maybe it is a magic, and I like it not.'

'Safer, then, to burn it,' suggested Thormod, and the old man nodded, as one giving a deeply considered judgement, and turned to throw the thing he held into the fire of spitting birch logs.

In that moment Aquila saw what it was, and flung down the load of salt-whitened driftwood and strode forward. 'No! Let you not do that! It is not magic—not dangerous.'

Bruni looked at him under the long wrinkles of his lids. 'You have seen this thing before, then?'

'I have seen many others of its kind,' Aquila said.

'So? And what thing is it?'

'It is a book. It is as though the words of a man were caught and set down on a long roll, in those small black marks, so that other men may take them up at another time and in another place—maybe long after the speaker is dead—and speak them again.'

'So it *is* magic,' Thorkel the younger boy said eagerly. 'Like our Runes.'

'You talk foolishness,' said his grandfather. 'The Runes are the Runes, and there is nothing else that is like them. They are the strongest of all magic, bought for men by the suffering of Odin, who hung for nine days on a tree to gain the secret of them.'

'None the less, it *is* magic of its kind,' Thormod said, and he looked up from the scroll in his grandfather's hands. 'But perhaps, after all, there is no harm in it. Can anyone read these dead man's words again?'

'Anyone who knows the signs,' Aquila said.

'Do you?'

'Yes.'

Old Bruni looked up from frowning at the magic marks, and frowned instead at Aquila, thrusting out the scroll. 'So. Then let you speak the words that are here, and maybe we will believe that what you say is true.'

Aquila hesitated for a moment of hot rebellion. Why should he lay the mind-riches of the civilized world before these barbarians who spat on their house-place floor and ate and slept like swine? Then he put out his hand and took the beautiful piece of scribe's work that the old man held out to him. The words looked up at him familiarly as he opened it. It was the Ninth book of *The Odyssey*—a Latin translation, fortunately, for despite Demetrius's patient tutoring he had never found it easy to read Greek. Now he translated again, haltingly, as he read, into the Saxon tongue.

' "My island stands deep in the sea, and nearer to the West than to its neighbours, which—which rather face the dawn and the sun. It is a harsh land, yet it breeds good men. But perhaps in every man's sight there is nothing better than his native land." '

The old man and the boys were leaning forward, their eyes moving from the scroll to his face and back again as though trying to catch the secret in flight.

'And who was it said that?' Bruni asked, when he reached the end of the passage.

'A man called Odysseus,' Aquila said, deciding to leave out the complication of Homer, who had put the words into Odysseus's mouth. 'A great seafarer, far from his own home.'

'So-o.' The fierce old warrior nodded. 'And hungry for his own landing beach. Aye, aye, we have all known the homing hunger, just as we have known the other hunger that comes when the birch-buds thicken and the seaways call again.' He settled himself more comfortably, stretching his great splay feet to the fire. 'Speak me more words of this seafarer who felt even as I have felt when I was young and followed the whale's road.'

And so, squatting in the firelight that leapt and fluttered across the papyrus, Aquila read on. ' " . . . Indeed that time I nearly came safely to my native land, only for the swell and the sea currents and a north wind which united against me as I worked round Cape Maleia and drove me wide of Cythera . . . " '

Suddenly the familiar words were sounding in his ears in Demetrius's deep and beautiful voice; and the roar of the firth outside became the roar of the summer gale sweeping up through a great forest; and he was back in the atrium at home, back in those last, oddly shining moments before the dogs began barking and the end of the world had come. He saw his father's hand with the great signet ring catching and losing the firelight as he fondled Margarita's head against his knee; and Demetrius's grey, gentle face bent over the scroll, and Flavia in the glow of the firelight, combing her hair.

He stumbled over the translating of a word, and the present closed down on him like the clanging shut of a prison door. Still he read on. There was nothing else to do, though something very like despair rose in his throat, and for a moment he was reading from memory, for he could not see the words.

The Lotus Eaters were behind them, and Odysseus and his crew had just reached the island of the Cyclops when Aude turned from the fire, her face flushed. 'Enough of this storytelling. Let you eat before the good food spoils.'

The moment was past, and Aquila let the scroll fly up, and laid it back in its box with the rest of the set, while his masters turned to the smoking food.

'When I was young and a warrior, I had a sword whose lightning none might stand against,' said Bruni, holding out his hand for his horn spoon to dip in the common porridge-bowl. 'Now that I grow old and only the things of the mind are left me, I have a thrall who can speak the words of long-dead men, only by looking at some little black marks. Truly I am still great among my kind.' He took a gulp of smoking porridge, spluttered messily, and spat most of it into the fire, for it was too hot, and gave Aquila a long, hard stare. 'Yet if I could have the strength of my sword hand again, and the lifting deck of a longship beneath my feet, my thrall might lie beneath seven galleys' lengths of sea, for aught that I should care!'

Aquila, closing the lid of the box, looked up. The bitterness and the anger rose within him, and the pain of the few moments when it had seemed that he was back in his own world made him reckless. 'And let you be very sure of this, Old Bruni,' he said, breathing quickly, 'that your thrall would be content to lie there, rather than be thrall of yours!'

For a long moment their eyes met, Aquila's dark and young and fierce, and the eyes of the old sea-rover that were mere glints of faded blue light under the wrinkled lids; while the two boys and the woman looked on as though they were watching a duel. Then Bruni nodded, with a fierce shadow of a smile on his bearded lips. It was almost the first time that Aquila had seen him smile. 'Sa, sa, sa, that was a fiery word, my thrall; but a flash of fire is not an ill thing in thrall or free,' and he ducked his head again to his porridge spoon.

From that time forward, few evenings went by that the old man, who seldom went up to the Hall now, did not call Aquila from among the farm-thralls to read to him of the journeyings of Odysseus. And so, evening by evening, crouching in the fireglow while the wind howled like wolves about the door, and the old man and his grandsons sat rehafting a spear or plaiting a bow-string as they listened, Aquila woke the magic of golden shores and distant seas as dark as grapes at vintage. He had never known those seas, any more than his listeners, but the magic was familiar to him, belonging to his own lost world.

On an evening on the edge of winter, Aquila squatted in his usual place, reading by the spluttering light of burning birch logs and the red glow of peat how Odysseus strung his great, back-bent bow, when the dogs sprang up quivering with pleased expectancy, and padded to the door.

'That must be Thormod,' young Thorkel said, for his elder brother was with the warriors in Hall that night. Two sets of footsteps crunched over the half-frozen first fall of snow. Someone was stamping in the fore-porch, the door opened letting in a blast of freezing air and crashed shut again; and Thormod appeared between the stalls, with someone else behind him.

He came into the firelight, shaking himself like a dog. 'See who is here! The *Sea-Witch* is back, and look now: I have brought Brand Erikson to sit by our hearth a while.'

The man who had come in behind him looked to Aquila as though Odysseus himself had come among them, save that his crisp, curly hair was sandy-grey instead of black. A man brown as a withered oak leaf and lean as a wolf, with a wily, sideways, sly, and daring face. Clearly he was an old friend, one well used to sitting by this hearth, and the others greeted him with the quick and casual gladness of long familiarity. Aude laid aside her spinning and rose and brought him the Guest cup of beechwood enriched with silver, brimming with the carefully hoarded morat that was made of honey and mulberry juice, saying, 'Drink, and be most welcome.'

The new-comer took the cup and drank, with the customary 'Waes-hael!' and gave it back to her. He drew a stool to the fire and sat down, rubbing the crimson stain of the morat into his grey beard, then looked about him with a cocked and contented eye. 'It is good to sit beside the hearth again, my friends; it is good to be through with the sea-ways until spring.'

'You are late back from your trading,' old Bruni said, huddling closer to the fire, his wolfskin cloak about him. 'We had given you up for this year, thinking that Guthrum must have run the *Sea-Witch* up some other landing-beach for her winter's sleep.'

'Na, na; as to that, the ways of trade may be more uncertain than the ways of the war keels.' The new-comer loosened his hairy woollen cloak and stooped to fondle the head of a hound pup that had rolled against his feet. 'Guthrum was minded to make Hengest's port in the North-folk territory our last trading call of the season. But when we made that landfall, what should we find but that Hengest and the main part of his people were gone south to some new hunting-run that the Red Fox had given them, to the island that the Romans called Tanatus— almost down to the White Cliffs. And our trade gone with them.'

Aquila, who had drawn aside into the shadows and taken up a broken seal-spear to work on, glanced up quickly as the familiar names fell on his ear. The Red Fox: did the barbarians, too, call Vortigern the Red Fox? And what could it mean, this sudden move of Hengest and his war bands? He was suddenly filled with an almost painful awareness of every word that was being spoken round the fire, as he bent again to his task.

'So south we went, coasting the shores of the Roman's Island—and none so easy at this time of year—until we too came to this Tanatus, and saw the great grey burg that the Romans built, across the Marshes. There we did good trading, and were welcome, so that when our trading was done, the season growing so late, it was in the minds of many of us to winter there at Hengest's camp. But the *Sea-Witch* was hungry for her home landing-beach; and so we set her head to the north-east; and truly a hard voyage we had of it, for half the time she ran before the gale until she leapt and twisted like an unbroken mare, and half the time we saw nothing beyond the oar-thresh but the freezing murk. Yet tonight Guthrum and the rest sit by the Chieftain's fire, and I before yours, before I go inland tomorrow to my own home; and it is good.'

'It is always good to sit by the hearth-fire when the voyaging is over,' Bruni said. 'But better to go down to the boat-sheds and hear again the dip of the oars when the spring comes back.' He looked up, his old face fiercely alert as a hawk's in the firelight. 'And what reason lies behind Fox Vortigern's gift of this new territory?'

But Aquila, his head bent low over the seal-spear, knew the answer to that a leaping instant before Brand Erikson gave it. 'A simple enough reason. The birds of the air brought him word of some plan that the followers of the old royal house had made, to rise up and call in the help of Rome and drive both him and our people into the sea. And Tanatus covers the way into the heart of the Roman's Island.'

'So. It seems that you know much concerning this thing.'

'It is a thing known to all the camp. Vortigern has taken an open enough revenge on any he could reach of those who were betrayed to him.'

The old man nodded. 'Aye, aye, it is a sad thing when there is one to betray his brothers—or was that, too, but the birds of the air?'

'Na, not the birds of the air.' The other cocked up

his head with a dry crackle of laughter. 'Indeed, I did hear that it was a bird-*catcher* they had the word from—a little, peaceful bird-catcher with a lantern and a basket. Ah, but be that as it may; the Sea Wolves have been busy, and there's more than one dead man that was alive when that message went to Rome-burg, and more than one hearth was warm enough then, that's cold and blackened now.'

Aquila, sitting suddenly rigid in the shadows, drew a sharp breath; he found that his hands were clenched on the spear-shaft until the knuckles shone white as bare bone, and carefully unclenched them. But nobody noticed the thrall beyond the firelight.

'And since when have we been the Red Fox's hired butchers?' old Bruni asked in a deep rumble of disgust.

The new-comer looked at him sideways. 'Nay, the thing was not done altogether in Vortigern's service. Do *we* want the Roman kind strong again in their old province? It is a rich land, the Roman's Island, richer than these barren shores to which our people cling, and Hengest will be sending out the call for more of us—more from all the tribes of Juteland, and the Angles and the Saxons also, come the spring.'

There was a gleam in old Bruni's eyes under the many-folded lids. 'Hengest—by Vortigern's wish?'

'By Vortigern's wish, or by what he thinks is his wish. Hengest is become a great man with the Red Fox. Aiee, a great man. He sits in his Mead Hall in the misty marshes, while the gleemen sing his praises, and he wears the gold arm-ring of an earl.'

Bruni snorted. 'And he naught but the leader of a war band!'

'Yet others besides his own band will follow him, come the spring.'

Thormod, who had sat listening in eager silence until now, broke in suddenly, his eyes brightening with excitement: 'The Roman's Island is indeed rich! Have I not seen it this past summer? On the downs many sheep could graze to the yard-land, and the corn stands thick in the ear, and there is much timber for houses and for ship-building——'

And young Thorkel joined his own voice to his brother's. 'When Hengest's call comes, why should we not answer it? We shall see Hengest's great camp, and there will be much fighting——'

Bruni silenced them both with a gesture of one great hand, much as he would have silenced the baying of his dogs. 'I also have seen the richness of the Roman's Island, though it was not this summer nor for more than five summers past. But I say to you that it is good to raid where the raiding ground is rich; yet no light thing to forsake for ever the landing-beaches that knew our fathers' fathers' keels, and the old settlements, and the old ways.'

In a while, though the two boys grumbled together with hunched shoulders, Bruni and the new-comer fell to talking of other things, telling one against the other of past raids and past voyages in search of new markets, while Aude spun her saffron wool in the firelight.

Aquila no longer heard them. He sat with his head in his hands and stared at a dry sprig of last year's heather among the strewing fern at his feet, and did not see that either. Somehow it had never occurred to him that the Sea Wolves who had slain all that he loved and left his home a smoking ruin had been anything but a chance band of raiders. He knew better now. He knew that there had been no chance in the matter. His father and the rest had died for the cause of the old Royal House and the hope of Britain. Died because they had been betrayed; and he knew who had betrayed them. And the thing that he was seeing was the little brown, pointed face of the bird-catcher . . .

That night he dreamed the old hideous dream again and again, and woke each time shaking and sweating and gasping in the darkness under the turf roof, with Flavia's agonized shrieks still seeming to tear the night apart.

5

Wild Geese Flighting

WINTER passed, and one morning the wind blew from the south with a different smell in it: a smell that tore at Aquila's heart with the memory of green things growing along the woodshores of the Down Country. The days went by, and the stream that had run narrow and still under the ice broke silence and came brawling down, green with snow-water from the moors inland; and suddenly there were pipits among the still bare birches.

As the spring drew on, a restlessness woke in the men of Ullasfjord. Aquila felt it waking, like the call that wakes in the wild geese and draws them north in the spring and south again when the leaves are falling. They began to go down to the boat-sheds, and the talk round the fire at night was of seaways and raiding. Just before seed time, the call came from Hengest, as Brand Erikson had foretold, and from many of the Jutish settlements, from Hakisfjord and Gundasfjord bands of settlers went in answer. But Ullasfjord still held to the old ways; the raiding summer and the return home at summer's end.

Aquila did not see the *Storm-Wind* and the *Sea-Witch* sail. He found something to do at the inland end of the settlement, and tried, with a sickening intensity, not to think. But afterwards he found young Thorkel disconsolately leaning against the fore-post of the lower boat-shed and staring away down the firth; behind him the brown, shadowed emptiness where the *Sea-Snake* had hung from the roof-beam, before him the churned tracks of the rollers in the sand. 'They wouldn't take me,' he said, scowling; 'not for another two years. Don't you wish you were sailing in the *Sea-Snake*?'

Aquila rounded on him with a flash of anger. 'Sailing down the Saxon wind against my own people?'

The boy stared at him a moment, then shrugged. 'I suppose they may try the Roman's Island, though Brand says that most of the richest parts are held by Hengest now, and so the Frankish lands make better raiding. I had forgotten about them being your people.'

'It is easy to forget an ill when it isn't in one's own belly,' Aquila said. 'Your kind under the Red Fox burned my home and slew my father and carried off my sister. I do not forget.'

There was a moment's silence, and then Thorkel said, awkwardly, as though in some way it was an apology, 'I never had a sister.'

Aquila was staring out along the line of dunes with their crests of pale marram grass brushed sideways by the wind. 'I pray to my own God that she is dead,' he said.

If he could know that, there might be some sort of peace for him as well as for Flavia; yet he knew in his innermost heart that if it were so, he would have lost the only thing that he had to hold to; and all there would be left to hope for in this world was that one day he might meet the bird-catcher again.

Without another word, he walked on, leaving young Thorkel still leaning against the boat-house.

Harvest came, and summer's end brought the men back from their raiding, with their own harvest of booty, without which the sparse, salty fields and poor pastures of Ullasfjord could never have supported its people. Winter passed, and seed-time came, and again it was harvest: the second harvest of Aquila's thraldom. That year the raiding season had gone ill, the *Storm-Wind* had suffered much damage from a pounding sea, they had gained little booty and lost several men, and so the war-keels with their crews had returned to lick their wounds even before the late barley was fully ripe to the sickle.

The harvest of the west coast of Juteland was never rich, but this year the sea-winds that had so nearly wrecked the Chieftain's war-keel had burned and blackened the barley, and it stood thin and poor, and beaten down in the salt fields like the staring coat of a sick hound. But such as it was, it must be gathered, and men and women, thrall and free, turned out sickle in hand to the harvest-fields, Aquila among them.

There was no wind from the sea today, and the heat danced over the coast-wise marshes; the sweat trickled on Aquila's body, making the woollen kilt that was his only garment cling damply to his hips and belly. Thormod, working beside him, looked round with a face shining with sweat.

'Ho! Dolphin, it seems that the women have forgotten this corner of the field. Go you and bring me a horn of buttermilk.'

Aquila dropped his sickle and turned, frowning, and made for the corner of the long, three-yardland field where the jars of buttermilk and thin beer stood in the shade of a tump of wind-shaped hawthorn tree. There he found old Bruni, who had come out to watch the reapers, leaning on his staff in the strip of fallow where the ox teams turned at ploughing time. There was a shadow on his old hawk face as he looked away down the field, that was more than the shade of the salt-rusted hawthorn leaves.

'It is in my mind that there'll be tightened belts and hollow cheeks in Ullasfjord before we see the birch buds thicken again,' he said as Aquila came up. But his voice was so inward-turning that for a moment the young man was not sure whether the old man spoke to him or only to his own heart. Then Bruni looked full at him, and he asked, with a glance back over the field where he had been working, over the brown backs of the reapers, the women with the big gleaning baskets and the poor thin barley, 'Is it often like this?'

'I have seen many harvests reaped, since first I took sickle in hand,' Bruni said; 'but it is in my mind that I have seen but two—maybe three—as lean as this one. We are seldom more than one stride ahead of famine, here on the west coast, and this year I think by Thor's Hammer that it will be but a short stride, and we shall feel the Grey Hag snuffling between our shoulder-blades before the spring comes round again.' The faded blue eyes opened full on Aquila. 'That makes you glad, eh?'

Aquila gave him back look for look. 'Why should I grieve that my foe goes hungry?'

'Only that you will go hungry with him,' Bruni growled, and there was a sudden twitch of laughter at the bearded corners of his mouth. 'Maybe that is why you work as hard as any man here, to get in what harvest there is.'

Aquila shrugged. 'That is as a man breathes. I have helped to get in many harvests, in my own land.'

'Your own land . . . Richer harvests than this, in the Roman's Island, eh?' the old man said broodingly, and then with a sudden impatience, as Aquila remained silent, 'Well, answer me; are you dumb?'

Aquila said levelly, 'If I say yes, it is as though I cried to the Sea Wolves, "Come, and be welcome!" If I say no, you will know that I lie, remembering the thickness of the standing corn you burned to blackened stubble in your own raiding days. Therefore I am dumb.'

The old man looked at him a moment longer, under the grey shag of his brows. Then he nodded.

'Aye, I remember the thickness of the corn. Once we grew such corn, in kinder fields than these. Our women sing of them yet, and our men remember in their bones. But that was before the tribes of the Great Forests over towards the sunrise started the westward drift, driving all before them.' His gaze abandoned Aquila and went out over the marshes to the low dunes that shut out from here the green waters of the firth. 'All men—all peoples—rise in the east like the sun, and follow the sun westward. That is as sure as night follows day, and no more to be checked and turned again than the wild geese in their autumn flighting.'

It seemed to Aquila that a little cold wind blew up over the marshes, though nothing stirred save the shimmering of the heat.

He took up a horn lying beside one of the jars and filled it with cool, curdled buttermilk, and went back to Thormod. The boy swung round on him impatiently, dashing the sweat out of his eyes.

'You have been a long time!'

'Your grandfather was talking to me,' Aquila said.

'What about?'

'Only about the harvest,' Aquila said, but he had an odd feeling that the thing they had really been talking of was the fate of Britain.

The harvest was gathered and threshed. They wove fresh ropes of heather to hold down the turf thatch in the autumn gales, and the gales came, and the wild geese came flighting south, and it was winter. A fitting winter to follow such a harvest. Snow drifted almost to the eaves of the settlement on the weather side, and lay there, growing only deeper as the weeks went by. Black frosts froze the very beasts in the byres; and for no reason that any man could give, the seals forsook the firth that winter, so that the seal-hunters returned empty-handed again and again. The deep snow made for bad hunting of any kind, and that meant not only less to eat now but fewer skins to trade with the merchants later.

There was always a lean time at winter's end, when the meal-arks were low and the fish grew scarce and the hunting bad; but in most years the first signs of spring were waking—a redness in the alders by the frozen stream, a lengthening of the icicles under the eaves—to raise the hearts of men and women for the last grim month before suddenly the promise was fulfilled. This year there was nothing save the lengthening of daylight to show how the year drew on. Indeed, as the days grew longer the cold increased. People's heads began to look too big for their gaunt shoulders, and even the children had hollow cheeks like old men. And still the ice clung grey and curdled along the shore, and under the frozen snow the ground was hard as iron. Ploughing would be a month late this year, and the seed, sown a month late, would not have time to ripen before the heat went from the short northern summer; and so the next harvest too was doomed.

Men began to look at each other, seeing each behind his neighbours' eyes the thought that had been growing in all of them ever since the harvest failed; the thought of their own barren, wind-swept fields, and the corn standing thick in some sheltered valley of the island over towards the sunset. Hengest still wanted settlers, not only for Tanatus, but for all the eastern and southern shores of the Roman's Island; still sent out the call each spring. Half of High Ness settlement had gone last year . . .

When Hunfirth the Chieftain summoned a council of all Ullasfjord to his great Mead Hall, the whole settlement knew what it was that would be talked of.

Old Bruni had been ailing for many days, but he was set like a rock on taking his place among his own kind at the Council. When the appointed night came, he turned a deaf ear to all Aude's protests, wrapped himself in his best cloak of black bearskin lined with saffron cloth, took his staff, and set out with Thormod over the beaten snow. Thorkel had wanted to go too, only to be told, 'When you are a man, then join with the men in Council. Now you are a bairn; bide therefore with the bairns and women.'

So he bided, scowling into the red heart of the fire, when his grandfather and his elder brother were gone. Aquila also crouched by the fire, rubbing down a new ox yoke against ploughing time—if ploughing time ever came again.

It seemed a long time since the last meal, but he did not feel as hungry now as he had done when the shortage started, which was as well, for he knew that there would be little enough to spare for the thralls, from the pot of thin oatmeal porridge which Aude was tending over the fire, against the men's return.

He worked on steadily, rubbing and rubbing at the creamy alder-wood, but without any idea of what his hand was doing; for all his thoughts were in the Chieftain's Mead Hall, all his awareness turned towards the thing that they would be discussing there; so that every rustle of falling peat ash on the hearth, every stirring of the beasts in the stalls, every beat of his own heart under his ribs seemed part of the fate of Britain. There was driftwood among the burning peat, white-bleached and salt-encrusted, burning blue and green with the shifting colours of distant seas. Driftwood was the right fire for these people, shifting, seaborn, rootless—for all their planted orchards and tilled fields—as the wild geese overhead.

Footsteps crunched and slithered over the frozen snow, and there was the usual stamping and beating in the fore-porch; the door-pin rattled as it was lifted, and the men of the steading were back, letting in a blast of bitter cold that seemed to make the very flames of the fire cower down, before the door crashed shut behind them. Old Bruni came up between the stalls, with his grandson at his shoulder, and looking at them, Aquila thought it would be hard to say whether the old man's eyes or the young one's were the brighter in their starved faces. Bruni stood looking down at them about the hearth.

'So, it is finished, and it is begun,' he said. 'When the spring comes, Ullasfjord also will answer the call.'

Aude looked up from the bubbling porridge-pot without surprise, for she had known like everyone else what Hunfirth's Council spoke of, and what would be the outcome. 'Who leads?' she asked.

'Young Edric. It is his right as Hunfirth's eldest son.'

'And who goes?'

'This year, the fighting men for the most part, and some of their women and bairns. Later, the rest of the settlement.' The old man glanced about him thoughtfully. 'From this steading, myself and Thormod—ah, and the

Dolphin; I am old and need my body-thrall about me. And besides, I am a great man and it is not fitting that I should clean and tend my own war gear.'

It seemed to Aquila, looking up from the fire, with his hand clenched on the ox yoke, that for a long moment everything stopped, even his own heart. Back to Britain! Back to his own land . . .

Then Thorkel sprang up with a furious cry. 'I also! Why should I be left behind? Always—always you leave me behind!'

'Peace, puppy,' Bruni rumbled. 'There will come another year.'

'For those who live through this one,' Aude said into the porridge-pot, while the boy, completely quelled by his grandfather as always, subsided glowering. She looked up at him kindly, but without understanding. 'Old foolish one, and do you think they will take *you*? They want the young ones, the warriors.'

Bruni stood rocking a little on his heels, and looking down at her; and there was a fire about him that Aquila had never seen before, though his face in the upward light of the flames was the face of a bearded skull. 'There are other things besides the strength of a man's sword arm; and even though that fail me—a little—I have my worth. I have more than seventy summers of garnered wisdom, of cunning in battle. I shall have my place when the long keels pull down the firth.'

'You spoke against the thing once, and now you would go yourself: I do not understand.'

'Did ever a woman yet understand ought beyond the baking of bread?' grumbled old Bruni. 'Whether I go this spring or not, the thing will go on. It is no more to be turned back than the flighting of the wild geese. In a few years this settlement will be dead—dead and hearth-cold;

and over towards the sunset, in better farming country, a new settlement will rise.' He looked round on them, contemptuous of their little understanding; and towering there with the smoke fronding about his head and the salty green and blue of the burning driftwood at his feet, he seemed to Aquila taller than any mortal man had a right to be. 'Aye, and before that new settlement rises there will be the fighting. Hengest knows that—a cunning warrior and a leader of men, for all that he has no right to wear the arm-ring. And I—I would take my sword in my hand once more, and smell again the oar-thresh and the hot reek of blood: I who was born a warrior and have lived beyond my fighting days.'

'Well, let you sit down now, before the porridge spoils,' Aude said. 'There will be time enough to talk of swords later.'

He made a great, impatient gesture, his head among the smoky rafters. 'Na, I am for sleep. There are other things than the need for porridge in my belly this night,' and he turned, lurching a little as though suddenly it was hard to hold up his own great height, to the box bed beside the hearth. Aquila, torn by a sudden raw and unwilling pity, laid aside the ox yoke and rose to help him.

That was the last time, save once, that he ever saw Bruni stand upright on his own huge feet; for next morning, when the old man would have risen, his legs would not carry him.

Aude scolded. 'Did I not say so? Going out to the Council when he was fit for nothing but his own fireside. These men, they must be for ever breaking their own bodies and the hearts of the women that are fool enough to care if they live or die!' and she opened the little kist of black bog oak in which she kept her herbs and simples, and brewed a strong, heady-smelling draught that she said would maybe drive out the sickness.

Bruni drank the draught, and by and by the sickness, whatever it was, seemed to go away. But no strength came back to the old man. He lay in the deep box bed beside the hearth, while the last days of the winter dragged by and the icicles began to lengthen under the eaves. Thormod and Aquila tended him, without a kind word between them, for he had never been one to speak kind words nor yet to listen for them. He lay under the wolfskin rug that his gaunt frame scarcely lifted. He seemed to be only dried skin lying lightly over the huge old bones, and the veins at his temples and on the backs of his great hands were blue and knotted like the painted worm-twists on the prow of a long-ship; and his lips, too, were blue. He had his sword beside him on the bed, and would lie fondling it as a man fondles the ears of a favourite hound; and often he would call for Aquila to read to him of the wanderings of Odysseus, that by now he knew almost by heart.

'A sad thing it must have been for this Odysseus,' he said once, when Aquila had come yet again to the end of the last scroll. 'A sad thing to know that the adventuring was over, and nothing left but his own fireside.' And his great hand moved on the amber-studded hilt of the sword lying beside him. 'As for me, glad I am that there will be one more adventuring . . . When the spring comes, I shall grow strong again, despite these black draughts of Aude's.' And then, as though to himself, 'By Thor's Hammer, I *will* grow strong again!'

But after the first few days he ceased to speak of the new settlement or the fighting that must come before it as something that he would have any part in. He made no complaint, spoke no word against his fate; grim old warrior that he was, he would have held proudly silent if he were being roasted before a slow fire. Yet Aquila knew that in the old man there was a furious rebellion. He could feel it, a high wind of rebellion that seemed to fill the whole steading with a sense of storm, though Bruni himself lay as still under his wolfskin, with his great sword beside him, as the pale snow-light that crept through the high windows at noon; as still as the shortening nights outside, beyond the first drippings of the thaw from the eaves.

They all knew that he was dying.

'One of these nights, when the tide runs out, he will go too, the Old One,' Aude said, and the old man himself smiled harshly at the puzzled look on his thrall's face. 'Aye, your folk can die at one time as well as another; but you have naught to do with the sea. We of the coast and the sea-ways cannot die in our beds save at low tide,' and he raised his sword and shook it. 'But there was a time when I never thought I'd lie in the straw waiting for ebb tide!'

In the grey of the next dawn, a great wind rose, a wild storm wind with sleet on its wings that rattled against the stretched membrane of the window-holes; but there was the smell of the south in it, and the sleet was half rain. Bruni slept most of that day, but about dusk he woke, with a wild, imprisoned restlessness on him that was like fever. But it was not fever, for his eyes under their heavy, crumpled lids were clear, and full of impatient and contemptuous laughter at the sight of the anxious faces about him. The wind was dying down now, and the sleety rain had almost ceased to spatter at the window membrane; but as the night drew on, old Bruni's restlessness seemed to rise like another storm, and blow down the whole length of the steading, making the very cattle stamp and fidget in their stalls.

When the other thralls had crawled away into their

own places in the hay-loft, Aquila remained crouching by the bed, held there by some feeling for the old dying warrior that he neither understood nor questioned. Aude was at her loom; he watched her shadow leaping all up the gable wall, the shadow of the shuttle as she tossed it to and fro; but the place was full of leaping shadows from the fire, for there was no seal oil to spare for the lamps. Thormod sat by the fire, his hands round his knees, his face strained and white under the tousled brightness of his hair; and Thorkel slept with his head on a hound's flank.

The fire had begun to sink, and the cold was creeping in. Aquila leaned forward to cast on another peat, and as he did so, and the sparks flew upward, a sudden movement from the box bed made him look round quickly.

Bruni had dragged aside the wolfskin covering and struggled into a sitting position, his tangled mane of hair shining round his head and shoulders, and his eyes full of cold blue light under the many-folded lids, and his great shadow bursting like a giant's all up the wall behind him.

'It is near to low tide,' he said. 'Bring me my shield and helm and my bearskin cloak.'

Aude let the weaving shuttle fall with a clatter, and came running to the bed. 'Let you lie down again and save your strength.'

The old man thrust her aside with a gaunt arm. Indeed there was strength in him again, an extraordinary flare of strength, like the last burst of smoky flame from a torch before it goes out. 'Save my strength? To what end shall I save my strength? I tell you I'll die on my feet. Not a straw death! Not a straw death for Bruni the Wave-Rider!'

She made some other protest, but nobody heard her, for the old man cried out in a great gasping voice, turning from his thrall to his grandson and back again: 'Thormod! Dolphin! My war gear!'

For a moment the eyes of the two young men met, blue gaze and dark gaze; and for the first and only time in their lives there was no feeling of any gulf between them. Then, while Thormod sprang for the black-and-gold buckler with its strange winged beast that hung from the house-beam, Aquila turned to the kist under the window and dragged out the bearskin cloak with its saffron lining and the helmet of bull's horn bonded above the brows with grey iron. The great sword with the amber studs there was no need to bring him, for it was already in his hands.

'Out of the way, my mother,' Thormod said; and while she stood against the wall with her hand on the shoulder of young Thorkel, who had woken at the sudden turmoil, the two of them armed old Bruni as though for his last battle, and supported him as he struggled, swaying, to his feet.

'Out!' Bruni said. 'I must have the wind on my face!'

And somehow, Aquila supporting him under one shoulder and Thormod under the other, they got him to the door and out through the fore-porch into the darkness and the failing storm beyond the firelit threshold.

The grey sky was hurrying overhead and the high-riding moon showed as a greasy blur of brightness, rimmed with smoky colours behind the drifting flocks of cloud. The tide was full out, and the brightness fell in bars of tarnished silver on the wet sandbanks beyond the dunes and the cornland, and the oily tumble of the water beyond again. The wind swung blustering in from the south-west and the sea, with the smell of salt in it and that other smell so long delayed, that was the promise of spring; and the whole night was alive with the trickle of melting snow.

Old Bruni drew in a gasping breath. 'Sa! That is better

than the hearth reek and the musty straw!' He shook off their hands and actually took one step forward alone, and stood unsupported, his head up into the wind, as though he waited. Aquila saw the proud old giant outlined against the grey, hurrying light, upheld by that sudden flare of strength, by his own terrible will to die on his feet as a warrior should, instead of woman-wise in the straw.

And suddenly, as he stood there, as though it were the thing that he waited for, they heard the wild geese coming—faint at first, far off in the hurrying heights of the sky, but sweeping nearer, nearer—the wild geese giving tongue like a pack of hounds in full cry down the storm wind.

Old Bruni looked up, raising his sword as though in salute to his kin. 'We also!' he cried. 'We also, in the spring, my brothers.'

The yapping of the geese was fading into the distance, and as it died, so it seemed that the last flare of the old warrior's strength was done. The iron-rimmed buckler crashed to the ground; but he was still holding his beloved sword as he fell back into the arms of the two young men behind him.

6

The Saxon Wind

WITH Bruni, it seemed that Aquila's brief hope of getting back to his own land died too, and must be laid in the old man's grave with his sword and buckler. He did not ask Thormod to take him for his shield-thrall in his grandfather's stead. That was partly pride, little as he could afford pride: a hot inability to bow his neck to ask anything of the blue-eyed barbarian kind; partly another thing that he would have found it hard to give a name to: an odd sense of fate. If Flavia was alive, she might be in Britain, but just as likely she might be in Juteland, or any other of the Saxon coast-wise lands. No action that he could take, no plan that he could make, would help him find her. If he was to find her at all, his only chance was to bide still, waiting for the wind—a little wind of God to rise and show him the right way.

So he waited, with something of the belief in fate, though he did not realize it, that he had caught from those very barbarians. And as it happened, he had not very long to wait; no longer than the day of the Arvale for old Bruni—the gathering that was at once funeral feast for the dead master of the house and heir feast for the man who came after him. There was little to spare for the feasting, but they spread the trestle tables before the house-place door with food that could be ill spared from the store kists, and brought out the heather beer and the dark, heady morat. And Thormod drank the Heir Cup, standing before all the hollow-cheeked gathering, and swore the great deeds he would do in his grandfather's place, according to the custom.

Later, when all the folk had gone home, he stood beside the cobbled hearth, and looked about him in the firelit quiet that was broken only by the stirring of a beast in its stall and the snoring of young Thorkel who slept already, in his favourite position with his head on a hound's flank, and more heather beer inside him than he had ever had at one time before.

'All this is mine!' Thormod said crowingly. 'The steading and the kine and the apple garth; the cloth in the kist and the honey in the crocks—what there is of it—and the thralls in the hay-loft.' He laughed, his eyes very bright. 'And I'm going to kick it behind me, and not come back! . . . No, not all, though . . . ' He began to cast up on his fingers, and Aquila, who had checked for an instant by the loft ladder, thought that he was a little drunk, but not as Thorkel was, with heather beer alone. 'I shall take my grandfather's good bearskin cloak, and his amber brooch, and the little kist with the carved worm-knots, and the red heifer to add to the breeding herd. Oh, and I shall take the Dolphin.'

Aquila, who had already turned again to the loft ladder, checked once more, and stood very still. Aude, beside the fire, braiding her hair for the night, looked up. 'Why the Dolphin?'

'For the same reason as my grandfather would have taken him. For my body-thrall, to carry my shield behind me.'

She laughed softly, scornfully. 'Large ideas for yourself, you have. Only the greatest warriors have their shield-thralls behind them.'

The young man laughed too, though his colour rose as always. 'And shall I not be a very great warrior? I am Thormod Thrandson, and my grandfather was Bruni the Wave-Rider, and my mother is sister to Hunfirth the Chieftain. It is fitting that I should have my shield-thrall behind me. And besides, not Hunfirth himself has a shield-bearer that can read the magic marks! Therefore, with the Dolphin behind me, I shall be the greater in the eyes of other men, because I have what they have not!'

Aude looked at Aquila by the loft ladder, seeing more deeply than her menfolk had done. 'And do you think that once landed on his own shore, he will not seek at all costs to escape?'

Thormod shrugged, breathing on his new dagger that had been his grandfather's, and rubbing it up his sleeve. 'It is none so easy to escape from the midst of the Jutish camp. Many of our folk in the Roman's Island have their Roman thralls. But to make yet more sure we will collar and chain him like a hound. I do not know why my grandfather did not put a thrall-ring on him years ago.'

The eyes of the two young men met and held, the moment when they had forgotten the gulf between them for old Bruni's sake now in its turn quite forgotten. Then Aquila turned again to the loft ladder and climbed up to his own place under the eaves. It was a long while before he slept, and when he did, he dreamed the old hideous dream again.

Spring came, full spring, with misty blue and green weather, and the pipits fluttered among the birches and the alder thickets where the buds were thickening. The bustle of preparation swole louder and more urgent as the days went by. Every year that thrum of preparation broke out as the time for launching the war-keels again drew near. But this year it was all different, more far reaching, for this year Ullasfjord was making ready not for a summer's raiding, but for a setting out from which there would be no return, and besides the men and their weapons, there were the women going, and the bairns, and a dog here and there, and the kine for breeding the new herds. There were extra stores and fodder to be loaded; the best of the seed-corn in baskets, even little fir trees with their roots done up in skins or rough cloth; and farm tools and household treasures—a fine deerskin rug, an especially cherished cooking-pot, a child's wooden doll . . .

On the last night before the setting out there was a gathering of all the men who were going from Ullasfjord in the Gods' House close by the Long Howe where the tribe laid its dead. And there in the torchlit dark a boar was slain and his blood sprinkled on the assembled warriors and smeared on the altar of blackened fir-trunks; and they swore faith to Edric the Chief's son who was to lead them, on the great golden ring—Thor's ring—that lay there; and swore the brotherhood in battle on ship's bulwark and shield's rim, horse's shoulder and sword's edge.

Aquila, being only a thrall, had no part in the gathering, but he crouched with the other thralls around the open door of the Gods' House, looking in. He was very conscious of the pressure on his skin of the heavy iron ring that a few hours earlier had been hammered on to his neck at Thormod's command. Old Bruni, he thought, would at least have made sure that it did not chafe; but Bruni had been more careful than his grandson would ever be to see that the yoke did not gall the neck of his plough-oxen, nor the collar rub the hair from the throat of his hunting dog. Yet in an odd way the chafe of the neck ring felt good to him. It was a promise, a constant reminder that where he was going it might be possible to escape. The little wind—God's wind—that he had been waiting for was blowing now. Suddenly he was sure of it.

With a confused idea that where other people had worshipped, though their gods were not his, must be a good place to pray, Aquila prayed now, silently and with a burning intensity, crouching heedless of the other thralls, with his hands clenched at his sides and his forehead against the bloodstained, serpent-carved door post of the Gods' House. 'Christus, listen to me—you must listen—— Let me find my sister if she yet lives, and let me be able to help her, or die with her if—there isn't any other way for her.'

The next morning the wind blew thin and cold from the east, and the waters of the firth were grey as a sword-blade; but the men laughed as they ran the long keels down over their rollers into the shallows.

'The Saxon wind blows strong; surely it is a good omen,' a young warrior cried, holding up a wetted finger. Aquila laughed too, a little, bitter laughter that strangled in his throat. He had thrown aside his honour, deserted all that he had been taught to serve, so that he might stand by Britain. And all he had done was to fall into the hands of the barbarians himself. He had served more than two years' thraldom on a Jutish farm, and now—he was to take an oar in this barbarian longship, his share in bringing her down the Saxon wind against his own land. The laughter in his throat knotted itself into a sob, and he bent his head between his shoulders and splashed down into the surf with the rest, feeling the galley grow light and buoyant as a sea bird as the water took her.

The cattle had already been loaded into the hold of the *Sea-Witch*, and at last it was over, the remaining stores loaded, the last farewells said; those who were to be left behind stood dry-eyed, for they were a people not used to weeping, on the landing-beach. Aquila was in his place at the oar. After more than two years among these people, he was no longer strange in the ways of boats as he had been the first time he felt the oar-loom under his hands. Wulfnoth the Captain stood at the steer-oar; and behind him, behind the high, painted stern of the *Sea-Snake*, the settlement with its dwindling figures on the landing-beach, and the dark line of the moors beyond, all grew fainter—fainter. Something that was over and done with, sinking away into the distance.

Presently, when they were clear of the shoal-water, Wulfnoth ordered, 'In oars. Up sail,' and the *Storm-Wind*, the *Sea-Witch* and the *Sea-Snake* slipped down the firth before the light north-east wind, the Saxon wind.

They lost the wind after two days, and had to take to the oars again, rowing almost blind in a grey murk mingling with the oar-thresh, in which they all but lost the rest of the squadron. Some of the young warriors grew anxious, though they made a jest of it, saying, 'Ran the Mother of Storms is brewing, and how may one find the way with so much steam rising from her vats?' But old Haki, the Chieftain's uncle, who was as wise as a grey seal in the ways of the sea, sniffed the mist with his wide, hairy nostrils and said, 'By the smell, children.'

Sure enough, when at last the mist gave them up, and at noon they were able to check their position by the dimly seen sun, with a spar set up on the half deck, they were not much off their course. There were other troubles on the voyage: many of the women were sick; a child was lost overboard; one night there was a sudden panic among the

cattle that all but capsized the *Sea-Witch*, and in the morning two of the best heifers were dead and one of the men in charge of them had a badly gored shoulder. But on the seventh day the gulls met them; and suddenly, towards sunset, there was a long, dark line that might have been a cloud-bank on the western rim of the sea, and a distant shout came back to them, thin as the cry of a sea bird, from the look-out clinging to the rigging of the *Storm-Wind*'s mast head.

'Land ho!'

Aquila, craning round to gaze over his shoulder as the galley lifted to the crest of the next sea, was suddenly blind with more than the salt hair whipping across his eyes.

For three days they ran down the coast, drawing in slowly, until, long after noon on the third day, they were nosing in towards the low, marshy shores of Tanatus. The wind had fallen light and they had had to take to the oars again to aid the scarcely swelling sails. They had hung the shields, black and crimson, blue and buff and gold, along the bulwarks just clear of the oar-ports, and shipped at their prows the snarling figureheads that had lain until now under the half-decks, safe from the pounding of the seas. And so, proud and deadly, the little wild-goose skein of barbarian keels swept down on Britain, and their appointed landing-beaches.

Aquila rowed with his chin on his shoulder, his gaze raking the tawny shore-line as it crept by, drawing always nearer, until, afar off, he caught the familiar whale-backed

hump with its grey crown of ramparts, and knew as
Wulfnoth put over the steer-oar that they were heading in
straight for Rutupiae.

Wulfnoth's eyes were narrowed in concentration as he
brought the *Sea-Snake* round in the wake of the *Storm-
Wind*, into the mouth of the winding waterway that cut
Tanatus from the mainland. And now the smell of the
marshes came to Aquila as he swung to and fro at his oar:
the sourness of marsh water, the sweetness of marsh
grass—a smell subtly different from the smell of the
Juteland marshes, that tore at something in his breast.
The sail came rattling down, and was gathered into a
bundle like a great, striped lily bud; and Wulfnoth's voice
came to them at the oars: 'Lift her! Lift her!' as the tawny
levels slipped by on either side. They ran the keels ashore
at last on the white landing-beach just across the channel
from Rutupiae and sprang overboard and dragged them
far up the slope of fine shells, out of reach of the tide.

Aquila knew that beach; he and Felix had used to bring
their birding-bows out here after wild-fowl. He knew the
wriggling trail of sea-wrack on the tide-line, the dunes of
drifted shell-sand where the yellow vetch and the tiny
striped convolvulus sprawled. Standing with panting
breast beside the *Sea-Snake* as she came to rest, he had the
feeling that he had only to look down to see the track of
his own feet and Felix's in the slipping white sand. He
caught a glance over his shoulder, and saw the tower of
Rutupiae Light rising against the sunset. There was a

great burst of flame above its crest, but it was only a cloud catching fire from the setting sun.

They had lifted the children out over the bulwarks. They were helping the women ashore now, and the man with the gored shoulder. Some of the men had turned already to the bellowing cattle in the hold of the *Sea-Witch*, anchored just off shore.

'Sa, we come to the landing-beach! We are here, my brothers, in this land that we take for our own!' Edric the leader said. And he scooped up a double handful of the silver sand, and raising his arms, let it trickle through his fingers in a gesture of triumph.

The stern of a big galley jutted sickle-shaped beyond the dunes round the next loop of the channel, and the gable end of a boat-shed reared stag's antlers against the sky; and there was a faint waft of wood-smoke in the air telling of human life that had not been there when Aquila and Felix shot mallard over Tanatus marshes. It seemed that scarcely were the *Storm-Wind* and the *Sea-Snake* lying above the tide-line with their crews swarming about them, before an inquiring shout sounded from the edge of the dunes inland, and a man came crunching down over the shingle towards them: a big man with a broad, ruddy face under a thatch of barley-pale hair.

'Who comes?'

'Jutes from Ullasfjord, north of Sunfirth,' Edric said. 'I am Edric, son of the Chieftain.'

'Welcome, Edric, Son of the Chieftain of Ullasfjord.' The man cast an eye over the women and children. 'Come to settle, seemingly?'

'Aye, to settle. The times are hard in Ullasfjord. A bad harvest, a hard winter, and the sons sail to find another land to farm. Always it is so. And the word blew to us on the wind that Hengest had room for good men at his back.'

'Umph.' The man made a sound at the back of his throat that was half grunt, half laugh. 'As to room—it is in my mind that if we pack much closer into this island of Tanatus we'll be ploughing the salt sea-shores and sowing our corn below the tide-line.'

'Maybe when we have spoken with Hengest we shall up-sail for some other part of the coast. But in any case'— Edric grinned, and jerked his chin towards the winding waterway—'are the Sea Wolves to lair for ever, this side of Tanatus channel?'

'That you must ask of Hengest when you speak with him.' The man flung up his head with a gruff bark of laughter; and the laughter spread, one man catching it from another. More men had appeared behind the first, and now two young women came running down the shingle, followed by a boy with a dog. Tanatus seemed very full of people, where the solitude of three years ago had been. And new-comers and old-comers together, they set about unloading certain of the stores, and getting the cattle ashore and penned, and rigging the ships' awnings; for it was settled that most of the Ullasfjord men should sleep on board with their gear tonight, while the women and bairns and the man with the gored shoulder were taken up to the settlement.

Later, when the full dark had come, and the men had eaten the evening food that the women brought down to them, and drunk deep of buttermilk and raw imported wine, and lain down to sleep beneath the awnings, Aquila, lying with the other thralls beneath the stern of the longships, raised himself to look out across the water again towards Rutupiae Light. The long chain by which he was secured for the night like a hound to a ring in the bulwarks rattled as he moved, and someone cursed him sleepily; but he scarcely heard them, any more than he heard the flapping of the awning in the little wind. Everything in him was straining out towards Rutupiae across the marshes and the waterways and the almost three years between; remembering that last night of all, when he had kindled the beacon for a farewell and a defiance; the night that the last Roman troops sailed from Britain. There was no beacon-light now in the windy spring darkness; even the huddle of the native town below the ramparts was dark. It had come into being to serve the fortress, in the way that such places always sprang up under the wings of the Eagles; and with the Eagles flown, the little town would have ceased to be.

To Aquila, torn by a sudden piercing desolation, it seemed that he was farther from his old happy world even than he had been in Juteland, because there the actual distance of sea between had hidden a little the greater gulf—the gulf that there was no crossing. He felt like a man who had been caught away into another world, and coming back to his own world at last, had found it dead and cold, and himself alone in it.

7

The Woman in the Doorway

SMALL settlements and single farms still raw with newness were scattered over the low, green land of Tanatus, mingling with the few native fisher villages. The core of this barbarian gathering was the great burg of Hengest, half a day's march northward of the place where the Ullasfjord band had made their landing: a vast camp within its bank and ditch and stockade; a vast huddle of reed-thatched steadings, wattle-and-daub huts, and even ship's awning tents that looked like crouching animals rather than living-places, all gathered about the great painted timber Mead Hall which, with its byres and barns, made up the home steading of Hengest himself. Here and there a line of bee-skeps against a house-place wall, here and there a plot of kale or a clump of ricks, their tops roped down against the wind; fair-haired women coming and going to tend the animals, carrying pails up from the milking, grinding corn in stone hand-querns in the doorways; children and dogs playing in the sunshine; men with their weapons; tethered cocks scratching on dunghills with their hens around them; half-wild spitfire cats in warm corners; cattle lowing, men shouting, the ring of hammer on anvil, the bright notes of a struck harp, the smell of roasting meat, and seaweed, and dung; and over all, the smoke of a hundred cooking fires. This was the great burg of Hengest.

Aquila, on his way to the swordsmith's bothie with Thormod's dagger, which had sprung a rivet, looked about him with a feeling of being a ghost in this huge, thrumming, rootless burg that had grown up in three years; and stepped aside yet again, this time for a cart loaded with grain-sacks coming up from the shore gate of the stockade. It was obvious that Tanatus could never yield the grain for all this horde; it must be tribute from the mainland—tribute paid by Fox Vortigern to the wolf within his gates. Aquila wondered whether the tribute-carts might perhaps be his means of escape when the time came. They came in full; did they carry anything on the return journey? If so, might it be something under which a man could hide?

At first, when they had run the keels ashore three days ago, he had been set on making a dash for freedom at the first chance, but Edric, leaving the women and bairns for the present, had swept his warriors straight up here to Hengest's burg, and there had been no chance to break away. That had given Aquila time to think. Now he understood that it would be foolish to try to escape before he had made sure that there were no tidings to be had of Flavia here in the great camp. So he laid plans for getting away when the time came, but in the meanwhile watched and listened and looked about him with an aching intensity.

He was not quite sure where he was in the vast camp, and checking a moment to look round him and make sure of his direction, he saw a woman sitting in the doorway of a wattle cabin close by: a dark woman in a kirtle of bright blue wool, her head-rail laid aside, her head bent low as she braided her hair, and at her feet a man child of about a year old, playing happily between the paws of a patient, grey-muzzled hound. She had begun to hum softly, to herself or to the child, he was not sure which, a thin, sweet, dark humming without words, at sound of which his breath caught in his throat. He couldn't see her face in the shadow of her hair—hair dark and fiercely alive as a black stallion's mane; the kind of hair that might give out sparks if she combed it in the dark. There was a queer, sick stillness in him; and yet he could not believe, he *would* not believe—until, as she flung out her hair, turning and parting it with her fingers, he caught the green flash of a flawed emerald in the windy sunlight, and knew his father's ring that he had last seen on the hand of Wiermund of the White Horse. And the unbelief that he had been desperately clinging to was torn from him.

He didn't think he made any sound, but she looked up quickly, as though startled; and he saw how all the blood drained out of her face, so that her eyes looked like black holes in the whiteness of it. She got to her feet and stood looking at him. The child pressed back against her legs, staring at him also with round, dark eyes; the old hound raised his head and whined softly in his throat; and it seemed as though all the sounds of the camp died away as the wind dies into a trough of quiet.

For a long moment it was clear that she did not quite believe, either. The time since they were last together had turned Aquila from little more than a boy into a thick-set, brown-skinned man, with dark hair and beard bleached sandy silver at the ends by the sun and the salt winds of Juteland; a man with a frown-line bitten deep between his brows, and a white scar running out of his hair to pucker the wind-burnt skin of his temple, and the heavy iron collar of a thrall about his neck. He saw the uncertainty in her eyes, and had the sudden aching thought that he should pull up the sleeve of his tunic and show her the dolphin . . . ('If I were away from home for a long time, and when I came back nobody knew me again, like Odysseus, I could take you aside and say, "Look, I've a dolphin on my shoulder. I'm your long-lost brother".' And she had laughed and said, 'I'd be more likely to know you by looking at your nose, however long it had been away.') Well, he knew the change that there must be in him, seeing the change that there was in her. She was grown up now, with so much in her face that had not been there in the old days, so much of the laughter gone from it, and she wore a Saxon kirtle of fine blue wool with bands of green and crimson needlework at throat and sleeve; the sort of kirtle that would not be given to a slave. His gaze took in all of that, without seeming for an instant to leave her face, and took in also the small man child clinging to her skirt.

Then, her lips scarcely moving, she said, 'Aquila.'

The blood was beating in Aquila's head, pounding in the old scar. 'Aye,' he said.

'They told me you were dead.'

'It is no fault of *theirs* that I am not,' Aquila said heavily. 'You remember how the wolves were howling that night—too close—too close for summer time. They left me tied to a tree on the wood-shore. The wolves did not come, but instead another band of raiders happened by. I have served nearly three years thraldom on a Jutish farm . . . And you, Flavia?'

She made a small convulsive gesture towards the child, as though that answered the whole question.

The silence hung between them. Then Aquila said, 'Does he—belong to the yellow-headed giant who carried you off across his shoulder that night?'

She nodded. 'You saw that, then?'

'Yes, I saw that. I heard you crying to me for help, and—I struggled to come to you. I've dreamed of that ever since.' He put up his hands, in one of which he still held Thormod's dagger, and pressed them to his face. And his words came muffled. 'I've been haunted all this while by the thought of you in Saxon hands; I've prayed harder than I thought a man *could* pray, for I was never much of a one for prayers, that if you yet lived I might find you again . . . ' He lowered his hands and looked at her once more. 'But, dear God! I never thought how it would be!'

'Isn't it always so?' Flavia said. 'The men fight, and after the fighting, the women fall to the conquerors.'

'Some women,' Aquila said bitterly. And then, seeing her flinch as though he had struck her, 'No, I—Flavia, I didn't say that—I scarce know *what* I am saying——'

'If I had known that you were alive, I think that I should have had the strength to kill myself,' Flavia said after a long, dragging pause. 'I thought there was no one left, and I was alone, you see.'

'Yes, I see, I—do see, Flavia.'

She remained a moment longer looking into his face, then, with one of her swift, flashing movements, turned half-away, and sitting down again on the stool, began to braid her hair. 'We must not seem to be talking so earnestly together; even now we may have been noticed . . . Aquila, you must escape!'

'Strangely enough, that idea has been in my mind also,' Aquila said.

'Ah, I know, I know; but don't you see, the thing is more urgent now? Wiermund of the White Horse is dead, but his sons are here, and they saw you slay his brother, and may know you again. If that happens, they will call for the full vengeance for the death of a kinsman.'

Aquila did not care. He felt that he would not care

much about anything, ever again. But he tried to force his mind in the direction she wanted it to go. 'Escape is a thing more easily said than done. Thormod, my—my lord, calls for me often through the day, and each night to tend his harness before he sleeps; and I must sleep at his feet just like a hound, with—my thrall-ring chained to the tent-pole.' He spoke the last words through shut teeth.

Flavia was silent a little, braiding the dark masses of her hair. Then she said, 'Listen. Two nights from now there will be a great feast in Hengest's Mead Hall; Vortigern himself is coming to it, and there will be much eating and drinking—mostly at his expense—and by midnight everyone will be too drunk to know whether their thralls are there or not, when they reel to bed—even if they get so far, and do not merely sleep among the rushes. That will be your chance.'

'And the guards on the gate?' Aquila said. He was fumbling blindly with his belt, with some confused and helpless idea of looking as though he were doing something to it.

Flavia tied the end of her hair with a thong and flung the heavy braid back over her shoulder before she answered, 'I will take care of the guards on the shore-gate. Also I will bring you a file to rid yourself of that ring about your neck. Come to the back of the woodwright's shop down yonder; you can't miss it, there's a carved figurehead for a galley just outside, and a thorn tree beside the door. Come when the merry-making is at its height, and if I am not there, wait for me. If I should be the first, I will wait for you.'

He did not answer at once, and she looked up quickly. 'You will come—you will come, Aquila?'

'I will come,' said Aquila.

She caught up the child clinging to her skirt. 'Come,

baba, it is time for food,' and rose and would have turned back through the house-place doorway, but Aquila stopped her, asking a thing that he felt was stupid and unimportant, and yet had to be asked. 'Flavia, how did you come by Father's ring?'

She checked, holding the solemn baby high on her arm, her head tipped far back to avoid the small, brown, starfish hand that patted her face. 'I told you Wiermund was dead. The ring came to his eldest son, and from his eldest son I had it for my bride gift.'

Then she was gone. The old hound lay still, head raised and watchful amber eyes on the face of the young man who stood there as though he had struck root. Then he got up and padded into the doorway, and lay down again across the threshold.

Aquila also turned away. He felt completely stunned, like a man so badly hurt that for the moment he feels only a numbness where presently there will be unbearable pain. Confusedly he remembered that he had been taking Thormod's dagger to have a sprung rivet seen to; and he went on his way in search of the swordsmith's bothie, because there was nothing else to do—nothing that would be any good.

Two nights later, Aquila sat on the beggars' bench before the door of Hengest's great timber Hall, with the hood of his rough cloak drawn forward to hide his face and the thrall-ring about his neck, and watched the scene before him. It would have been more sensible to have lain up in some quiet corner until the time came to go down to the woodwright's shop, he knew, but invisible strings had drawn him to the feasting in Hengest's Hall, whether he would or no, and all evening he had been looking for Flavia, with a sick dread of finding her there among the other women. But now the eating was over—odd to see so much food again—and the trestle tables had been taken down and stacked against the gable wall; and he knew that she was not here. At least she was not here, pouring mead for these golden hogs and for the Red Fox.

All evening, too, he had been looking for a man he had seen only once before, the man who had given Flavia their father's ring for a bride gift. But he remembered him as something horrible, something not properly human; maybe, after all, he only looked like a big, blond man—and there were so many big, blond men in Hengest's Mead Hall, he could not be sure.

He still felt numb, and the numbness left him free to look about him, and watch with a kind of remote, hill-top clearness the scene before him: the long hall swimming in heat and smoky torch-light, the women moving to and fro with the great mead jars, the hounds among the rushes, the harper by the fire, the warriors sprawling on the benches with their drink-horns slopping. He saw Hengest's hearth companions, and the darker, slighter, redder men who were of Vortigern's company; Saxon and Briton mingling on the same bench, leaning on each other's shoulders, drinking from the same horn; a joyful scene that sickened him. He knew who most of the great ones were. That big, broad-faced, broad-bellied warrior was Horsa, Hengest's brother. That other with a white, proud face, carrying even in Hengest's Mead Hall a hooded falcon on his wrist, was Vortimer, the King's eldest son. But close behind him lounged a man in a tunic of chequered silk, who caught at Aquila's interest, and to whom he could give no name. He muttered to the little, wizened thrall beside him, 'Who is the man behind Vortimer—the man with a face like a dark dagger-thrust?' And the thrall said, 'A kinsman of the Red Fox, Guitolinus

I think they call him. If you want no more of that beer, give it to me.'

Aquila passed the horn pot that he had been holding unconsciously on his knee, and his gaze went on from Guitolinus, whose name meant nothing to him now, though he would know it well enough one day, and returned, as it had done again and again that evening, to the two men sitting side by side in the carved High Seat, midway up the hall.

Hengest was a huge man, huge in more than body, so that to Aquila, remembering the scene afterwards, it seemed that his head was upreared almost to touch the firelit under-belly of the house-beam way up where the firelight ended and the smoky darkness began. A greying-golden giant, whose eyes, turned just now on the harper beside the fire, were the shifting grey-green of a wintry sea. He leaned forward, wide kneed, one hand curved about his drink-horn, while with the other he played with the string of raw yellow amber about his neck—an oddly womanish trick that somehow made him seem yet more terrible than he would otherwise have done.

Beside him, and dwarfed by him in every way, sat Vortigern the Red Fox, King of Britain; a long, lean, red-haired man with a thin beard, with rings on every finger of his narrow hands, rings set with jewels as brilliant as the dark eyes that flickered about the hall unceasingly as he talked with the giant beside him, never resting more than a few moments in one place or on one person. Aquila, looking at him with that coldly detached interest that had no feeling in it, wondered what he would feel if he knew that the son of a man he had murdered—for the murder had been Vortigern's, no matter who struck the blow—was watching him from the beggars'. bench by the door, watching the place where the life beat in his long

throat and thinking how simply it could be let out, with a little dagger, or even with one's naked hands. He was probably a good deal stronger than Vortigern.

What were they talking of, he wondered, those two who were breaking Britain between them? What were they talking of under the song of the harper and the rising and falling surge of voices? What was the real meaning behind this great feast? Whatever it was, it could make little difference now, he supposed. The cause of Rome in Britain and the old Royal House was dead; it had been dead nearly three years; but all the same, he would like to know what they were talking of; what was passing in Vortigern's mind. He was more interested in Vortigern's mind than Hengest's, because Hengest was only the enemy without the gates, but Vortigern was the traitor within them.

Vortigern was also wondering, a little, what lay behind this great feast; but not so much as he had done at first, because of the wine. It was difficult to get imported wines inland in Britain now, but Hengest's wine was good, though they drank it like barbarians from ox horns. Probably it was the fruits of piracy, but still . . . He drained

the gold-mounted ox horn so quickly that a little of the thick red wine trickled into his beard, and set it down empty on his knee. As he did so, the girl who had been sitting on the steps of the High Seat rose to pour for him again. A tall, red-gold girl, fiercely proud in her crimson kirtle and the fillet of twisted goldsmith's work that bound her hair. The wine that was as crimson as her gown splashed into the ox horn, and the bubbles rose thickly. Vortigern looked up at her, seeing her through a faint haze; everything was growing a little hazy, but it was a golden haze, golden as the girl's hair. One heavy braid swung forward and brushed his hand, and as she straightened from her task, she smiled at him, only with her eyes that were the same shifting grey-green as Hengest her father's. Mermaid's eyes, he thought, and was pleased because the thought was pretty—worthy of a poet.

The girl poured for her father also, and then seated herself once again on the step, setting the tall wine-jar down beside her, and Hengest raised his horn again.

'Waes-hael! I drink to you, my King. May the sword of power never fall from your hand.'

'I drink to you,' Vortigern returned, and laughed a little. 'Truly I think that it will not—now that the menace of Rome and of young Ambrosius is past.' He did not usually like speaking of such things openly, but the wine seemed to have loosened his tongue.

Hengest laughed also, looking about him with an air of jovial and slightly drunken contentment. 'For me, and for the men that follow me, that menace of Rome and Ambrosius has been a fine thing, and that I'll not deny. This is a better and a fatter land than our North-folks' territory; and here we are your household men. And yet——'

He let the end of the sentence drift into silence; but

Vortigern pounced on it. 'And yet? Man, what else would you have of me?'

'Na, na,' Hengest said hurriedly, and yet with seeming unwillingness, staring into his wine. 'It was but that at times my mind misgives me as to the safety of the King's northern borders. The King set me and my war bands to guard the door of the north against the Picts, and we flung back the Picts, and the Pict menace passed a little; and the King called us south to stand in the southern gateway, against another menace. But sometimes now, I think that if the Painted People should one day swarm in from the north again, there would be but a thin defence and no strong leader to withstand them.'

Vortigern was alarmed and wary. 'What, then, is the answer? If I send you and even half of your war bands north again, the other danger may wake once more. While young Ambrosius lives among the mountains, he will always be a possible rallying point.'

'Na, na.' Hengest made a gesture as though to brush something away. 'The thought was but a thought—such as men think in the dark of the night, when the evening meat sits heavy under the breast-bone . . . Yet it might be no bad thing to settle some other leader there with his war bands around him; men bound by loyalty, even as we are, to Vortigern the King whose mead they drink and whose golden ornaments they wear.'

Vortigern looked at him a moment, his nostrils widening, as though just for that moment he caught the smell of a trap. Then he said, 'So? And if this leader were for you to choose, who would he be?'

Hengest stared, as though he had never given the matter a thought, until that moment. 'Nay then, let me think. I should choose—whom should I choose? There is Octa, my son, of course. He has his own war bands, his own

victories, across the Great Sea; but if the thing were made
worth his while . . . ' He broke off with a wide, impatient
gesture. 'Ah, but no matter. Forget what I said, Vortigern,
my hearth lord. My tongue ran away with me—it is the
fault of wine. And talking of wine——' He frowned round
at the girl in the crimson kirtle. 'Hey! my maiden, you
neglect your duty! Do you not see that the King's horn is
not full? Pour again for your guest and your father.'

She looked up quickly, then rose, taking up the wine-jar,
and stooped again to pour for the red Celtic King. 'It is
not my duty that I neglect, but my heart's pleasure. I crave
forgiveness that I did not see my lord's horn was empty.'

'It is good to have the horn empty, so that it be filled by
so fair a maiden,' Vortigern said courteously.

She raised her eyes to his in a flash, then lowered them
again before he could see what lay under her golden
lashes. 'My lord the King is most kind to his handmaiden.'

Hengest swung round to his gleeman sitting beside the
central fire and strumming idly with the air of a man who
knows that he is not being listened to. 'Sing up, man,
strike that harp and give us "The Battle of Goths and
Huns"! What is a feast without harping?'

The man grinned, and flung up his head like a hound
before it bays, then broke into the swift, fierce word-music
of the old lay, beating out the leaping rhythm on the
twanging strings of the little harp. The bright harp-notes
flew up like the sparks from the fire into the rolling smoke-
cloud overhead, and the man's full, strong voice, half
singing, half declaiming, filled the hall so that little by little
men who had been arguing, talking, laughing, bragging
against each other, grew silent to listen. Vortigern listened,
leaning back in the High Seat, one hand playing with the
horn on his knee, the other, elbow propped on the carved
side-piece, cupping his bearded chin, his restless, brilliant

gaze moving as always here and there about the smoky, crowded, firelit hall.

When the last flight of notes had thrummed away into the silence, and the ragged burst of approval that followed it had fallen quiet, Hengest turned to his guest and asked, 'How does my lord the King like our Saxon harping?'

'It is well enough,' Vortigern said, 'but to my ear harsh, and I can find no tune in it.' He smiled as though to take the sting out of his words; he seldom smiled, and when he did it was a pleasant smile save that it showed too many pointed teeth in the thin red of his beard. 'To every people its own music. I am of another people, and to me the music of my own mountains is sweetest.'

Hengest smote his knee with an open palm. 'The King speaks truly; to every man the songs of his own people! Well, let the King but speak, and it may be that even here he will find singing to bring him the very scent of his own mountains.'

'So? Have you then some Cymric harper among your household thralls?'

'Nay, not a Cymric harper, but one skilled in the harp, none the less.' Hengest made a small gesture towards the girl in the crimson kirtle, still standing beside the High Seat. 'For see now, so deeply does Rowena my daughter long to please you that she has been learning a song of your people, from such a harper as you speak of, hoping that you will let her sing it to you. Say then, shall she sing? If she may give you any pleasure, you will make her very happy.'

Vortigern looked again into the mermaid eyes of Hengest's daughter. 'To look at her, singing or silent, is enough to make any man happy,' he said. 'But let her sing.'

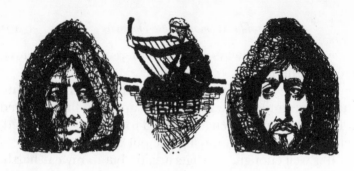

8

Singing Magic

T HEIR earlier talk, under the cheerful tumult and
the gleeman's thrumming, had been private
to themselves, but this, spoken into the silence
following the close of the ancient Saga, was spoken as it
were before every soul in the great hall, and as Rowena,
carrying her head as though the goldwork fillet were a
crown, moved across to the fire and took the slim, black
harp from her father's gleeman, every eye in the place
was upon her, even to the frowning gaze of the man on
the beggars' bench before the door, who sat with the
hood of his cloak pulled so far forward that no man
might see his face.

For a great lady to take a gleeman's harp and sing
before all her father's crowded Mead Hall was a shameless
thing, more shameless even than it was for a Saxon
woman to appear with her hair uncovered; and yet
Aquila, who had known that she was shameless in wearing
no head-rail, forgot that she was shameless in this also. He
only knew that she was beautiful, the most beautiful thing
he had ever seen, and that he hated her.

She sank down beside the hearth, settling the harp on
her knee and into the hollow of her shoulder, and
remained a few moments gazing into the fire that seemed

to leap up to meet her as though there were a kinship between her and the flames, fingering almost silently the horsehair strings. She looked far remote, as though she had no need to be aware of the mead-flushed faces turned towards her, for she and they were in different worlds. She began to pluck the strings more strongly, conjuring up a strange music of long silences and single, singing notes that sprang up, each separate and perfect as some infinitely small silver bird that leapt up like a lark towards the smoky rafters, and hovered a little, and was gone. Gradually the notes spun closer together until the bright shadow of a melody began to emerge; and then suddenly, still looking into the fire, she was singing.

Aquila, watching her, had expected her voice to be hard and high and clear. It was clear, but with a clearness of depth, not height, a dark voice.

> 'The apple tree blooms white in the Land of the Living:
> The shadow of the blossom falls across my door stone:
> A bird flutters in the branches, singing.
> Green is my bird as the green earth of men, but his song is
> forgetfulness.
>> Listen, and forget the earth.'

British born and bred as he was, Aquila could speak the native tongue as easily as the Latin: and though this was a dialect unfamiliar to him, he caught the gist of the song, and his pulses stirred with a strange magic. And by the light of that magic, it seemed to him that the great firelit hall, the warriors leaning forward on their benches, even the two men in the High Seat were no more than a background for the woman harping beside the fire.

> 'The petals fall from my apple tree, drifting,
> Drifting down the wind like snow: but the snow is warm:

And a bird flutters in the branches, singing.
Blue is my bird as the blue summer sky, over the world of men.
    But here is another sky.'

She had turned from the fire now, to look up at Vortigern the King, as he sat forward beside her father, his restless gaze still at last, resting on her face. Watching her under the shadow of his hood, Aquila thought, 'She is a witch! Surely she is a witch! Flavia used to talk of a singing magic . . . ' Rowena had risen, and moved, drifting as though on the slow, haunting notes of her song, to the foot of the High Seat; and sank down again, still looking up at the thin, red-haired man.

> 'The apples are silver on the boughs, low bending;
> A tree of chiming, of singing as the wind blows by:
> But the bird flutters through the branches, silent.
> Red is my bird, crimson red as the life of my heart is.
>   Will you not come to me?'

It seemed to Aquila that the last, lingering notes clung for a long time to the smoky rafters; that they were still hanging there when the singer rose without another word, without another look at Vortigern, and went, sweeping her crimson skirts after her through the rushes, to set the little harp back in the hands that her father's gleeman held out for it.

Hengest sent one glance after her; it might have been in triumph, quickly hidden under his down-drawn, golden brows. But Vortigern did not see it, for his eyes also were following her. 'They will always follow her now,' Aquila thought, with a sudden flash of clear seeing. 'She has crossed over in his mind from the Saxon folk, and become part of his childhood and his own hills and the songs his people sing and the beautiful crack-brained dreams they dream.'

The silence was torn apart by the harsh scream of a peregrine, as the falcon on Vortimer's fist bated wildly, with a furious clapping of wings. The young man rose, striving to calm the bird. He was whiter than ever as he bowed with all courtesy to his father and his host, murmuring his excuses: 'My falcon—not properly manned as yet, it seems. I crave your pardon,' and drew back into the shadows, making for the upper doorway.

The spell that had bound the whole gathering, holding even the Saxons silent, was broken, and the tumult burst upward again, louder than ever. At the lower fire, Thorkel and another young warrior, both very flushed with mead, had started a bragging match that would probably end in a quarrel.

'Once I fought three men one after another, and beat them all!'

'That is nothing. Once I fought three men all at the same time——'

Time to be on his way, Aquila thought. He rose, and stood taking a last look at the scene in the great Mead Hall. All these two days past he had been too numbed really to understand that tonight he was going to try to escape; that in one way or the other, this was the end of his years among the Saxon kind, and by dawn he would be either free or dead. But now, in the moment of setting out, there was a breathless tightening at his heart as he stood by the open doorway, with the smoky torchlight in his eyes and the harp-song in his ears. Then he turned, and slipped out from Hengest's hall into the night.

He had eaten all that came his way, not knowing when he might get the chance to eat again, and drunk little, that he might keep a clear head. But even so, his head seemed full of wood-smoke and the fumes of other men's mead, and he stood for a few moments breathing deeply in the night air to clear it. Then he set off for the woodwright's shop. He was surprised to find how light the world was, for he had forgotten that there was a full moon and it would be up now. A still, white night, with a faint mist rising from the water, glimmering, gauzy between the timber halls and the tents that seemed now more than ever like crouching animals. Behind him the sounds of feasting fell away, and around him Hengest's burg lay quiet between the mist and the moon, for by now all those who did not feast with Hengest and the King were asleep or taking their ease around their own hearth, with house-place door or tent-flap drawn close against the chill of the mist.

Once a cat ran like a striped shadow across his path, and turned to look at him with eyes that were wide and hostile in the moonlight; otherwise he met no living thing until he came in sight of the woodwright's shop close to the shore-gate of the burg. He had made sure of the place in the daylight, a solitary spot in some waste land that seemed to belong to the marshes rather than the burg, though it was within the stockade, and easily recognized from the description that Flavia had given him. The mist was thicker down here, so near the water, wreathing and drifting like wet, moonlit smoke about the hump-backed shape of the bothie and the ancient thorn tree beside it. The dragon-head of a galley prow stood against the thorn tree, its snarling mask upreared as though some living monster were trying to crest the mist like a fantastic sea. For a moment, as he came down towards it, Aquila thought that that was all. Then something else moved in the mist, and he saw that Flavia was there before him.

'You have come, then,' she said, as he halted beside her.

It was such an obvious thing to say, but sometimes it was better to stick to the obvious things.

'I have come,' he said, and sent a swift glance towards the stockade gate, just visible in the mist.

She saw the glance, and shook her head. 'There are none there to overhear us. Did I not say that I would take care of the guards on the shore-gate?'

There was a sudden chill in him. 'Flavia, you don't mean——What have you done to them?'

'Oh no, I am not a poisoner. They will but sleep a few hours.'

'But how——?' Aquila began, but she cut him short.

'It was a simple thing to do. They were glad enough of the mead cup that I brought down to them from Hengest's Hall. See now'—she brought a bundle from under her cloak—'here is some food, and a dagger, and a good sharp file that I stole. With the food, you can lie up for a day or so until you are free of that cruel thrall-ring, before you go among men again.'

Aquila took the bundle from her, mumbling something, he did not know what. They stood looking at each other; and suddenly the ordinary things were no good, after all. Aquila said hoarsely, 'I have seen—I have heard a singing magic tonight, Flavia. The Lady Rowena made it for the Red Fox. But she did not comb her hair. I do not think that she could comb sparks out of it in the dark.'

Flavia caught her breath. 'Aquila, no! It hurts too much. I never made *my* singing magic because I could not bear that you should—that you shouldn't feel the same about me any more; and now . . . '

'Come with me,' Aquila said—it felt like a sudden impulse, but he knew that it wasn't really.

'—and leave the babe?'

Silence again. Then Aquila said, 'Bring him too. We'll

find somewhere—a place for ourselves. I'll work for both of you.'

'For the child of a Saxon father?'

Aquila looked down at the hand in which he held the bundle, and forced it to relax from the clenched and quivering fist that it had become. 'I will try to forget his Saxon father, and remember only that he is yours,' he said carefully.

She drew closer, lifting her face to his. It was very white in the moonlight and the wreathing mist; and her eyes had again that look of being mere black holes in the whiteness of it. 'Aquila, part of me would lie down and die tomorrow and not think it a heavy price to pay, if I might come with you tonight. But there's another part of me that can never come.'

'You mean, you can't leave the man either.'

'Our Lord help me! He is *my* man.'

After a few moments she moved again, and held out something. 'You must go. But first—take this.'

'What is it?'

'Father's ring.'

Aquila made no move to take it. 'What will *he* do when he knows that you have given his bride gift away, and in what manner you gave it?'

'I shall tell him that I lost it.'

'And will he believe that?'

'Maybe not,' Flavia said. 'But he won't beat me.' How strange and luminous her eyes were, all at once, in the moonlight. 'I am quite safe, my dear. He is a brave man in his way, but he won't beat me.'

Aquila put his free hand on her shoulder, and looked down at her, trying to understand. 'Is it love, with you, or hate, Flavia?'

'I do not know. Something of both maybe; but it

doesn't make any difference. I belong to him.' Her low voice was completely toneless. 'Take Father's ring, and—try to forgive me.'

He dropped his hand from her shoulder, and took the ring, and slid it on to his bare signet finger. The numbness that had helped him was wearing thin, and the black, appalling misery was aching through. Somewhere, hidden at the back of his mind, he had thought until now that she would come with him; he hadn't quite accepted that what had happened was for ever. He said in a voice as toneless as her own, 'If I escape by your help, and take Father's ring at your hands, then I must forgive you, Flavia.'

And without another word between them, they turned to the gateway. The guards lay tumbled beside it in uncouth attitudes, the mead cup between them; and Aquila was struck by a sudden fear. 'Flavia—they'll tell, when they wake, who gave them the mead!'

'No,' Flavia said. 'The moon was not up then, and I took pains to change my voice. They will not know who came.' She had gone to the bar that held the gate; but Aquila put her on one side, and raising the heavy timber himself, drew the gate open just enough to let him through. Then, in the narrow gap, he turned again to Flavia, for the last time; the last time of all. She looked very remote and still in the darkness of her cloak, with the mist smoking about her; and here in the shadow of the gateway he could scarcely see her face at all. At the last moment he made a half-movement towards her; but she made none towards him, and he checked and let his arm fall to his side. 'God keep you, Flavia,' he said.

'And you,' Flavia whispered. 'God keep you always. Remember me sometimes—even though it hurts to remember.'

Aquila made a small, harsh sound that was like a sob,

and turned away into the glimmering mist that veiled the boat-sheds and the long keels drawn up above the tide-line. He did not look back, but as he went he heard the soft, heavy creak of the gate being urged shut behind him.

There were some small fishing coracles on the tide-line, but he did not want to leave any trace of his escape route behind him. The tide was ebbing, and soon there would be no more than a narrow channel between Tanatus and the mainland; and a few miles south towards Rutupiae he knew the channels as a man knows the lines of his own hand. Simpler to swim for it. He turned southward, following the edges of the farmed land, and after some miles' walking, came down on to saltings that he knew well. The mist had cleared and the wild-fowl were stirring. There was no hint of day as yet in the sky.

On a spit of blown dune-sand and shingle where he and Felix had often run their coracle ashore he stripped, and making his tunic, with the things that Flavia had given him, into a bundle in his rough cloak, tied it on to his shoulders with its own ends, and took to the water. The channel had shifted in three years, but he got across without much trouble, and waded ashore among the mainland dunes, shaking himself like a dog. He untied his bundle and dragged his tunic on again over his wet body; his cloak also was wet in the outer folds, but the thick oiliness of the wool had kept out most of the water, and the food was quite dry. He bundled it up again, scarcely aware of what he did; he was not aware of anything very clearly, simply doing each thing as it came, because it was the next thing to do. And because it was the next thing to do, he set out towards the dark shore-line of the distant forest.

The moonlight was fading and the day was coming fast, the cirrus cloud already beginning to catch light from the hidden sun; and a skein of wild duck went overhead against the high, shining dapple of the morning sky. The cool daylight of marsh country was washing over the levels behind him as he reached the first fringes of squat, wind-shaped oak and whitethorn, where the great forest of Anderida swept to within sight of the sea. He pushed in a little way among the trees, found a clearing among brambles and hazel scrub, and sitting down with his back to an oak tree, untied the bundle of food that Flavia had given him. He ate a little without knowing what it was, then took out the file and set to work to rid himself of his thrall-ring.

It did not take him very long to realize that it couldn't be done, not by the man wearing the thing. You couldn't get any force on the file, and you couldn't see what you were doing. Well, it did not matter much. By and by, when he was well clear of the Saxon hunting runs, he would go to a smith and get it cut off. Meanwhile, that left nothing to do but rest a little before he pushed on again. He thrust the useless file back into the bundle, and lay down, his head on his arm. The glints of sky through the young oak leaves were like a thousand eyes looking down at him; blue eyes, mocking him because he had prayed to God that he might find Flavia, and God had answered his prayer; and he did not think that he would ever pray to God again . . . He had said that he forgave Flavia, but he hadn't been able to make the words mean anything. Just words. And Flavia knew that. He knew that she knew. He felt lost and adrift in a black tide of bitterness, and the last thing that he had to hold to was gone. No, not quite the last thing—there was still the hope of finding again the man who had betrayed his father.

He would have given up that hope for Flavia's sake, if she had come with him, because the quest for vengeance

was a trail that no man should follow with a woman and a
child dependent on him. But Flavia had not come.

He thought about it coolly and carefully. He would go
on westward until he was sure that he was clear of the
Saxon's reach, and get rid of the thrall-ring on his neck,
and then turn back towards the barbarians again; because
most likely, he thought, the little bird-catcher would be
found clinging to the hem of the Sea Wolves' garments.
At any rate, a Saxon camp was the most likely place to get
word of him. And word of him he would get, if it took
twenty—thirty years.

Had he but known it, it was to take just three days.

9

Forest Sanctuary

A FTER a while he must have slept, for suddenly it was long past noon, and the sunlight fell slanting through the branches to dapple the brown of last year's leaves. He got up, ate a little more of the food, and then, wrapping it up again, set off westward.

There were few roads through the forest, but next day he struck one of the native trackways that had been old before the Legions' roads were thought of; and since it led in roughly the right direction, he turned into it for the sake of easier travelling and followed it along. By the evening of the next day it had led him into higher and more rolling country, an upland world of long, forest ridges, where the ground was sandy underfoot, and the trees grew taller and more cleanly than the damp oak scrub that he had left behind. The fine spell had broken and soft, chill rain was blowing down the wind. Aquila was wet through and blind weary, for he had scarcely rested since he set out westward; if he rested, the little bird-catcher might draw farther away from him; so he kept on—and on . . .

It was already dusk among the trees when, as he came trudging up the long slope of yet another ridge, he caught a waft of wood-smoke on the sodden, forest-scented air, and as he checked, sniffing, the warm saffron flicker of firelight reached him through the hazel and wayfaring trees that fringed the track. He must go to men some time and be rid of the betraying thrall-ring about his neck. Also he must have food. He had finished the last scraps in his bundle at dawn, and the emptiness in his belly drew him towards the fire. Almost without knowing that he did so, he turned to a gap in the wayside scrub, beyond which the faint gleam of fire-light beckoned.

Parting the hazel boughs, he found himself on the edge of a little clearing—in daylight it must be full in sight from the track—and saw before him a plot of what looked in the dusk like bean-rows and kale; and in the midst of it a knot of daub-and-wattle huts squatting under deep heather thatch, a wisp of hearth-smoke rising against the sodden yellow of the afterglow, and the fire-light shining softly through an open door. He hesitated a moment on the edge of the clearing, wondering whether he was yet clear of all shadow of the Saxon kind. Then he saw, hanging from a birch sapling close beside the huts, outlined against the fading daffodil light of the west, something that could only be a small bell. There would be freedom from the Saxons here, where a Christian bell was hanging.

He walked forward between two dripping bean-rows to the firelit doorway. The fine rain hushed across the clearing behind him, but within the hut a fire burned on a small raised hearth, with something boiling in a pot over it, and the warm, fluttering light flushed the little bothy golden as the heart of a yellow rose. There was a stool beside the fire, and a bench with a pillow of plaited straw on it pushed back under the slope of the roof. Otherwise the place was quite bare, save that on the gable wall hung a small cross of rowan wood with the bark still on it, and before it a man in a rough brown tunic stood with arms upraised in the attitude of prayer. Aquila wanted to say, 'It isn't any good, you know: God only laughs at you.' But the rags of a gentle upbringing made him prop himself against the door post and wait, rather than interrupt the holy man until the prayer was done.

He did not mean to make any sound, but it seemed that the man before the rowan-wood cross had sensed that there was somebody behind him. Aquila saw him stiffen, but he made no move until he came to the end of his prayer. Then he turned and looked at Aquila drooping in the doorway. He was a small, thick-set man, with immensely powerful shoulders, and the quietest face that Aquila had ever seen.

'God's greeting to you, friend,' he said, as though Aquila were an expected guest.

'And to you,' Aquila returned.

'Is it food and shelter that you seek? You are most welcome.'

Still leaning against the door post, Aquila thrust back the shoulder folds of his wet cloak. 'Those too, if you will give them to me: but firstly, to be rid of *this* about my neck.'

The man nodded, still without surprise. 'So, a Saxon thrall-ring.'

'I have a file. It isn't possible to use the thing on oneself.'

'That, I should imagine.' The man had come to Aquila in the doorway, drawing him in, a steadying hand under his elbow as though he knew better even than Aquila himself how far spent he was. 'Eat first, I think, and we will see to the next thing later.'

Aquila found himself sitting on the stool beside the fire,

his wet cloak fallen at his feet, while the man in the brown tunic was ladling a mess of beans from the pot over the fire into a bowl of finely turned birch wood. And in a little he was supping up the scalding hot beans, with a wedge of brown barley bread dripping with honey-in-the-comb waiting on the floor beside him, while his host sat on the bench and watched him with an air of quiet pleasure, asking no questions. It was not until he was more than half-way through that he realized that the bean pot was now empty, and stopped with the horn spoon poised on its way to his mouth.

'I am eating your supper.'

The older man smiled. 'I promise you that in eating my supper you are doing me a kindness. I strive after a disciplined life, superior to the pull of the flesh. But alas! the flesh pulls very hard. It is good for my soul that my body should go hungry, but I fear that I find it hard to carry out that particular discipline unless I can prevail on some fellow man to aid me as you are doing now.' His quiet gaze went to the bowl which Aquila had firmly set down on the corner of the hearth, and returned to his face. 'Let you finish the good work, friend, so that I may sleep with a glad heart this night.'

After a long moment's hesitation, Aquila took up the bowl again.

When the beans were gone, and the bread and honey also, the man in the brown tunic rose, saying, 'I think that you have walked a long way, and you are far spent. Let you sleep now. Tomorrow will be time enough to be rid of that thrall-ring.'

But Aquila shook his head stubbornly. 'I would not lie down another night with the Sea Wolves' iron about my neck.'

The other looked at him searchingly. Then he said, 'So

be it then. Give me the file, and kneel here against my knees.'

It must have been close on midnight when the file broke through the last filament of metal with a jerk that seemed to jar Aquila's head on his shoulders. The monk wrenched the thing open, and with a satisfied sigh laid it on the floor, and Aquila, lurching to his feet, stiff with long kneeling, drunk and dazed with weariness, stood swaying with a hand on the king-post to steady himself, and looked down at the small man who had laboured so many hours for his sake. The monk looked as weary as himself, and there was a red tear in his thumb, where the file had gashed it as it broke through. Surely his host might sleep with a doubly glad heart tonight.

The other man had risen also, and was looking at his neck, touching it gently here and there with square-tipped fingers. 'Aye, the iron has galled you badly, here—and here. I was expecting that. Bide while I salve it; then sleep, my friend.'

And in a little, Aquila did sleep, lying on a bed of clean fern in a tiny wattle bothy behind the main one, that made him think of a bee-skep.

When he woke, the hut was full of sunlight that slanted in through the doorway and quivered like golden water on the lime-washed wall beside him. He realized that he must have slept through the night and most of next day; a sleep that was a black gulf behind him with nothing stirring in it, not even the old hideous dream that had woken him so often with Flavia's screams in his ears. But he was never to have that dream again.

He lay still a few moments, blinking at the living golden water on the wall, while little by little the thoughts and events from across the black gulf fell into place around him. Then he sat up, slowly, and remained for a while squatting in the piled fern, feeling the galled places on his neck with a kind of dull relief because the pressure of the thrall-ring was gone. But it was time to be away, down towards the coast and the Saxon kind again, while there was still some daylight left for travelling, and before the man in the brown tunic could ask questions. Last night the man had been merciful and asked no questions, but now that his guest had eaten and slept, surely he would ask them; and everything in Aquila flinched from the prospect, with a physical flinching, as though from a probing finger too near a raw place.

He sprang up and went to the doorway of the cell. Yesterday's rain was gone, and the still-wet forest was full of a crystal green light. In the cleared plot before the huts, the man in the brown tunic was peacefully hoeing between his bean-rows. Aquila pushed off from the door post and walked towards him. The beans were just coming into flower, black and white among the grey-green leaves, and the scent of them was like honey and almonds, strong and sweet after the rain. The man in the brown tunic straightened up as he drew near, and stood leaning on his hoe.

'You have slept long,' he said, 'and that is well.'

'I have slept over-long!' Aquila returned. 'I thank you for your food and shelter, and for ridding me of this,' he touched the sore where the thrall-ring had pressed on his neck. 'And now I must be away.'

'Where to?'

Aquila hesitated. What if he said, 'Back towards the Saxon kind, to look for the man who betrayed my father'? Doubtless this little monk with the quiet face would try to make him leave his search, say to him that vengeance was for God and not for man. 'I am not sure,' he said. And that was true, too, in its way.

The man looked at him kindly. 'To journey, and know not where, makes uncertain travelling. Stay until you *are* sure. Stay at least for tonight, and let me salve your neck again; it is not so often that God sends me a guest.' And then, as Aquila made a swift gesture of refusal, he shifted a little to lean more comfortably on his hoe, his gaze resting on Aquila. 'I will ask you no question, save by what name I am to call you.'

Aquila looked at him in silence for a moment. 'Aquila,' he said at last, and it was as though he lowered a weapon.

'So. And I am Ninnias—Brother Ninnias, of the little Community that used to be in the woods over yonder. And you will stay here at least for tonight, and for that my heart rejoices.'

Aquila had not said that he would stay; but he knew that he would. He had known it when he told Brother Ninnias his name. There was something about this place, a feeling of sanctuary that stilled a little his driving restlessness. He would take one night from following his vengeance, and then no more until he found the bird-catcher and the debt for his father's death was paid. But he would take this one night. He remained silent, staring along the bean-rows.

The little amber bees were droning among the bean-blossom, and at that moment one fell out of a flower, the pollen baskets on her legs full and yellow. She landed sizzling on her back on a flat leaf, righted herself, and made for another flower. But Brother Ninnias stooped and pointed a reproving finger at her. 'That is enough for one journey, little sister. Go back to the hive.'

And the bee, seeming to change her mind, abandoned the bean-flower and zoomed off towards the main hut. Aquila, following her line of flight with his eyes, saw that against the wall stood three heather-thatched bee-skeps. 'It is as though she knew what you said to her,' he said.

Brother Ninnias smiled. 'They are a strange people, the bees. I was bee master to our little Community before the Sea Wolves came. It is so, that I am alive.'

Aquila glanced at him questioningly, but the bargain to ask no questions must work both ways.

Yet Brother Ninnias answered the question as though he had asked it, none the less; and most willingly. 'I was away in the forest after a swarm of bees that had flown away, when the Sea Wolves came. I was angry with myself for having lost them; but since—I have thought that maybe God meant that one of us should be saved. The bees smelled my anger; bees will always smell anger; and so it was a long time before they let me find them. And when at last I found them—just here, hanging on a branch of the oak tree yonder—and came back to the Community with them in my basket, the Saxons had passed that way, and it was black and desolate, even to the bee-skeps along the wall. Only I found the Abbot's bell, quite unharmed, lying in the ruins.' He broke off to pick a bee gently off his rough brown sleeve. 'It was a common enough happening then. At least we do not see so many burned homes in these years; not in the three years that Hengest and his war bands have been squatting in Tanatus, eating from the Red Fox's hand.'

'It does not suit Hengest to have others despoil the land before he swarms out over it himself,' Aquila said harshly.

'Aye, I have often thought that myself. And when I think it, I pray; and when I have prayed, I go and plant something else in my physic garden that it may perhaps flower, and I may perhaps make a salve or a draught from it and heal a child's graze or an old man's cough before the Saxons come.'

There was a silence, full of the peaceful droning of the bees, and then Aquila said, returning to the earlier subject, 'What did you do after you came back to the Community?'

'I said the last prayers for the Abbot and my brethren, and then I took an axe that I found, and the Abbot's bell, and my swarm of bees in their basket, and came away, back to this place where I had found my lost swarm. And here I built a skep for the bees, and hung the Abbot's bell from that birch tree. And then I gave thanks to God, before I set to building my first hut.'

'Why?' Aquila said harshly.

'That I was spared to preach His word.'

'And who do you preach it to? Your bees and the bush-tailed squirrels?'

'A man might preach to worse hearers. But I have others besides. There is a village of iron-workers down yonder, one of many in the Great Forest, and some among them listen to me, though I fear that they still dance for the Horned One at Beltane. And sometimes God sends me a guest, as he did last evening . . . And if I am to feed more guests, I must finish this hoeing lest the weeds engulf my beans.'

And so saying, he returned peacefully to his task.

With some idea of lessening his debt for food and house room, Aquila began to help him, gathering the raked weeds into a willow basket and carrying it up to the place at the far end of the clearing that Brother Ninnias pointed out to him, ready for burning. From that side of the clearing, the land dropped unexpectedly towards the east, and through a gap in the trees the blue distance opened, ridge beyond ridge of rolling forest country fading to the far-off, misty flatness that might be coastwise marshes, or even the sea. Aquila, straightening up from emptying his basket, stood at gaze. The light was fading now, and the forest ridges rolling into the distance were soft as smoke. He must be looking towards Rutupiae, he thought, towards Tanatus and the Saxon kind, and maybe his vengeance. He had been a fool to say that he would stay one more night in this place, just because it had the smell of sanctuary. He would go back and tell Brother Ninnias that he must go now, this evening, after all. There would be the remains of a moon later, and he could be a few miles on his way, a few miles nearer to finding the little bird-catcher, before he lay down to sleep.

The shadows were creeping among the trees, and somewhere an owl hooted softly as he stooped to take up the basket again.

Brother Ninnias's voice spoke just behind him. 'I used to come out here every evening, just at owl-hoot, to watch for Rutupiae Light.'

Aquila looked round quickly at the square, brown man with the hoe on his shoulder. 'Can you see so far from here?' he asked, startled, because in a way it was as though the other's thoughts had been moving with his.

'Sometimes. It must be upward of forty miles, but I could see it in clear weather. And when there was mist or rain I knew that it was there . . . And then one night it was very late in coming; but it came at last, and my heart leapt up to see it as though it were a friend's face. And the next night, though I looked for it three times, it did not come at all. I thought, "The mist has come up and hidden it." But there was no mist that night. And then I knew that the old order had passed, and we were no more part of Rome.'

Both of them were silent awhile; then Brother Ninnias spoke again. 'It came to me later—news travels swiftly along the forest tracks—that the last Roman troops had already sailed, before that last beacon fire shone from Rutupiae. A strange thing, that.'

Aquila shot him a quick glance. 'Strange enough. What did men believe to lie behind it?'

'Ghosts—omens—all kinds of marvels.'

'But you did not believe that, I think?'

Brother Ninnias shook his head. 'I will not say that I did not believe; I should be the last man to disbelieve in marvels; but I have sometimes wondered . . . It has seemed to me that it may so well have been some poor deserter left behind when his comrades sailed. I have even thought of him as someone I know, and wondered what his story was.'

'Why should a deserter take the trouble to light Rutupiae Beacon?' Aquila demanded, and his voice sounded rough in his own ears.

'Maybe in farewell, maybe in defiance. Maybe to hold back the dark for one more night.'

'To hold back the dark for one more night,' Aquila repeated broodingly, his mind going back to that last night, after the galleys sailed, seeing again the beacon platform in the dead silver moonlight, the sudden red flare of the beacon under his hands. And two days' march away this man had been watching for it, and seen it come. In an odd way, that had been their first meeting, his and the quiet brown man's beside him; as though something of each had reached out to make contact with the other, in the sudden flare of Rutupiae Beacon. 'That was a shrewd guess,' he said.

Brother Ninnias's quiet gaze returned from the distance to rest on his face. 'You speak as one who knows.'

'I was the deserter,' Aquila said.

He had not meant to say it. He did not know that he was saying it until he heard the words hanging in the air.

But in the same instant he knew that it did not matter; not to this man.

Brother Ninnias said, 'So,' without surprise, without any questioning, simply in acceptance of what Aquila had told him.

Aquila had been so afraid of questions; but now, because Brother Ninnias had asked none, because of that odd feeling that they had reached out to each other in the last flaring of Rutupiae Light and were somehow old friends, suddenly he was talking—talking in small, bitter sentences, standing there with the willow basket forgotten in his hand, and his gaze going out over the forest in the fading light.

'You said that you wondered what his story was—the deserter who lit Rutupiae Beacon that last time . . . He found that he belonged to Britain, to the things that Rome-in-Britain stands for; not to Rome. He thought once that they were the same thing; but they're not. And so at last he deserted. He went back to his own place—his own people. Two days later, the Saxons came. They burned the farm and slew his father and the rest of the household. The deserter they bound to a tree and left for the wolves. The wolves did not come, but instead a raiding party found him and took him for a thrall. He served three years on a Jutish farm, until this spring half the settlement came to join Hengest in Tanatus, and among them the man who owned him. So he came again to Britain.'

'And from Hengest's burg, he escaped,' Brother Ninnias said.

'A man helped him to escape,' Aquila said after a moment. And the words caught a little in his throat. To no living soul, not even to this man, could he speak of Flavia in the Saxon camp.

Brother Ninnias seemed to know that he could ask a question now, for he said after a while: 'You spoke of these men who took you thrall, as a raiding band, as though they were different in that from the men who burned your home.'

'The men who burned my home were no mere raiding band,' Aquila said bitterly. 'No chance inland thrust of the Sea Wolves, that is.' He was silent a moment, his hand tightening convulsively on the plaited rim of the willow basket. 'My father was heart and soul with the Roman party who stood behind young Ambrosius. They appealed to Aetius in Gaul for help to drive out both Vortigern and the Saxons. You will know that, as all men know it, now. You will know that all the answer they ever had was that the last Roman troops left in the province were withdrawn. But Vortigern was brought word of the plan, and took no chances. He called Hengest and his war bands down from their old territory and settled them in Tanatus at the gateway to Britain; and he took his revenge on all he could reach of those who were—betrayed to him.'

He was aware of a sudden odd stillness in the man beside him. 'Among them, your father,' Brother Ninnias said.

'Among them my father; betrayed to his death by a little rat-faced bird-catcher.' Aquila almost choked.

Brother Ninnias made a small, quickly suppressed sound, and Aquila whipped round to face him. For a long moment they remained looking at each other. Then Aquila said, 'What did you say?'

'I do not think that I said anything.'

'You cried out—you know something of that bird-catcher. Something that I don't.' His eyes widened in the dusk, his lip stuck back a little over the dryness of his teeth. 'Maybe you know where he is! Tell me—you shall tell me——'

'So that you may be revenged on him?'

'So that I may repay the debt,' Aquila said in a voice suddenly hard and quiet with the intensity of his hating.

'You are too late. The debt has been repaid.'

'What do you mean? You're trying to shield him because of your monkish ideas—but you know where he is, and you *shall* tell me!'

He flung the willow basket aside, and caught the other man by the shoulders, shaking him, thrusting his own distorted face into the one that looked back at him as quietly as ever. 'Tell me! By Our Lord, you shall tell me!'

'Let me go,' Brother Ninnias said. 'I am as strong as you, possibly stronger. Do not make me put out my strength against one who has eaten my salt.'

For a few moments Aquila continued to drag him to and fro; then he dropped his hands, panting. *'Let you tell me where he is!'*

Brother Ninnias stooped and picked up his hoe and the willow basket. 'Come over here,' he said, and turned towards the nearest trees.

Aquila hesitated an instant, staring after him with narrowed eyes. Then he strode forward after the broad, brown back. A wild suspicion of the truth woke in him, even before they halted among the first of the forest shadows, at a gesture from Brother Ninnias, and he found himself looking down at a long, narrow hummock of mossy turf under an oak tree.

For a long time he remained, staring down at the grave. All the fury, all the hate, all the purpose had gone out of him. After a while he said in a dead-level voice, and still without looking up, 'Tell me what happened.'

'I told you that sometimes God sends me a guest,'

Brother Ninnias said. 'Nearly three years ago—aye, only a few nights after Rutupiae Light went out—God sent me one, sore pressed and very near to his end. A man escaped from the hands of Saxon torturers. I took him in and did for him what I could, but there is a limit beyond which the body cannot be hurt and live . . . For two nights he raved in fever, so that, sitting with him, I learned that he had been one of those who followed Ambrosius, one who had carried messages among the others, passing as a bird-catcher. And again and again he cried out against Vortigern's torturers, that he could bear no more, and cried out that he had betrayed his fellows. On the third night, he died.'

'Other men have died under torture, without speaking,' Aquila said after a moment, in a hard, level voice.

'All men's spirits are not equally strong. Are you sure of the strength of your own?'

Aquila was silent a long time, still staring down at the long hummock that seemed dissolving into the dusk. The grave of the man who had betrayed his father under torture, a man who had died because flesh and spirit had been torn apart by the Saxon torturers, and also, perhaps, because he did not wish to live. 'No,' he said at last. He had lost everything now—all that he had to love, and all that he had to hate—in three days. He looked up at last, and asked as a lost child might ask it, 'What shall I do?'

'Now that you are robbed of an old hate; robbed of the tracking down and the vengeance?' Brother Ninnias said, with a great gentleness.

'Yes.'

'I think, if it were me, that I should thank God, and look for another service to take.'

'I am not one for the holy life,' Aquila said, with an ugly bitterness in his voice.

'Nay, I did not think that you were. If you believe, as your father believed, that the hope of Britain lies with Ambrosius of the House of Constantine, let you take your father's service on you.'

For a long moment they stood facing each other across the bird-catcher's grave. Then Aquila said, 'Is it there to take? Surely the cause of the Roman party was finished nearly three years ago.'

'It is not so easy to kill a cause that men are prepared to die for,' Brother Ninnias said. 'Come back to the evening food now, and eat, and sleep again; and in the morning let you go to young Ambrosius in Arfon.'

Aquila turned his head to look westward, where the afterglow still flushed behind the trees and the first star hovered like a moth above the tree tops.

'To Arfon,' he said. 'Yes, I will go to Arfon, and seek out this Ambrosius.'

10

The Fortress of the High Powers

A LITTLE before sunset on an autumn evening, Aquila was leaning against the trunk of a poplar tree beside the gate of the principal inn of Uroconium, idly watching the broad main street, and the life of the city that came and went along it. Inn courtyards were good places; often there were odd jobs to be done for guests and a few coins to be earned. He knew; he had hung about inn courtyards all across Britain in the past few months. A yellow poplar leaf came circling down through the still air past his face, and added itself to the freckled, moon-yellow carpet already spread around his feet. But the evening was as warm as summer, with the still, backward-looking warmth that returns sometimes when summer is long past; and the little group of ladies who came out from the Forum gardens across the way wore only light wraps, pretty and fragile as flower petals, over their indoor tunics. One of them carried a late white rose-bud, and another sniffed at a ball of amber in her hand, and they laughed together, softly, as they went on up the street. A man came out through the Forum gate, with a slave behind him carrying his books. Maybe he was a lawyer. How odd that there were still towns where the Magistrates sat to administer the laws and discuss the water supply, and women walked abroad with balls of amber in their hands for its delicate fragrance. The town was shabby as all towns were, the walls that had gleamed so white against the distant mountains of Cymru, stained and pitted here and there with fallen plaster, the streets inclined to be dirty. But there were things to buy in the shops, and on the citizens' faces a look of unawareness that made Aquila want to climb on to the mounting-block and cry out to them, 'Don't you know what is happening all round the coasts? Haven't you *heard*?'

'I suppose this is so far inland that they have never felt the Saxon wind blowing. But what hope can there be for us if only our coastwise fringes understand?'

He did not realize that he had spoken the thought aloud, until a voice behind him said in heartfelt agreement, 'The same question occurs to me from time to time,' and he swung round to find a man standing in the courtyard gateway; a big man, with a plump, pale face spreading in blue, shaven chins over the dark neck-folds of his mantle, and eyes that were soft and slightly bulging like purple grapes.

'You speak, I think, as one who has felt the Saxon wind blow somewhat keenly?' said the man.

'Aye,' Aquila agreed.

The full dark eyes moved in leisurely fashion from the white scar of the thrall-ring on his neck, down to his feet bound in dusty straw and rags, and up again to his face ' . . . And have walked far today.'

'I am on a journey, and since I have no money for horse hire, I walk.'

The man nodded, and slipped a hand into his girdle, and held out a sesterce. 'So. This will at least give you a meal and a night's shelter before your next march. I also have little love for the Saxon kind.'

Aquila stiffened. He was hungry, and he had been hanging round the inn in the hope of earning the price of a meal; but earning, not begging. He could not afford pride, but it rose in his throat all the same. 'Tell me what I may do to earn it.'

The other smiled, raising his brows a little. 'Some days ago I left a piece of broken mule-harness to be mended at the saddler's by the West Gate; and since tomorrow I continue my own journey, I am in need of it. Do you go and fetch it for me.'

'What name shall I tell them, so that they will give it to me?'

'Say that Eugenus the Physician sent you to collect his mule-bridle that he left three days ago.' He fished again in his girdle. 'Here is some more money to pay for the mending. Now take the other without hurt to your pride.'

And so, with the price of a meal stowed in the breast of his ragged tunic, Aquila set out for the West Gate.

The saddler had not finished his work, so he got a meal in a cheap cook-shop while he waited; and it was near to dusk when he came again up the broad main street towards the inn, the mended bridle in his hand chiming with every step he took, for the fine crimson leather was hung with tiny bronze and silver bells. He had expected to hand the thing over to one of the inn slaves and go his way, but when he came into the courtyard, the man he spoke to jerked a thumb towards the outside stair that led to a kind of gallery and said with obvious disapproval: 'You're to take it up yourself, he says. It's the first door at the head of the stair; you can't miss it.'

So Aquila went up the stairs, and turned to the first door he came to, and a few moments later, having knocked and been bidden to enter, he stood in a small chamber shadowy with mingled dusk and candlelight, that looked into the inn courtyard. Eugenus, who was standing at the window, looked round as he entered. 'Ah, you have brought it, then.'

'Did you think that I had run off with it? It must be worth quite a handful, with all those little chiming bells.' Aquila laid the gay harness across the foot of the sleeping-couch, and a small bronze coin on the table beside the wine-flask that stood there. 'I would have come back sooner, but it was not finished, and I had to wait. There is a denarius change from the money that you gave me to pay for it.'

Eugenus took up the coin, looked at Aquila a moment, as though wondering whether to offer it to him, and then returned it to his girdle and reached instead for the wine-flask and a cup of faintly honey-coloured glass. 'I did not think that you had run off with it, no. I think that you have eaten since I saw you last, and therefore it will do you no harm to drink before you go.'

Aquila was suddenly on his guard, his reason telling him that Eugenus was not the type of man to be asking every chance, dusty wayfarer he met into his chamber to drink with him. He demanded bluntly, 'Why did you leave word that I was to bring the harness up to you myself, and why do you seek to keep me here, now that I have brought it?'

Eugenus poured out the wine before he answered, and pushed the wine-cup across the table. 'For a very simple and a very innocent reason. I am interested in people—in interesting people, that is to say.'

Aquila frowned. 'You find me interesting?'

'I—think so, yes.' The physician lowered himself on to the couch and leaned back, fingering his stomach as gently and sensitively as though it were somebody else's, with a pain in it. But his eyes never left Aquila's face. 'You have a very bitter face, my young friend, and I think that it was not always so. Also there are about you certain contradictions. You are—forgive me—extremely ragged and dusty, and carry what looks very much like the scar of a Saxon thrall-ring on your neck; you are without the price of a meal; yet when I proffer you a sesterce in charity, you stiffen, and give me to understand that if you may earn it, and not otherwise, you will do me the favour of accepting it. And all the while you wear on your hand a signet ring that would pay for many meals.'

'It was my father's ring, and it is not for sale,' Aquila said.

'Your father being dead, I take it? Maybe at the Saxons' hands?'

Aquila was silent a moment, facing the questing interest in the full, dark eyes. His mouth was tight and hard. 'My father was killed by the Saxon kind, three years ago,' he said at last, 'and I was carried off into thraldom. My father's ring came to me again in a way that does not matter to anyone save myself. I escaped from the Saxon camp on Tanatus and now I am on a journey. Does that answer all your questions?'

Eugenus smiled; a smile that was big and slow like himself; but there was all at once a new alertness in his gaze. 'What an inquisitive creature I am. This journey— where does it lead you?'

'Westward, into the mountains.'

'So. That is a long journey. *It is all of two hundred miles from Venta to the Mountains.*'

Aquila, who had taken up the cup of wine, set it down again with great care, as though he were afraid of spilling it. He felt exactly as though he had been jolted in the stomach, and the memory of the terrace steps at home and the sharp brown face of the bird-catcher sprang out before his inner eye. There was a long silence, and then he looked up. 'Why did you say that?'

'To see if the phrase meant anything to you, and it does, doesn't it?'

'My father was one of Ambrosius's men; it was so that he died by Vortigern's order,' Aquila said harshly. 'What made you guess that the old password would mean anything to me?'

Eugenus made a deprecating gesture of one hand—a plump hand, unexpectedly small for such a big man. 'Oh, it was nothing so definite as a guess. Merely the wildest arrow loosed in the dark, that could do no harm if it missed its target.'

'Who are you?' Aquila demanded.

'I was personal physician to Constantine when he ruled in Venta Belgarum. Now I serve Ambrosius his son in the same capacity, and occasionally, as at present, as a strictly unofficial envoy.'

There was another silence, and then Aquila said, 'Do you believe in blind chance?'

'Meaning, do I believe it was by blind chance that you, on your way, as I take it, to lay your sword—if you had one—at Ambrosius's feet, should fall in with Ambrosius's envoy in the gateway of the Golden Grapevine at Uroconium?'

Aquila nodded.

Eugenus puckered his lips a little. 'Blind chance has about it, somehow, the ugly sound of despair; a world without form or meaning. Let us say that if it was chance, it was a kindly one. For me a most fortunate one; for tomorrow, having completed my mission here, or rather, failed to complete it with any success—as you say, this is so

far inland that they have not felt the Saxon wind
blowing—I return to Ambrosius in the mountains. And
since I am by nature a sociable creature, I shall be
delighted to have company on the road.'

The river rushed and sang and dawdled beside the
track, and on either side the mountains soared upwards,
out of the tawny woodlands into bare, mist-scarfed rock
and fading bell heather. The clop of the mule's hooves
and the jingle of little bells that seemed out of place in the
great solitude nagged at Aquila's ears as he trudged beside
the beast on which Eugenus rode. Eugenus sat slumped in
the saddle, sighing and snorting. He was soft; one of those
unfortunates who never seem to get hardened by the
things that harden and toughen most people; but his spirit
rose above the flabbiness of his big body: Aquila had
learned that in the week and more that they had travelled
together.

A week and more that had brought them up from
Uroconium among its orchards and water-meadows, into
the wild heart of the Arfon Mountains. 'Eryri, the Home
of the Eagles,' Eugenus had said when first they saw the
distant mass of interlocking peaks against the sunset, with
Yr Widdfa standing like a king in their midst, and Aquila
thought that the name was a fitting one.

Presently the valley opened before them, and the track
dipped to skirt the alder-grown fringes of a lake. Faint
mist hung over the water, rising already among the
alders, and creeping up the glens and corries of the far
mountain-sides that were already blue with the first
twilight of the autumn evening. Rising out of the mist, as
he looked away southward beyond the foot of the lake,
Aquila saw a great, round hill standing boldly out from
the mountains behind, as though to close the valley; and

caught even at that distance the trace of rampart walls that lay like a coiled snake about and about and about the huge, up-thrusting mass of it.

'Ah-h-h!' Eugenus heaved a gusty and heartfelt sigh of relief. 'Dynas Ffaraon! And never did I see a more welcome sight, for I am saddle-sore from the crown of my head to the soles of my feet.' And then, glancing about him at the mist creeping up over the matted heather and bog myrtle, 'Also I think that we have arrived just in time, for poor, fat, comfort-loving creature that I am, I have no liking for riding blind in one of our mountain mists.'

Aquila nodded, his gaze fixed on the fortress hill that seemed to close the valley. 'And so that is Ambrosius's stronghold,' he said, and there was both wonder and a faint distrust in his tone.

'That is Ambrosius's stronghold from the autumn round again to the spring. It was old before the Legions drove their first road through the mountains to build Segontium on the coast, and has served many princes in its time.' Eugenus gave him a glance of amused understanding. 'You find it not to your liking?'

'Maybe it was well enough for some wild mountain princeling of the old time,' Aquila said.

'But not for Ambrosius the son of Constantine, the last hope of Britain? You must realize that this old hill fortress has always been the ruling-place of the Lords of Arfon, and as such it has a power in men's minds that Segontium of the Legions could never have; though it is to Segontium that he calls his young men for training in the summer. Not for nothing is it called Dynas Ffaraon, the Fortress of the High Powers . . . Also let you not forget that it was from this hill fort that Constantine came down in his day, to drive the Saxons into the sea.'

Aquila looked up at the big, weary man on the mule's

back, and asked the question that he had been on the edge
of asking many times since Uroconium. 'Will Ambrosius
ever come down from the mountains as his father did? Is
it a living cause, Eugenus, or a dead one that men serve
because they loved it when it was alive?'

'Speaking for myself,' Eugenus said after a moment, 'I
think that I might die for a dead cause, but I do not think,
I really do *not* think, my young friend, that I could bring
myself to ride up and down the world on anything so
uncomfortable as a mule, in its service.'

And they went on in silence, the mist thickening little by
little about them. Aquila had accepted what Eugenus had
said, but his uneasiness remained. He had thought of
young Ambrosius as the leader of men like his father, but
now he began to realize that the son of Constantine was
something very much more complicated than that. Not
only the leader of the Roman party, but the Lord of
Arfon, a man belonging to two worlds. Was he, after all,
only another Vortigern?

Slowly the fortress hill drew nearer until it towered right
above them in the mist and the lake was left behind;
Aquila saw that it did not after all close the valley, but left
a narrow pass through which both the track and the river
ran on. A rocky path swung right-handed, rounding some
stone-walled cattle enclosures, and took the steep upward
slope at a bound; and as Aquila took hold of the mule's
head-gear to help the poor brute, suddenly out of the mist
that was growing thicker every moment there loomed on
either side of them the great, rough-hewn walls of the first
defences. The path squeezed its way through, and
plunged on upward. In the softer and more level places it
was a slithering quagmire, at others it ran out on to bare,
mist-wet rock. Other great ramparts, part man-made, part
natural outcrop, loomed through the drifting whiteness as

the path went leaping and looping upward; and Aquila sensed people near him, and glimpsed the crouching shapes of turf-roofed bothies among the rocks and hazel scrub, for it seemed that all up the slopes of the fortress hill, wherever there was foothold for a bothy, men had their living-places. But they met nobody until they were about half-way up. Then a young man with a couple of huge, rough-coated hounds in leash came round the next corner out of the mist, and stopped at sight of them. 'Sa ha! Eugenus! I thought it must be you when I heard that fairy chiming of mule bells. What news of the outer world?'

Eugenus brought his weary mule to a halt. 'None that cannot wait until I have first seen Ambrosius. What news of the world here, Brychan?'

The other shrugged. 'What news is there ever, here in the mountains? You have come in a good time, though. Belarius has had his thigh laid open by a boar, and that fool Amlodd doesn't seem able to do much about it.'

Eugenus sighed. 'Other men may rest at their journey's end, but so sure as I return weary from distant parts, somebody waits for me with a fever or a gored leg! Where is he?'

'In his hut.'

'I'll go round and take a look at him as soon as I reach the top—if I ever do. I swear by Æsculapius's Rod, this track grows steeper and longer as the years go by.'

Eugenus was already urging his mule on again; but the young man still stood directly in his path. A very tall young man in a close-fitting tunic of many-coloured plaid, with a smooth cap of darkly golden hair and a laughing, insolent face. He flicked a long finger towards Aquila. 'Who is this that you have collected on your travels?'

'A friend,' Eugenus said. 'Maybe he will tell you his name himself, later, if you ask him.'

The young man looked at Aquila, and Aquila looked back. 'So? I may ask him—some time, if I chance to remember,' the young man said coolly.

The frown that was always between Aquila's brows deepened. 'If you do, I would suggest that you ask in a more courteous manner.'

Again they looked at each other, with a quarrel smouldering between them; and then suddenly laughter won in the young man's face. 'It may be that I will even do that!' He stepped aside, flinging up his hand in greeting and farewell to Eugenus, and went on down the track.

Aquila stood a moment, still frowning, looking after him as he merged into the twilight and the mist, then turned once more to the steep climb as Eugenus, saying blandly, 'Shall we go on?' shook the reins and urged his tired mule into movement again.

The track levelled for a few yards, then swung inward and upward, cutting through the side of a sheer outcrop of black rock, and looking up Aquila saw the innermost ramparts close above him, and a tall man leaning on a spear in the gateway, with nothing but the wet, smoking mist behind him.

A short while later he was walking over the hill crest into that mist, alone, while Eugenus, tumbling from the mule's back like a sack of peat, went to tend his patient.

'Go up to the Fire-hall,' Eugenus had said. 'You can see the roof ridge over the lift of the ground yonder. It must be close on supper time, and Ambrosius may be there already. If he is not, wait for me.'

But the mist had become a dense whiteness, salt tasting on his lips, that wreathed about him like a wet smoke out of which the huts and bothies loomed and were lost in the fading light. The roof ridge of Ambrosius's Fire-hall had dissolved into the mist, as though it had never been. Maybe he had been a fool to refuse when the man who took over the mule had offered to come with him. It had been a friendly offer, and once he would have accepted it gladly. But he turned away from all things that were friendly now. He held on in what he thought was the right direction. There was peat reek in the air, and the tang of horse-droppings and the fat smell of cooking; he heard cattle lowing in the mist, and knew that people were coming and going about their usual business, but saw no one of whom to ask his way. Suddenly the ground dipped beneath his feet, and he found himself on the edge of a little hollow with the gleam of water at the bottom of it. He halted, and as he stood there his ear caught very faintly the struck notes of a harp that seemed to rise from that gleam of water. Through the mist, he made out the crouching shapes of a cluster of huts; and from the doorway of the largest came the faint, amber gleam of firelight. At all events there must be someone down there to tell him where he was. So he turned his steps down into the little hollow.

A few moments later he stood on the threshold of the largest hut, between the swirling mist and the firelight. The fire burned on a raised hearth in the midst of the big, round house-place, and all the place was fragrant with the smoke of peat and wild apple logs that hung in a blue haze under the crown of the roof, and the fluttering flame-light showed Aquila, at that first swift glance, the glint of weapons along the walls and hanging from the king-post, and that for the most part they were the long swords and small, round bucklers of Roman Cavalry. But if the hut was an armoury, clearly it was a living-place as well. On the creamy, spread ram-skins of the bed-place an old man sat with his harp on his knee, his head bent over it as though he slept, and his fingers plucking the shining strings so softly and wanderingly that it was as though he played in his sleep. And beside the hearth a man with a pouchy face and a general air of having run to seed, but something in the set of his shoulders that made Aquila instantly think of the parade-ground none the less, stood looking down at a third who crouched on one knee, tracing something with a charred stick on the flagged floor beside the hearthstone. A slight, dark man, this, of about Aquila's own age, in a rough, home-spun tunic, and a sheepskin with the fleece inside belted about his waist for a mantle, but a narrow gold fillet round his head, such as Aquila had seen the Celtic nobles wear before now.

'Aye, it is well enough, though the bend of the Tamesis should be somewhat sharper,' the man with drilled shoulders was saying. 'If you make that map many times more, I am thinking that you will be able to make it blindfold.'

'There is always something new, Valarius,' the dark young man said, speaking in Latin with an accent that was somehow just a little too pure, as though it were not quite his native tongue. 'And I must be able to carry it in my head, so that I have but to shut my eyes to see it all here on the hearth, as a Royal Eagle in the sky must see the whole of Britain spread below him.' He looked up, and saw Aquila in the doorway, and rose, the charred stick still in his hand. 'I greet you, stranger. Have you some message for me?'

Aquila shook his head. 'I seek Ambrosius, Prince of Britain, and was told that I might find him in the Fire-hall. But I have lost the Fire-hall in this fiend's brew of a mist—and seeing your firelight and hearing your harper——'

The young man tossed the charred stick into the flames. 'It is early yet, and Ambrosius will not have gone to the Fire-hall. What is it that you want with him?'

'If I had a sword, I should say "To lay it at his feet".'

For a moment they stood looking at each other in the firelight, while the old harper still fingered the shining strings, and the other man looked on with a gleam of amusement lurking in his watery blue eyes. But Aquila was not looking at him. He was looking only at the dark young man, seeing that he was darker even than he had thought at first, and slightly built in a way that went with the darkness, as though maybe the old blood, the blood of the People of the Hills, ran strong in him. But his eyes, under brows as straight as a raven's flight-pinions, were not the eyes of the Little Dark People, that were black and unstable and full of dreams, but a pale, clear grey lit with gold that gave the effect of flame behind them.

'But you have no sword,' the dark young man said.

'I had once.'

'Tell me how you lost it.'

Afterwards, Aquila never knew how it was that he neither questioned the dark man's right to ask, nor guessed the truth about him. Maybe the mist had got into his head—mists were notoriously unchancy things. He came in from the doorway without knowing that he did so, and standing beside the hearth with the fragrant smoke of the burning apple logs fronding across his face, he gave account of himself in a few brief, harsh sentences, much as he had done to Eugenus. 'So I came west to take my father's service upon me if that may be,' he ended, 'not loving greatly either the Saxon kind or the Red Fox.'

'Not loving greatly either the Saxon kind or the Red Fox,' the dark young man echoed broodingly. 'Yes, there are things easier to forgive than the murder of one's father.' He stood looking at Aquila for a few moments; a long look, a hard look. Then he turned and took down from among the weapons that hung on the king-post a long cavalry sword in a rough, wolfskin sheath. He drew it with a swift, controlled gesture—swiftness and control were in all he did—ran his eye along the brightness of the blade, and sheathing it again, held it out, hilt foremost. 'Here is your sword.'

Aquila's hand moved involuntarily to close round the familiar grip. But in the act, he checked, his head up and the frown deepening between his brows; and then a sudden suspicion of the truth dawned on him. 'Do you usually decide who Ambrosius shall take into his service?'

The dark young man smiled—a swift flash of a smile that seemed to kindle his whole narrow face. 'Usually—I *am* Ambrosius, Prince of Britain.'

Aquila was silent a long moment. Then he said, 'Yes, I should have known that . . . May I serve you as truly as my father did, my Lord Ambrosius.' He put out his hand again, and his fingers closed round the plain, workmanlike bronze hilt.

So Aquila took his father's service upon him. It wasn't as good as love; it wasn't as good as hate; but it was something to put into the emptiness within him; better than nothing at all.

The Young Foxes

ON a day in early spring, Aquila came up from the
level valley to the south of Dynas Ffaraon, where
the wild, leggy two-year-olds singled out from the
horse herds were gathered for breaking. The Celts were all
horse-breeders and breakers, and now it seemed that
every sheltered glen in Arfon had its herds of brood
mares, its long-legged, tangle-maned colts who would one
day be the horses of the British Cavalry. Aquila, cavalry
trained as he was, had worked with the breakers all winter.
If he worked hard enough and long enough, spending
mind and strength and skill in the battle with some
wild and whirling young stallion, and came back to
Ambrosius's Fire-hall so tired that sleep closed over him
almost before the evening meal was eaten, it was easier
not to think, not to remember.

The snows were melting on the high southern face of
Yr Widdfa, and the sound of running water was everywhere, mingling with the wild, sweet, bubbling call of
curlews from the high heather slopes above the valley; and
the hazel scrub along the skirts of the fortress hill was
dappled mealy gold with catkins. The strangeness was
gone from the fortress hill, no mist hung above it now save
the faint blue haze of cooking-fires, as Aquila looked up at

it. It was just a place that he knew, as he knew other places, with people that he knew in it: old Finnen the Harper, and Valarius with his pouchy red face and watery blue eyes, who had been of Constantine's body-guard in his better days; fat Eugenus, and the lean and fiery little priest Eliphias, with his prophet's eye; Brychan with his two great hounds—the men, mostly young, who formed a kind of inner circle, a brotherhood, round Ambrosius, and whom he called his Companions.

He headed for the winding cleft in the hillside where the trickle from the fortress spring in its little hollow came down. It was a climb for goats, but it saved going round to pick up the track on the north side of the hill. There was a thin warmth from the sun on the back of his neck as he climbed, and a flittering of tits among the still-bare black-thorn bushes that arched over the little thread of water, and the small purple flowers of the butterwort cushioned the wet, starling-coloured rocks. More than half-way up, where the cleft widened and the freshet had worn a tiny pool for itself among rocks and tree-roots, he found a small boy and a hound puppy very intent on a hole under a brown tumble of last year's fern. He would have passed by without speaking and left them to it, but the small boy sat up and grinned at him, thrusting back a shock of hair the warm, silvery-mouse colour of a hayfield in June, and the puppy thumped its tail; there was something so irresistibly friendly about both of them that he stopped, without meaning to, pointing at the hole.

'Is it a grass snake?'

The boy nodded. 'We have been watching for him a long while, Cabal and I. He came out yesterday. A monster!' He hooked an arm round the puppy's neck. 'When he comes out again, I am going to catch him and take him up to show Ambrosius.'

Artorius—Artos, most people called him, meaning a bear—was Ambrosius's nephew, bastard son to his brother Utha; and when Utha died, Ambrosius had taken him. From that day, Ambrosius had become Artos's private God.

Suddenly he remembered something which in his concentration on the grass snake he had forgotten; Aquila saw his eyes darken with excitement in his square, brown face. 'Did you hear the messenger come?'

'No,' Aquila said, his foot already on the next step of the climb. 'What messenger was that, then?'

'From Canovium. His horse was all in a smother. He said that Vortigern has put away his real wife and married Hengest's daughter instead, and given Hengest a *huge* piece of land, that wasn't his to give, for a bride piece!'

Aquila brought his foot down again. 'Since when have Ambrosius's messengers told their news to Artos the bear cub?'

The boy nodded, gravely vehement. 'He didn't tell me, of course. But it is true! All the Dun is buzzing with it.' He sat up straighter, his eyes fixed on Aquila's face. 'They say she's very beautiful—Hengest's daughter.'

'She is,' Aquila said.

'Have you seen her?'

'Yes, when I was a thrall in the Jutish camp.'

'What is she like?'

'A golden witch in a crimson gown.'

'Oh,' said Artos, digesting this. He brushed the hair of the puppy's neck up the wrong way, parting it between his fingers as though in search of ticks. 'It's sad for Vortigern's real wife,' he said gruffly, and then, his excitement quickening again, 'What do you think will happen now? Something is *bound* to happen now!'

'Is it?' Aquila said. He stood silent a few moments,

staring at the little dark hole under the ferns, while the boy and the puppy watched him expectantly. 'Yes, I suppose it is . . . Good grass-snake hunting to you.' And he stepped over the puppy and went on up. Rowena had made her singing magic well, he thought; she had caught the Red Fox in a net of her golden hair; and what would happen now? What would the three Young Foxes do about their mother's wrongs? So much might depend on that.

But there was little time for wondering in the days that followed. For with spring running through the glens, Ambrosius was making ready to go down from Dynas Ffaraon to the coast.

The grey stone fortress of Segontium, that crouched on its low hill with its seaward ramparts reflected in the narrow straits of Môn, had been abandoned by the Legions long before they marched from Britain, and the tribesmen had taken from it all of Rome that could be carried off, and left it to the mountain foxes. But now it had been pressed into service again to help defend the coast against the Scots from Erin who swarmed all along the western shores in the raiding season, its broken walls patched up, its fallen roofs replaced with bracken thatch. There was fire again on its cold hearths and horses in its stable rows. Here Ambrosius made his headquarters while spring drew on, and day by day the old grey fortress became fuller of crowding life as the young men of the little standing army that he had been gathering in the last few years came in for their summer training. And in the grain-lands of Môn across the Straits men ploughed, and sowed the barley, while the coastwise guards kept watch westward for the first dark sails of the Scots raiders.

But the Scots were late that year, and still there had been no sign of them, and no more news of the outside world, when Ambrosius went north for a few days, with a handful of his chosen Companions, to Aber of the White Shells, at the place where the northern road from Canovium came down through the mountains to the coast.

On the third day that they were at Aber, they had been out with Dogfael the Chieftain and some of his warriors, trying their horses against each other on the hard, wave-rippled sands that stretched towards Môn; and now they were heading back towards the dunes that fringed the coast. The wind blustered in from the sea, setting the horses' manes streaming sideways, and the gulls wheeled mewing against the blue-and-grey tumble of the sky; and Aquila, riding a little aside from the rest as usual, caught for a moment from the wind and the gulls and the wet sand and the living, leaping power of the young red mare under him, something of the joy of simply being alive that he had taken for granted in the old days. He still wasn't certain how he came to be there, one of the inner circle, one of Ambrosius's chosen Companions; it was a thing that had grown naturally through the winter. But suddenly for that one moment he was glad that it was so.

As they swept inland, a gap widened in the dunes where the stream came down. He could see the bracken-thatched huddle of the village now, at the mouth of the valley that licked like a green flame into the dun and grey and purple of the mountains; and beyond it the Legion's road that came plunging down from the high mountain saddle. And far up that road he could see a puff of dust with a seed of blackness at its heart; a seed which, even as he watched, became a horseman riding at full gallop.

The others had seen it at the same moment. Ambrosius spoke to Dogfael riding beside him, and urged his black stallion into a canter, the rest following. Aquila, driving his heel into the red mare's flank, found himself riding beside Brychan—Brychan of the two great hounds, who could take the harp from old Finnen and charm a bird off a tree with his playing, but whose chief joy in life was the picking of quarrels. Brychan had come to him, a while after their first encounter, and asked his name with an elaborate show of deference, long after he must have known it perfectly well, and Aquila had longed to put the puppy across his knee and teach him manners with the flat of his hand. But he was used to Brychan now, and there was a kind of armed peace between them, within which they got on well enough together. Brychan cast a quick glance at him over his shoulder, and grinned. 'If it is news that must travel at that pace, then surely it is news to melt the snows of Yr Widdfa!'

They lost sight of the road for a few moments among the dunes, and when they swept through on to the landward side, the wild rider was already past the village and coming on towards them at the same tearing gallop. A few moments later he had brought his rough-coated pony to a plunging halt, and dropped from its back; a young, round-faced warrior, looking from Dogfael to Ambrosius and back again, his breast panting.

'My Lord Ambrosius—Dogfael the Chieftain—there is a band of men on the road from Canovium. They were past the Mark Stones when I saw them, and I have galloped all the way to bring you word.'

'It is not the first time that men have come down the road from Canovium,' Dogfael said.

But Ambrosius looked at the panting young warrior. 'What is different about these men?'

'My Lord Ambrosius, the three who lead them carry green branches like an embassy that comes in peace, and the heads of all three shine red as foxes' pelts in the sunshine!'

He checked, almost choking with the hugeness of the

thing he had to say. 'My Lord Ambrosius, it is in my mind that it is—the Young Foxes!'

For a moment there was absolute silence save for the crying of the gulls. Then Ambrosius said, 'I wonder if you are right,' and turned to the others about him. 'Well, we shall soon know. Valarius, Aquila, follow me.'

'I also, and some of my warriors,' Dogfael said quickly.

'Neither you, nor any of your warriors, I think.'

But Valarius seconded the Chieftain, his watery eyes full of urgent trouble. 'Sir, you should have more of us with you. It may be a trick!'

Before Ambrosius could answer, Brychan flung up his head and laughed. 'Valarius the cautious thinks maybe of his own skin! Best take me in his stead, sir.'

The old soldier swung round on him with his hand on the hilt of his sword. 'Why, you—you young whelp! Let you say that again——' His face was darkly mottled and he breathed through flaring nostrils with a rage that seemed to Aquila, watching, to be out of all proportion to what had called it up. Surely the fool had known Brychan long enough to understand that this was merely Brychan being himself!

'If you want to fight me, I am most joyfully all yours, when we ride back again,' Brychan said lightly. 'Don't drink any more before then; it makes your sword hand unsure.'

Ambrosius's voice cut quietly into the flaring quarrel. 'Peace, my brothers! I have other things to do than beat up your swords, either now or later. Brychan, your manners grow worse as the days go by. Valarius, have you not sense to make allowances for a half-broken cub?' And while Brychan shrugged, and Valarius sat gnawing his lower lip, he turned to Dogfael. 'If these men come in friendship, I should do ill to ride to meet them with a swarm of armed men about me.'

But it was Valarius who answered, grimly sticking to his point. 'And if they do *not* in truth come in friendship?'

His voice was shaking, and Aquila, glancing at his bridle hand, saw that it was shaking too, and realized that there was something here that he did not understand.

Ambrosius was already wheeling his horse towards the road; he looked round at them. 'One man with a dagger under his cloak would be as like to succeed as three men with a war band behind them . . . If it is God's will that I am to lead Britain, then I shall not die as my father did at a murderer's hand, with my work undone. If I die so, then you and Eugenus and old Finnen with his harp had all your pains for nothing, when you carried me off that night, and after all it is not God's will that I should lead Britain.'

He struck his heel into the black stallion's flank, and the great brute broke forward from a stand into a canter; and he was away, his dark cloak lifting and spreading behind him. Aquila and Valarius heeled their own horses to a canter after him, and so, with only his two chosen Companions, Ambrosius rode up towards the mountain pass, to meet the three red-haired riders.

The road swept on and up, the great mountain mass that thronged about Yr Widdfa towering dark as a gathering thunder storm on either side. Presently they were in a different world from the green valley and the white sands of Aber left far behind, a high, wide-skyed, empty world, with no sound beyond the beat of their horses' hooves save the wind through the tawny mountain grasses, and the sharp cry of a golden eagle that hung circling above the crags. Then the road lifted over the mountain shoulder, and the next long, looping stretch lay clear ahead, with a distant knot of horsemen sweeping towards them along it.

'So, here we meet our guests,' Ambrosius said, and striking his heel again into the black's flank, broke forward into a full gallop, Aquila and Valarius behind him. And so the two knots of horsemen thundered towards each other, with the dust of early summer rising behind them. Aquila saw three men riding ahead of the stranger band; three men whose flying cloaks made points of vivid colour in the pale mountain air, one saffron, one emerald, and one, whose wearer rode at the very point of the arrowhead of wild riders, glowing violet; and the heads of all three shone red as a fox's pelt in the sunshine. Nearer and nearer they swept, until the two dust-clouds were almost one, and Ambrosius reined the black stallion back on its haunches, in full gallop, plunging and snorting, the great round hooves scraping along the ground. There were a few moments of trampling chaos as the sweating horses plunged under their riders, fighting for their heads; and then the dust sank a little, and the two knots of horsemen were facing each other with a spear's length of road between. The man in the violet cloak wheeled his tiger-spotted mount with superb horsemanship, and brought him out from among his companions, almost with a dancing step; and Aquila, still soothing his own red mare as she fidgeted under him, recognized the white, proud face under the flaming crest of hair, and the hooded falcon he carried on his fist, just as he had carried it in Hengest's Mead Hall a year ago.

'I greet you, strangers. Who are you that come over the mountains with green branches in your hands?' Ambrosius asked, as the last of the dust-cloud drifted away.

Vortimer lowered the spray of birch leaves that he held in his bridle hand, and sat for an instant lithe and haughty in the saddle, looking Ambrosius full in the face; and, watching him, Aquila thought suddenly of a purple saffron crocus—the same pride, the same silken sheen. Then he said, 'We three are the sons of Vortigern the High King, and we would speak with Ambrosius Aurelianus, Lord of Arfon.'

Ambrosius, sitting his fidgeting black stallion, looked back with a quieter and cooler pride. 'I am Ambrosius Aurelianus, Prince of Britain,' he said; and then, 'To all who come in friendship, I give welcome; to a kinsman most of all.'

Aquila looked at them quickly. He had forgotten that they were cousins, the dark man and the red ones.

Vortimer bent his head in acknowledgement of both rebuke and welcome. 'My Lord Ambrosius, Lord of Arfon and Prince of Britain, we come to lay our swords at your feet and be your men if you will have it so.'

'Deserting the standard of Vortigern your father, to serve under mine?'

There was a low, angry muttering from the men behind. The two younger brothers stared straight before them, frowning. Vortimer spoke for them again, his head up and the mountain wind lifting the red hair on his forehead. 'My Lord Ambrosius will maybe have heard that our father has put aside Severa our mother, to take in her place the golden Saxon witch who is Hengest's daughter. My lord will have heard also that he has given much land east of Tanatus to the Saxons for a bride-gift. Therefore with our mother's wrongs burning upon us we come to lay our swords at your feet. Also we do not come alone and empty-handed. With us here are seven Chieftains who were our father's men; they will bring over their clans; and there are others besides, more than half of those that followed him—for the sake of our mother's wrongs and for the sake of British lands given over their prince's head to the Saxon kind.'

So Vortigern had gone too far, Aquila thought. Hengest, that giant with the shifting, grey-green eyes, had over-reached himself. Between them they had split the Celtic party from top to bottom, and sent more than half of them to Ambrosius. If Ambrosius would take them— and Ambrosius must take them; it would be madness to refuse; but they might be a weakness as well as an added strength.

'Are the Saxon kind, then, become yet more hateful to you than Rome has always been?' Ambrosius said levelly.

The silence held for a long moment, broken only by the soughing of the wind through the heather and the jink of a bridle-bit as a horse flung up its head. Then Vortimer spoke again for his fellows. 'My Lord Ambrosius, we are a free people, taking hardly to any yoke; but for us, now, the Saxon yoke is unthinkable above all others. Therefore we stand with you against the menace of the Saxon kind. Let you speak one word, and we will ride back with it by the road that we have come, to gather all the fighting men we may. Then, before summer's end, look for our spears against the sunrise.'

'How may I be sure that all this is not a trick to bring an army through our defences?'

'One of us three, whichever you choose, will remain here in your hands as a hostage for our good faith,' Vortimer said proudly.

Ambrosius shook his head. 'Nay, I ask no hostage.' He had come to his decision, and he was smiling. Aquila, close behind him, could hear both the decision and the smile in his voice. 'I speak the word, Vortimer my kinsman; let you ride back with it to those that follow you. But not yet. First there are many things on which we must take counsel together. I have no need of more men here in the mountains, nor space, nor fodder; my need is to

know that I can call upon them when the time comes. All
that we must speak of. Meanwhile come back with us now,
and feast among my Companions tonight, that we may
seal the covenant in mead from our mountain heather
honey.'

Vortimer looked at him a moment, not speaking. Then
he thrust the spray of birch leaves into his belt, and swung
down from the saddle, and with the bridle over his arm
and the tiger-spotted horse pacing beside him, came to set
his hand on Ambrosius's thigh, and take the oath of
allegiance on him.

'If we break faith with you, may the green earth gape
and swallow us, may the grey seas roll in and overwhelm
us, may the sky of stars fall on us and crush us out of life
for ever.'

It was an ancient oath, well suited to the mountains and
the wild scene. The two younger brothers, who had also
dismounted, came and took it after him. They would keep
faith, the Young Foxes, Aquila thought; but what of those
who followed them? Out of the knot of Chieftains,
another face looked back at him, a dark, reckless face as
dangerous as a dagger-thrust; Guitolinus somebody had
said his name was. His eyes were dark blue, and the sun
made raw turquoise flecks in them, the eyes of a fanatic,
beyond the binding of any oath.

That evening Ambrosius with his Companions and the
Young Foxes with their following feasted side by side in the
bracken-thatched hall of Dogfael. The fire cast a web of
leaping, tawny light over the ring of alert faces; over fine
wool the colour of jewels, and pied and dappled sheepskin, the blink of Irish gold from the hilt of a dagger, the
green, unwinking eyes of a hound, the fiercely flecked
breast of the hooded falcon secured by its jesses to the
back of Vortimer's seat. And all round the long hearth ran

a kind of shining, jagged thorn garland, where every man had drawn his sword and laid it before him in full view of all the rest. By ancient custom no man should bring his weapons to such a gathering, but on the coast in these days no man went unarmed.

Aquila's neighbour was a middle-aged man, Cradoc by name, with sandy hair like the ruffled feathers of a bird in a high wind, and a face full of old regrets. He was a Chieftain from farther south, and found all things here in the north of Cymru to be less good than in his own mountains.

'In Powys,' he was saying, 'where I have my hall, the turf is richer even at mid-winter than this valley is now; and the soil is red and strong. I have an apple orchard running to the river, and in the autumn every tree in it bows to the ground under its weight of apples.' And then, looking regretfully into his cup, 'Our mead is better than this, too.'

Ambrosius rose in his place, that on other nights was Dogfael the Chieftain's, holding high his golden cup, and turned to Vortimer beside him. 'I drink to our friendship, and the new bond between us.'

He drank, and gave the cup to the Young Fox, who took it from him with a bend of the head, and stood for a moment spear-straight in the firelight with the great cup shining between his hands. Then, almost in the act of drinking, he checked, and his head whipped up, as, clear in the hush that had fallen on the hall, from somewhere seaward beyond the village rose a long-drawn cry.

There was a moment's tingling silence, while the men about the fire looked each into his neighbour's eyes, and then a scatter of shouting broke out in the village itself.

'It is in my mind that the Scots wind blows again from Erin,' Ambrosius said, and stooped for his sword.

As though the action had broken a spell of stillness, a splurge of voices burst up in the hall; and every man had sprung to his feet, catching up his weapons, when a man burst through the doorway into the firelight, crying, 'The Scots! They're close in shore, heading for the bay!'

Ambrosius whirled about on them, his light eyes blazing, his sword naked in his hand. 'We are to fight our first battle together sooner than we thought! Come, my brothers!'

The big, silver-fringed clouds were drifting overhead before a light sea wind as they headed for the shore, joined as they ran by every man and boy in Aber of the White Shells, and the moon rode high in the deep blue of the sky between. The tide was in, covering the sand where they had raced their horses a few hours earlier, and out on the tossing, quicksilver surface of the bay three vessels showed dark: low amidships, high at stem and stern like venomous sea creatures with head and tail upreared to strike: many-legged creatures, for the sails were down and they were creeping in under oars.

'Down into the cover of the dunes,' Ambrosius ordered. 'Let them not see you until the ships are fairly beached and I give the word. So maybe there shall be three Scots ships the less to come raiding our shores in another summer.' And the order ran from man to man. 'Get down—keep out of sight!'

As he crouched in the lee of the furze tangle, Aquila's view of the shore was cut off by the shoulder of the long dune where the stream came through, but that made no odds: there was nothing to do but wait until Ambrosius gave the word . . . He found that Cradoc was still at his shoulder, suddenly much happier and with the superiority of the south quite forgotten.

'Sa! This is better than feasting!' Cradoc said softly.

Aquila nodded, shifting his hand a little on the grip of his buckler. Better than feasting; there was not much pleasure for him in feasting, these days; but in that moment of waiting there was a keen, cold pleasure as sharp as the blade in his hand. The moments passed, silent save for the sea wind in the furze and the creamings of the tide beyond the dunes. Then, very faintly, his straining ears caught the dip of oars; and a shiver of expectancy ran through the waiting men. A few moments more, and there came, faint but unmistakable, the light splash of men slipping overboard and the grating of a keel on the beach. A pause, and then the sounds were repeated as the second galley was run up the sand, the third following so close that Aquila could not tell where one ended and the other began. There was a grumble of orders, and a low, daring laugh. He could hear men splashing ashore through the shallows now; and he drew a deep, slow breath, his body tensing under him like that of a runner in the instant before the white garland falls. And then, on the very crest of the dune before him, Ambrosius rose with a yell, his sword above his head.

'Now! With me, my brothers!'

They saw him stand for an instant against the drifting sky; then they rose like a wave and swept after him, across the crest and down over the slipping sand.

The three raiders lay in the shallows, their dark bows on shore like so many stranded sea-beasts, and men were swarming up the beach, the moon on their weapons and the lime-whitened discs of their shields. The sea-raiders and the British—for all those who followed Ambrosius were British in that moment, with no thought of Celt or Roman—came together above the tide-line in the soft sand at the foot of the dunes, sword to sword, shield to shield, in a ragged burst of shouting. The Scots, taken by surprise when they had thought the surprise to be on their

side, attacked furiously
at first, shouting their
battle-cry as they closed
buckler to buckler and
strove to break through;
and for a time the fight
hung in the balance,
as now one side drove
forward and now the
other, the whole skir-
mish wavering this way
and that like a banner
streaming in the wind.
Aquila's ears were full
of a great yelling, and
the clash and rasp of
weapons. The soft,
shifting sand clogged his
feet and the fine lime-
dust from the enemy
shields rose white in the
moonlight. Cradoc was
still at his shoulder,

shouting some wild, rhythmic battle-song of his own
people that rose and rose above the tumult of the fighting
into a kind of triumphant raving that was horrible to hear.
From the swaying line of warriors a tall Scot leapt in with
war-axe upswung, and Cradoc's war-song ended in a
grunt. Aquila was aware of the place at his shoulder
suddenly empty, and the moonlit flash of the axe blade
raised to finish the work it had begun, and in the same
instant he had sprung astride the fallen man, who was
already struggling to his elbow among the trampling feet
of the mêlée. He took the blow, as it came whistling down,

on his upflung buckler, and the axe blade sheared through the bull's hide and beaten bronze, so that it was hacked almost in two. He bore down with all his force on the shield with the axe blade still embedded in it, and stabbed wildly with shortened sword point, and saw the Scot fling wide his arms and stagger back, gaping stupidly, as the blow went home.

He realized suddenly that the Scots were beginning to give ground, the wavering of the fighting line going all one way. Stubbornly, valiantly, fighting for every step before yielding it, they were back into the shallows now, the trampled spray sheeting up all about them in the moonlight, falling back more swiftly: no aim left them but to win back to their ships. But around the stranded ships also there was fighting, as more of the British, led by the Young Foxes, flung themselves upon the men who had been left to guard them; and suddenly, from one of the galleys, from another, from the third, yellow tongues of fire shot up, licking about the masts. Someone had brought a fire-brand from the village, and there was to be no escape for this band of raiders. A yell, a howl rose from them as they saw the flames, and they turned as a doomed boar turns at bay, to make their last stand in the shallows about their blazing ships.

The silver of the moon was ousted by the angry gold of the burning vessels as the flames leapt higher, and there was gold in the hollow of every ripple that spread shoreward; gold, and then red . . . It was over at last, and the glare of the blazing galleys shone on dead men lying like sea-wrack along the tide-line; and the sea wind and the hushing of the tide sounded clear again. The British were taking stock of their own dead and wounded, and Aquila knelt over Cradoc, helping him staunch the blood that ran from the base of his neck.

Cradoc looked up at him with a twisted smile. 'Sa! It seems that they teach men to fight under the Eagles! It was a good fight; and that I am here to say so instead of lying in the sand with my head smitten from my shoulders is a thing that I owe to you. Also it is a thing that I shall not forget.'

'In the heat of battle it is no more to ward a blow from a comrade than to ward it from oneself,' Aquila said. 'Hold still or I cannot stop this bleeding. It is not a thing for remembering afterwards.'

A few paces off, in the full glare of the flames that leapt from the snarling prow of the nearest galley, Vortimer, with his gay crocus tunic gashed and stained and sodden about him, leaned on his reddened sword and smiled at Ambrosius as he stood in the gilded foam-fringe, starkly outlined against the flames. 'It is a good covenant, and we have sealed it in blood, which is better than the mead of feasting.'

12

Brown Sister, Golden Sister

CRADOC had exaggerated the richness of his own valley, Aquila thought, as he rode down from the low saddle of the hills, following the track that the man at the ford in the last valley had pointed out to him. The place was mostly under bracken—bracken beginning to turn now, and patched with bright buttercup gold where it had been cut for litter and not yet carried; and the hall that he glimpsed below him in the bend of the valley, with its huddle of turf bothies around it, was the usual squat, heather-thatched hall of every petty Chieftain, lord of a few mountain valleys, a few hundred cattle, a few score spears. But maybe one's own valley, when one was away from it, was always richer than anyone else's; one's own orchard bore sweeter apples. Maybe even his own valley in the Down Country . . . He reined back his mind from the memory as he might have reined the red mare Inganiad back from a pit in the track before them.

It was almost a year since he had come up with Eugenus the Physician to take service with the Prince of Britain. A year in which he had made some kind of mended life for himself, some kind of place among Ambrosius's Companions, some kind of name for himself—and the name, he knew, was not altogether a pleasant one. The dark man with the scarred forehead and the frown always between his eyes had no friends. He went always in a kind of armour, and a man who does that cannot have friends. They called him the Dolphin, as old Bruni had done, because of the pattern on his shoulder; and they called him the Lone Wolf. Felix could have told them that he hadn't always been like that; Felix, with whom he had laughed, and shot wild fowl over Tanatus Marshes. But Felix was like enough dead by now in the Padus marshes in defence of Rome. They said the Vandals were pressing down Italy again.

Automatically he gathered the mare, steadying her for the stony, downward plunge of the track; but his thoughts went wandering back over the summer that had gone by since the Young Foxes had come in with their Chieftains behind them; the summer that he had spent training men as he had spent winter breaking horses, striving to hammer into wild, mounted tribesmen some idea of what made disciplined cavalry. It was odd to find himself something like a Decurion of Horse again.

Only a few weeks ago they had heard that Vortigern, deserted by his sons and most of his followers, had fled north, to the lands held by Octa and his war bands, and now Ambrosius rode south to hold counsel with his new allies. It was so that Aquila, sent ahead of the main party, was riding down into Cradoc's valley this still autumn day, to warn him that Ambrosius would be there by dusk, claiming lord's shelter for himself and his Companions as they passed by.

The Hall and its huddled bothies was drawing nearer,

and he saw the hearth-smoke rising blue against the tawny flank of the mountain beyond, and a few people moving about the kale plots and the cattle-byres. The track swung right hand, towards the village, skirting a small orchard, an orchard cradled in the loop of the river, the apples ripe on the dipping branches of the little half-wild trees; and the bright shadow of a song came into his mind.

> 'The apples are silver on the boughs, low bending;
> A tree of chiming, of singing as the wind blows by.'

But these apples were homely russet, not silver, and no wind stirred the branches; only the still, autumn sunlight slanted through the orchard, casting each tree's shadow to the foot of the next. But there was movement among the trees, a girl's laugh, and the flicker of colours under the leaves, dark red and saffron and tawny, and a deep, living blue like a kingfisher's mantle, and he realized that a group of girls were at the apple-picking.

It seemed that they became aware of the rider on the track at the same moment as he became aware of them. Their laughter stopped, and there was a moment's hush among the trees, and then two of the girls broke away from the rest, and ran back towards the Chieftain's Hall as though to carry word of his coming.

He rode on slowly, the bridle loose on Inganiad's neck. He heard the chink of a smith's hammer on anvil as he came up between the bracken-thatched bothies, and a woman coming from the weaving-shed with a piece of new cloth over her arm, the long threads still dangling where it had been cut from the loom, turned to watch him as he rode by; and a child and a hound puppy were struggling for possession of a wild cherry branch with the coral and scarlet leaves still upon it. Then, as he rode out into the open space before Cradoc's hall, he saw the two girls again, waiting for him in the doorway, and realized that they must be Cradoc's womenfolk and had run ahead to receive him as a stranger should be received, on the threshold of the house.

The taller of the two held a cup between her hands, and as he reined in and dropped from the saddle, she came forward, holding it out to him, saying in a very soft and gentle voice, 'God's greeting to you, stranger. Drink, and forget the dust of the journey.'

Aquila took the cup and drank as custom demanded. It was an ancient cup of flame-grained birch inlaid with gold and age-blackened silver, and the drink was mead; a thin mead with the aromatic tang of heather in it. He gave the cup back into her hands, looking at her for the first time, and saw that her hair was bright in the sunshine, brighter than the gold clasp at the shoulder of her tawny kirtle, and he supposed vaguely that she was pretty.

'God's Grace upon this house. The dust of the journey is forgotten.' He made the customary reply with cold courtesy. 'Is Cradoc the Chieftain here, that I may speak with him?'

'Cradoc my father is out hunting, and the other men with him,' the girl said. 'Let you come in, and be most welcome, while you wait for his return.'

'I will come in,' Aquila said. 'But since my business cannot wait for Cradoc's hunting, it seems that I must tell it to you. Ambrosius, Prince of Britain, is on the road here, and sent me ahead with word that he will be on your threshold by dusk, claiming lord's shelter for the night, for himself and eight of his Companions.'

The girl's eyes widened. 'Ambrosius? Tonight? Oh, then we must kill the pig.'

'Must you so? You have my sympathy,' Aquila said, with a flicker of contemptuous laughter.

The girl blushed scarlet, and he saw her gathering her dignity about her as though it had been an embroidered mantle. 'We must indeed. But that need not concern you. Let you come in now, and I will bring you warm water, for you are dusty and must be weary besides.'

'What of my mare?' Aquila asked.

'I will take your mare and tend her,' another voice answered him, a harder and lower voice, and looking round, he saw that the other girl had gone to Inganiad's head. He had forgotten about the other girl; a little fierce, nut-brown creature who seemed even browner by contrast with the kingfisher blue of her kirtle. Seeing his look, she smiled, but her gaze was challenging. 'I am used to horses, and I promise you that I am quite trustworthy.'

Aquila's hand tightened on the bridle. For the golden sister to bring him the Guest Cup in welcome, to bid him in and promise warm water after the dust of the journey, was no more than the duty of the mistress of the house towards the stranger within her gates; but, in some odd way, for the brown sister to take his mare and rub her down seemed a more personal thing.

'Cannot one of the men take her?' he said.

'Did you not hear Rhyanidd my sister say that our father and the men have ridden hunting?'

'All the men of the village?'

'All who are not busy in other ways. Shall I call Kilwyn from his shoeing, or Vran from his own hut where he nurses a broken ankle?'

'Ness, how *can* you?' the elder girl put in in soft distress, but neither paid any heed to her.

'I will take and tend her myself, if you will tell me where I may find the stable,' Aquila said.

'And let it be said that in my father's house a stranger must stable his own horse at the journey's end? This is so poor and outlandish a place that we must kill a pig to feed the Prince of Britain—though I daresay that pigs have been killed for him before—but at least no guest need tend his own horse.'

He realized that she was angry with him because he had laughed at her sister about the pig—no, not because he had laughed, because of the *way* he had laughed—and he liked her the better for that. Her hand was beside his on the head-stall now, and he had no choice but to let his own hand drop.

'Then it seems that I can only thank you and give you your will,' he said stiffly.

He stood a moment watching as she led the red mare away, then turned back to Rhyanidd. She was still flushed foxglove pink, and he wondered if she were going to make some sort of apology for her sister. But she did not. She said only with gentle dignity, 'And now come you in and rest, while we make all things ready for Ambrosius.' They were loyal to each other, those two.

At cow-stalling time, Ambrosius and the hunting party arrived almost together. And that night there was feasting in Cradoc's hall, and next day they rode out after wolves—Cradoc was proud of the hunting in his runs—and brought home three grizzly carcasses to be shown to the women and hung up for trophies in the hall before they were flayed and the meat given to the hounds. That night, when the feasting was over and the time came for sleep, Ambrosius sent for Aquila to attend him, instead of his armour-bearer, who, being young and weak-headed and proud of his part in the wolf hunt, had drunk too much of the thin, heather-flavoured mead, and was asleep under one of the hall benches.

The guest place reminded Aquila of the little beehive hut of Brother Ninnias, where he had slept with the gall of the Saxon thrall-ring still smarting on his neck. Only there were fine roe-deer skins on the bed-place, and feather-stuffed pillows of blue and violet cloth; and someone had set a bowl of apples on the stool beside it; apples whose smooth gold was flecked and feathered with coral colour, and the scent of them mingled with the aromatic breath of the herbs burning in the white, honey-wax candle.

Ambrosius, sitting on the bed-place, had taken an apple from the bowl, and sat turning it in his hands, examining the delicate flecking and feathering of the skin. 'What a beautiful thing an apple is. One so seldom notices . . . ' He looked up suddenly at Aquila, where he stood against the central king-post, rubbing up the bronze boss of the light wicker hunting shield that his lord had carried that day. 'Does it seem very strange to you, this life among the mountains, Dolphin?'

'Yes,' Aquila said, 'but not so strange as it did a year ago.'

'It is so familiar to me. The only life that I have known since I was nine years old.' He had returned to the apple in his hand, turning and turning it. 'It seemed strange enough to me then . . . I was brought up to wear a Roman tunic and read with a Greek tutor. I remember the baths at Venta, and the high, square rooms, and the troops of Thracian Horse trotting down the street looking as though all the world were a bad smell under their noses. It is an odd thing to belong to two worlds, Dolphin.'

'But a thing that may be the saving of Britain,' Aquila said in a moment of clear seeing. He breathed on the bronze boss and rubbed harder to get out a spot of wolf's blood. 'A leader who was all Britain, or all Rome, would be hard put to it, I'm thinking, to handle such a mixed band as we are, when the day comes for fighting.'

'When the day comes for fighting,' Ambrosius said broodingly. 'It is in my mind that next spring comes all too soon.'

There was a sudden silence. Aquila raised his eyes quickly to Ambrosius's face, finding there a white gravity which startled him, after the harp song and the easy merriment in Cradoc's hall. His hand checked in its burnishing.

'Next spring?'

'Aye, with the Saxons already beginning to hum like a swarming hive, we daren't delay an attack any longer.'

Aquila's heart was suddenly beating a little faster. So it was coming at last, the thing that they had been waiting for so long. But something that he sensed in the other man puzzled him, and he frowned. 'Daren't? Why do you wish to delay longer?'

'I suppose I sound as creeping cautious as an old man.' Ambrosius looked up again. 'Dolphin, I am as eager to be at the Saxon's throats as the wildest hothead among us. But I have to be sure. If Aetius in Gaul had sent us one legion, we could have done it; when Rome failed us I knew that it must be years before we were strong enough to take up the fight alone . . . I have to be sure; I can't afford to fail once, because I've nothing in reserve with which to turn failure into victory.'

'Have the Young Foxes not bettered things by coming over to our standard?' Aquila said after a moment.

'If I could be sure of them, yes,' Ambrosius said. 'Oh, I'm sure of the Young Foxes themselves, their personal loyalty. For the rest—I don't know. I am seldom quite sure of my own kind; we dream too many dreams, and the dreams divide us . . . That is why we must make closer ties between ourselves and these new friends of ours.'

'What sort of ties?'

Ambrosius set the apple back in the bowl with the air of coming to a decision. 'Dolphin, let you take one of Cradoc's daughters for your wife.'

At first Aquila thought it was a jest, and then he realized that it was not. Along with the rest of the Companions, he had been waited on by Cradoc's daughters; he had spoken a few words with them, but that was all.

'I have had no thought of taking any woman from her father's hearth,' he said after a moment.

'Think of it now.'

There was a long silence. The two men looked at each other levelly in the candle-light.

'Why should Cradoc give me a daughter from his hearth?' Aquila said at last. 'I am a landless man, owning nothing but my horse and my sword, both of which you gave me.'

'Cradoc will give you his daughter if you ask, because you are of my Company, and because he would have died at Aber of the White Shells, if you had not turned the blow that was meant for him.'

Aquila said, 'If it seems to Ambrosius good that there should be such ties between his folk and Vortimer's folk, then surely it is for Ambrosius himself to take a wife from the hearth of some greater prince than Cradoc.'

Ambrosius raised his head slowly, and there was a look in his eyes as though he were seeing something at a great distance. 'To lead Britain is enough for one man; with a whole heart and no other ties.'

Aquila was silent. Because of Flavia he wanted nothing to do with women, ever. They were dangerous, they could hurt too much. But he hoped that if Ambrosius had asked him to walk out of the candle-lit guest place to certain death, because in some way his death could help to bind Britain together and drive the barbarians into the sea, he would have done it. Had he any right to refuse the lesser thing?

Ambrosius smiled a little, looking into his eyes. 'Rhyanidd is very fair—cream and heather-honey.'

Aquila never knew what made him say it, hanging the hunting shield from its peg on the king-post with great care as he did so. 'Cream and heather-honey may grow to be a weariness. If I must take one, when I want neither, I'll take the little brown sister.'

13

The Empty Hut

NEXT morning, with the bustle of preparations for departure already beginning to rise, Aquila sought out Cradoc the Chieftain and asked him for Ness, that he might take her with him for his wife when he rode north again. He did not quite believe, even while he asked, that Ambrosius had been right. But when he had finished asking, he found that Ambrosius had been perfectly right. There was no escape.

When he and Cradoc had done talking together, and everything was settled, he did not at once go to join the rest of the Companions. He should have gone, he knew; they were already gathering, the horses being walked up and down, but he had to be alone for a little. He turned aside into the orchard and walked to and fro under the trees, with his sword gathered into his arms. The gold was gone from the orchard, even the apples had lost their warmth of colour, and the branches swayed in the small, chill wind that turned up the leaves silverly against the drifting, sheep's-wool sky. He turned at last to go back to the others—and found Ness standing at a little distance, watching him.

He went towards her slowly, and they stood and looked at each other. 'What is it that you do here, Ness?' he asked at last, in a tone as grey as the morning.

'I came to look at you. I must be forgiven if I am a little interested, seeing that I am to go with you among strangers and live the rest of my life in the hollow of your hand.'

'Cradoc your father has told you, then?' Aquila asked.

'Oh yes, my father has told me. That was kind of him. It makes no difference in the end, of course; but it is nice to be told these things at the time, not left to find them out afterwards.' She looked at him with the cool challenge in her eyes that had been there the first time he saw her, but without the smile. 'Why do you want to marry me?'

If it had been the golden sister, Aquila knew that he would have had to make some kind of lie for kindness' sake, but not for Ness; only the truth for Ness. 'Because unless we can become one people, we shall not save Britain from the barbarians,' he said. It sounded stiff and pompous, but it was the truth, the best he could do.

Ness studied him for a moment, and there was a twitch of laughter at the corner of her mouth. 'So it is by Ambrosius's order! And to think that we killed the pig for him!' And then, suddenly grave again, she asked curiously, 'Then if it does not matter which of us it is, why me, and not Rhyanidd?'

'I don't know,' said Aquila simply.

There was a little silence, and then Ness said, 'I wonder if you ever will. How long have I, to make ready for my wedding?'

'We shall be in the south upward of a month. Be ready to ride with me when we pass this way on the road north again.'

Ness took her eyes from his face for the first time since he had turned and found her watching him, and looked about her, back towards the thatched roof of her father's Hall, up through the shivering apple branches to the dark lift of the mountains against the sky. And her look hurt him sharply with the memory of a valley in the Down Country with the trace of old vine terraces on the southern slopes.

'I have known this orchard for sixteen years,' she said. 'And now there's only a month left.' But she was not talking to him.

Aquila realized that the prospect of the marriage must be far more overwhelming for her than it was for him, because for her it meant being torn away from all that she knew and loved. But he shut his mind to that thought quickly. Once he began to feel sorry for the girl the whole thing would become unbearable. And he also had been torn away from all that he knew and loved, and more harshly than this.

He heard one of the others calling him. 'Dolphin! Hi! Dolphin! Are we to wait all day?' and he turned without another word, leaving her standing under the dipping branches of the apple trees, and strode back to rejoin his fellows.

When Ambrosius and his Companions returned to their winter quarters at Dynas Ffaraon, Aquila no longer had his regular sleeping-place among the young men in Ambrosius's Hall, but was lord of a turf-roofed bothy below the western rampart, where Ness spread fine skins on the bed-place and fresh bracken on the earthen floor, and cooked for him when he chose to eat at home, and spun wool by herself in the firelight, in the long winter evenings. Aquila was not often there. In this last winter before the great attack there was so much to do, so much to think about, that for most of the time he managed to forget about Ness altogether. She seemed as far away from him as though she had never ridden up from the south in the curve of his bridle arm; and he found it quite easy to forget her.

Winter passed, and spring came to the mountains, the snipe drumming over the matted bog myrtle at the head of the lake, and the purple butterwort in flower among the rocks of the cleft where the little stream came down. Dynas Ffaraon was humming, thrumming with preparations for the march; and all the broad valley below the Dun was an armed camp.

On a close, still evening Aquila sat beside Valarius at supper in the Fire-hall, his legs outstretched beneath the table on which he leaned, his platter of cold bear ham almost untouched before him. The great hall, crowded with leaders from the camp, was hot, despite the earliness of the year; too close and airless to eat, with the heavy, brooding closeness of coming storm. Also there were things in his stomach that came between him and food. Only a few hours since, he had ridden in with his squadron from Segontium, and all evening he had been with Ambrosius and his captains in council. Everything was settled now, as far as it could be in advance. The Cran-tara had been sent out days ago, the stick dipped in goat's blood and charred at one end, whose summons no tribesman might disobey. They were to host at Canovium, four days from now. That was for northern Cymru. Powys and the south were to join them later on the line of march. Aquila glanced again at the strangers sitting beside Ambrosius in the High Place, men in Roman tunics and with clipped hair and beards. They too had ridden in only a few hours since, bringing Ambrosius word from the Roman party of the support that waited for him in Venta and Aquae Sulis, Calleva and Sorviodunum, the cities of his father's old lowland territories. Bringing also word of another kind from the world beyond the mountains; word that for the second time Rome had fallen.

They had known for years that there was no more help to be had from Rome, that they were cut off. But now they were not merely cut off, but *alone*—the solitary outpost of an empire that had ceased to exist. Aquila's thoughts were suddenly with his old troop from Rutupiae garrison, the men of his own world whom he had known and served with; the old optio, who had taught him all he knew of soldiery and whose teaching he was now sweating in his turn to hammer into his wild mountain tribesmen; Felix, dead under the blazing walls of Rome. He jibed at himself for a fool; Felix and his troop might have been dead any time these four years past, they might have been drafted to the Eastern Empire, and be feasting safe in Constantinople tonight. But still the sense of loss was with him.

A woman bent over him to refill the cup that stood empty by his hand. He looked up, vaguely expecting it to be Ness, for the women generally poured for their own men in hall, but it was the wife of one of the other captains; and when he came to think of it, he had seen no sign of Ness in Hall this evening. The woman smiled at him, and passed on. He realized suddenly that men were beginning to leave the Hall, rising as they finished their meal, and taking their weapons and going. There was so much to be done; no time for sitting and staring at nothing. The waiting time was over.

He began to eat again, hurriedly.

'Sixteen years we have waited for this coming down from the mountains,' Valarius said beside him, rather thickly. 'Sixteen crawling years since Constantine was murdered.'

Aquila looked round at him. 'You were one of those who got Ambrosius and his brother away to safety after that happened, weren't you?'

Valarius took a long, loud drink from his mead cup, and set it down a little unsteadily, before he answered. 'Aye.'

'That must be a proud thing for you; now that the waiting time is over and he comes down to take his father's place.'

'Proud? I leave pride to the other two—to old Finnen with his harp and Eugenus with his draughts and stinking salves.'

There was a kind of raw, jeering bitterness in his voice, under the thickness of the mead, that startled Aquila, and he asked quickly, 'What do you mean?'

'Eugenus was Constantine's physician, Finnen was Constantine's harper; not to them the shame,' Valarius said dully after a moment. '*I* was one of Constantine's bodyguard—yet Constantine died at a murderer's hand.'

There was a small silence. Aquila was suddenly remembering the scene of Aber of the White Shells, remembering that rage of Valarius's that had seemed out of all proportion to Brychan's jibe. Odd, he thought, how little one knew about people. He had lived and worked with Valarius for more than a year, and never known anything about him but that he drank too much and was the ruins of a good soldier, never known that for sixteen years he had carried shame with him as a man might carry a scar, a bodily hurt hidden from the eyes of other men. Maybe it was because the waiting was over and they stood on the edge of a great struggle and that somehow loosened things, maybe it was because of his own feeling of loss for Felix—something in him reached out to the older man, stiffly, rather painfully because it was so long since he had reached out to another human being, and he said with unaccustomed gentleness, 'Assuredly Ambrosius has not thought of the thing in that way.'

'But I have,' Valarius said. And it seemed that there was no more to be said.

Aquila finished his own meal quickly, and went out into the dusk. He went first to make sure that all was well down at the horse-lines and with his troop; then made for his own bothy. The skin apron was drawn back from the doorway and there was fresh bracken on the floor; a tallow candle burned low and guttering on the carved kist that held Ness's clothes, and his own; everything in readiness for him, but no sign of Ness here either.

He stood for a while with his hand on the door post and his head ducked under the lintel, thinking. He was bone weary, and on any other night he would simply have slipped his sword-belt over his head and flung himself down on the piled fern of the bed-place, to sleep. But tonight, because Rome had fallen and Felix was dead, because of Valarius's shame, the empty hut seemed horribly lonely, and there was a small aching need in him for somebody to notice, even if they were not glad, that he had come home. That frightened him, because it was only as long as you did not need anybody else that you were safe from being hurt. But after a few moments he pinched out the candle and went in search of Ness, all the same.

He thought he knew where to find her: in the little hollow of the bush-lined cleft where he had once found Artos and his hound watching for a grass snake. He had found her there once before, and she had told him, 'It is a good place. It looks south, and if I close my eyes to shut out the mountains in between, I can see the apples budding in my father's orchard.'

It was full dark now, though the flat-topped clouds massing above the pass to the coast were still touched with rose-copper on their under-bellies. The air was without freshness, lying like warm silk over one's face, and the stars were veiled in faint thunder-wrack. Certainly there was a storm coming, Aquila thought, as he made his way round the curve of the hill below the inner rampart, and plunged into the twisting cleft among the rocks. The thin, silver plash of the water under the ferns sounded unnaturally loud in the stillness, and the faint honey scent of the blackthorn breathed up to him. Looking down as he scrambled lower, he saw the pale blur of the blossoms like foam on dark water, where the thorn trees leaned together over the little hollow in the rocks—and the pale blur of a face suddenly turned up to him.

'Ness! What are you doing here?' he demanded, slithering to a halt just above her. 'There's going to be a storm.'

'I like storms,' said Ness composedly.

'And so you come down here to meet this one, instead of being in Hall this evening?'

He could not see her face, save as a paleness among the cloudier paleness of the blackthorn blossom, but he heard the old challenge in her voice. 'Why should I be in Hall? I have not the second sight to know that my lord would ride in tonight.'

'But you did know it, didn't you, before you came out here? You left all ready for me in the bothy.'

'What is it, then, that you complain of? Did no one feed you?'

'A woman brought me cold meat and bannock and kept my wine cup filled,' Aquila said, coldly angry now, and not quite sure why. 'And when I looked up, it was Cordaella, Cenfirth's wife, and not you.'

'I wonder that you noticed the difference.'

Aquila leaned down towards her over his bent knee. 'There is a simple reason for that,' he said, repaying her in her own coin. 'Cordaella smiled at me, so I knew that she could not be you.'

Ness sprang up to face him with a movement as swiftly fierce as the leap of a mountain cat. 'And why should I smile at you? For joy that you took me from my father's Hall?'

'You know why I took you,' Aquila said after a moment.

'Yes, you told me. For the strengthening of a bond between your people and mine.' She was breathing quickly, the fierce white blur of her face turned up to his. 'Oh, I know that you did not want me, any more than I wanted you. The thing was forced on both of us. It was not that you took me, but the *way* that you took me——' She began to laugh on a hard, mocking note that made him long to hit her; and as though her wild laughter had called it up, and there was some kinship between her and the coming storm, a long, dank breath of wind came sighing up the cleft, thick with the smell of thunder and the thin, honey sweetness of the blackthorn flowers, and a flicker of lightning played between the dark masses of the mountains. 'It was not that you laughed at Rhyanidd about the pig, but the *way* that you laughed. It is never the things that you do, but the way that you do them. You took me from my father's hearth as you might have taken a dog—no, not a dog; I have seen you playing with Cabal's ears and gentling him under the chin—as you might have taken a kist or a cooking-pot that you did not much value. Did you never think that I might have knifed you with your own dagger one night, and been away in the darkness? Did you never think that there might have been someone of my own people whom I loved, and who—might have come to love *me*?'

There was a long silence, filled with the soft uneasy fret of that swiftly rising wind. Aquila's anger ebbed slowly out of him, leaving only a great tiredness behind. 'And was there, Ness?'

The fire had sunk in her also, and her voice was spent and lifeless. 'Yes,' she said.

'I am sorry,' Aquila said stiffly, awkwardly.

'Oh, it doesn't matter now. He is dead. He was killed hunting, nine days ago. Rhyanidd sent me word by the messenger for Ambrosius that came up yesterday.'

'I am sorry,' Aquila said again. There seemed nothing else to say.

He knew that she was looking at him intently, as though for her the darkness was daylight. 'I wonder if you are,' she said at last. 'I wonder if you have it in you to be sorry about anything—or glad . . . '

'I had once,' Aquila said harshly. He made a small, helpless gesture. 'We march against the Saxons in two days' time, and maybe you will be loosed from me soon enough. Meanwhile, come back to the bothy before the storm breaks.'

She drew away a little. 'Let you go back and sleep dry in the warm deerskins. I like storms; did I not tell you? This is my storm, and I am waiting for it. It will be bonnier company than you are to me.'

The wind was blowing in long, fitful gusts now, the blackthorn branches streaming like spray; and a white flicker of lightning showed him Ness with her unbound hair lifting and flying about her head as she crouched against the rocks behind her. She looked like something that belonged to the storm; and how he was to deal with her, now that he had lost his anger, he simply did not know. But deal with her he would; the determination not to be worsted by her rose in him, mingled with a kinder feeling that he could not leave her here to be drenched and beaten by the storm; and he reached out and caught her wrist. 'Come, Ness.' He pulled her towards him and caught her other wrist, not at all sure that if he left it free she would not indeed try to knife him with his own dagger.

She struggled wildly for a moment, and then suddenly it was as though all her fighting was spent. She was leaning weakly against him, and if it had been Rhyanidd, he would have thought that she was crying, the quiet crying of utter desolation. But surely Ness would not know how to cry. The first low rumble of thunder was muttering among the mountains. 'Come, Ness,' he said again. He released her one wrist, and still grasping the other, turned back to the steep climb; and with a little harsh, exhausted sigh, Ness came.

But he had no feeling of victory.

14

The Honour of First Blood

IN front of Aquila the main street of Durobrivae ran uphill, deserted in the evening sunlight. The town must have been growing emptier for years, falling gradually into decay, as happened to most of the towns nearest to the Saxon country, until now, before the threat of the Saxon inrush, the few people who were left had streamed away westward. The utter, heart-cold emptiness made Aquila think suddenly of Rutupiae on the night the last of the Eagles flew from Britain. Nothing left alive in Durobrivae but a half-wild yellow cat sitting on a wall; a stillness so complete that the shadow of a wheeling gull sweeping across the cobbles seemed important.

That was in front. Behind Aquila and the knot of champions who stood with him at the town end of the bridge was the ring of axes on heavy timbers, and a hoarse shouting of orders; all the sounds of desperate activity, of labour against time. Time. Aquila sent a swift glance over his shoulder to see how the bridge-felling was going forward. Men were swarming over the long, timber-built bridge, townsmen and Celtic warriors labouring side by side. He saw the blink of axes in the evening light, as they rose and fell, crashing into the bridge timbers; and Catigern, the second of the Young Foxes, standing in the midst of his men, directing operations, the sunset turning his red hair to the colour of fire. It was a wild sunset, beyond the low, wooded hills, touching woods and marshes and mudflats with its own singing gold, and kindling the water to flame. It seemed to Aquila, in that one swift glance before he turned face forward again, somehow fitting that they should fight with the sunset behind them.

The road that led back from the bridge climbed slowly, gold-touched like all the rest, over the brow of the hill, and into the brightness beyond; and Aquila, facing the Saxon lands again, was aware of it behind him, leading back and back, to Deva, to Canovium, to the ancient fortress among the mountains of Arfon. At Deva the three Young Foxes had come in to the hosting. And there, knowing that Hengest would have word of their advance almost as soon as it was begun, and therefore speed was all important, Ambrosius had divided his host in two, and unloosed his swift-moving cavalry and mounted archers under the Young Foxes directly against the barbarians, while he himself, with the slower foot-soldiers, swept south to Glevum and on through his father's old territories, gathering the troops that waited for him there, on his line of march. That was the last that they had heard of Ambrosius; the last that they could possibly hear for many days. And meanwhile it was for them to hold the river line.

The Saxons, already on the move themselves and fully warned (for news always travelled faster in wild places than a horse could gallop) of British hooves drumming towards them down the Legion's road from Deva, had come swarming out to finish with the British cavalry before the main host could come up with them, if that might be: at all events to reach the river-line before the British reached it. Durobrivae River, cutting its broad valley through the downs, had only two crossing places between its estuary and the place where the almost impenetrable forest of Anderida closed its own barriers to friend and foe alike. How often Aquila had seen its course drawn out with a charred stick beside the hearth in Dynas Ffaraon. His mind went to the hurried council of war this morning, in the lee of a dripping hazel copse, with the British leaders gathered about the little dark forest man who had foundered a stolen pony to bring them word of the Saxons' nearness.

'A day's march from the river,' Catigern had said, his face full of reckless laughter. 'Well, so are we, but horses march quicker than men.'

'We cannot hold the river at both points, however many hours we may be ahead of them,' Vortimer said; Vortimer for once without a falcon on his fist, and looking strangely incomplete without it. 'Look at us—we are a meagre handful!' And then with a sudden resolve, 'But if we can be in time to cut the bridge at Durobrivae, it is in my mind that we can hold the upriver ford.'

So they had split forces again, and while the main band, with the little forest man for their guide, had struck off through the scrub for the ford six or seven miles inland, where the ancient track under the North Chalk crossed the river, the smaller squadron had followed Catigern, forcing their weary horses to one last desperate burst of speed, down the road to Durobrivae.

And now, with the Saxons God knew how near, Aquila and his knot of champions stood their guard on the Saxon bank, while their comrades strove desperately against time to cut the bridge behind them.

'How many men do you want?' Catigern had

demanded when he had volunteered for the task three hours ago. And Aquila had said, 'Horatius is supposed to have done it with two, but that leaves nothing in reserve. Give me nine—nine who choose to stand with me.'

He had meant men from his own squadron; and indeed the men of his own squadron had been quick enough to come crowding round him, Amgerit and Glevus and grim little Owain and the rest, many times nine. But before he could make his choice from among them, Brychan, of all unlikely people, had come shouldering through the press, crying, 'Hai, hai! Make way for your betters, my children!' to stand beside him.

It was odd, that. There had never been any warmth between them from their first meeting on the track up to Dynas Ffaraon, yet now Brychan came as though by right to stand with him at the doomed bridgehead, and he, Aquila, had accepted his coming as something that fitted as a well-worn garment fits. He glanced aside at the young Celt now. Brychan looked very happy. He came of a people to whom fighting was the very flowering of life. Aquila, coming of another people, could not feel that, only a cold, knife-edged sense of waiting, but something leapt between them all the same, binding them for the moment into a brotherhood.

Steps pounded along the quay, and a man came into sight, running as though all the hounds of hell were behind him. He was shouting as he ran; they could not hear what, but there was no need.

'So, I think they come,' Aquila said, and drew his sword with quiet deliberation. He caught one more glance over his shoulder. The bridge had a lopsided look, and the whole fabric shuddered and jumped with every stroke of the axes. It could not hold much longer, he judged, but the Saxons would be here before it went.

The scout was right upon them now, and checked, panting. 'The Saxons are out of the woods.'

'How many?' Aquila snapped.

'Only an advance party, but more than we are, and the rest will be hard behind.'

Aquila nodded. 'Get back and report to Catigern.'

As the man plunged on, his feet drumming hollow on the crazy bridge timbers, the ten resolute men at the Saxon end of it closed up shoulder to shoulder, their drawn swords ready in their hands, their eyes turned in the direction from which the enemy must come. Behind them the ring of axes took on a redoubled urgency. In the tumble of bright clouds above Durobrivae a lake of clear sky shone blue, a faded harebell colour with the shadow of dusk already upon it; and the gulls swept and circled by with the sunset on their wings. And then, from away south-eastward beyond the silent town, a Saxon war-horn boomed.

Aquila braced himself, tensing like an animal ready to spring. He felt the slight movement run through the men with him, the tautened body and the softly indrawn breath.

'Brothers,' he said, almost wonderingly, 'whoever, in the years to come, strikes the last blow in this fight for all that we hold worth fighting for, to us—to us ten—is the honour of first blood.'

Behind him he heard a panting shout of orders, and the splintering crash and splash as one of the huge timbers went down, and the bridge shuddered under his feet like a live thing in torment. And now there was shouting before them as well as behind, and the yellow cat streaked along the wall with tail bristling, and the stillness was gone from Durobrivae, as the advance guard of Hengest's host came pouring down the quay, the last fiery light of the sunset jinking on iron helmet and spear-point and ring-mail byrnie. At sight of the bridge, the foremost checked an instant, then they broke forward, yelling as they ran, storming down upon the little knot of champions who waited grimly to receive them.

As the fight joined, Aquila, who had known only that cold, knife-edged sense of waiting in the moment before, suddenly caught fire. He had known more than one skirmish with Scots pirates in the past year, but this was the first time since Wiermund of the White Horse had burned his home that the man at the other end of his sword had been a Saxon; and for Flavia's sake he hated every Saxon with a sickening hate; a hate that seemed now to spread wings within him and lift him up and fill him with a terrible red delight as each blow went home. Twice a man beside him was struck down, and twice somebody sprang into the empty place, but he was not aware of that, not aware of anything but the faces of the Sea Wolves that thrust upon him, blue-eyed and snarling, behind their bright blades. His own blade was bright, too, and growing red. Aquila killed that day, killed and killed again: and each time his sword struck home, sweeping aside the guard of a Saxon blade or thrusting under the rim of a buckler, his heart cried out within him that this was for his father, that that was for Demetrius, for Kuno, for Gwyna, even for the old hound Margarita. But though it was Flavia who had put that tempest of hate in him, he did not give her name to any of the blows he struck that sunset.

Someone was shouting to him. 'Fall back! In the Christus' name fall back! The bridge is going!' And he woke to the world around him again, and to the fact that he was not there simply to kill Saxons so much as to hold them back while their line of march was cut. He took one long step back, two steps, and the others with him—those that were left of them—their chins tucked down into their shields, their blades biting deep as the Sea Wolves came thrusting after them. The whole bridge felt lax and limber under his feet, swaying above the water as he moved back, and back. Swaying more wildly . . . He heard a voice above the tumult shouting to his comrades to break off the fight, and never knew that it was his own. There was a

whining and rending of timbers, as the others lowered their blades and sprang back, and for one splinter of time that seemed to broaden into an eternity, he stood alone in the face of the Saxon flood. Then he had a sudden sense of a gulf, an immensity of nothingness opening behind him; the hills and river and ragged, darkening sky seemed to heel over in a vast half-circle, and with a shout of triumph he sprang back and down.

A falling beam caught him on the temple just over the old scar, sending jagged splinters of light through his head. He was aware of a great falling and crashing down, a rending uproar, and the shock of cold water that engulfed him and closed over his head. Then there was darkness—no, never true darkness; a kind of rolling cloud of confusion that never quite shut out the world.

It lifted at last, and he realized dimly that he was lying on his side on grass, and had just vomited up what felt like about half the river. The river must be tidal at Durobrivae, he thought, for the taste of it was still salt in his mouth. He rolled farther on to his face and propped himself up a little on his hands, remembering after a while to open his eyes. He found himself staring down at his own hands in a pool of sharp golden light, one spread-fingered on the rough turf of the river bank, one still cramped about the hilt of his sword, which he must have clung to throughout. In the almost acid radiance every grass-blade stood out distinct and glowing, and a tiny yellow-banded snail-shell was a thing to marvel at, living a life of its own and casting a shadow that was as complete and perfect as itself.

'Sa, that is better,' said Brychan's voice above him; and he made a great effort and got a leg under him, and Brychan helped him to his knees. The world swam unpleasantly in the light of a torch that someone was holding above him; there was a numbed aching behind his forehead, and he hoped vaguely that he wasn't going to be sick again. But after a few moments the world began to steady. It was dusk now, dusk full of movement. He saw other torches, and men moving about him, and horses. A group of men already mounted went past him in the crowding shadows, and he had a confused impression of the black, stark lines of the bridge running out into the cold paleness of the water, jagged and driven askew, and ending in a skeleton tumble of beams, and then nothing. A vague impression also of flames springing up on the farther bank. The barbarians had fired Durobrivae.

'How many of us got—back?' he demanded thickly, with an arm on Brychan's shoulder to steady himself. Brychan was dripping with river water, too, and something in Aquila registered the fact that it was probably Brychan who had hauled him out of Durobrivae River.

'Five. You and I, Struan and Amgerit and Owain. But Amgerit is about done for. They've taken him up to the fisher huts with the rest of the wounded. Anyway, we accounted for a fine lot of Saxons, what with the fight and those that were swept away when the bridge went.'

Aquila said after a moment, 'Five—six out of ten. Well, I suppose that is not a heavy price for the bridge.' He realized for the first time that somebody else had checked beside them. He looked up and saw that it was Catigern himself; and with a hand still on Brychan's shoulder, he lurched unsteadily to his feet. 'First blood to us!'

Catigern nodded. 'First blood to us! That was a most noble fight, my friend . . . Can you ride yet?'

'Yes,' Aquila said.

'So, ride then. We head for the ford now,' and he was gone, swinging his cloak behind him.

Someone brought him a dry cloak to fling round him

over his dripping tunic, and someone brought Inganiad. She whinnied, pleased and calling to him, when she caught his smell. He groaned as he hauled himself into the saddle. There had been a few hours' rest for the horses, none for the men.

He knew, when he came to think back over it later, that they pushed on up-river through the short spring night and reached the ford and the British camp before dawn; that there were a few hours' rest, and then more fighting, as the Saxons, baulked of Durobrivae Bridge, swept inland to attack the ford: the first full battle of the long struggle for Britain, and at the day's end the first British victory; to be remembered long after the cutting of Durobrivae Bridge was forgotten. But to Aquila it was all no more than a dream; something seen dimly through the aching numbness in his head, moving like a painted curtain with the wind behind it.

It was not until the fighting was over and sunset came again that reality broke in on him once more, and he found that he was in a charcoal-burner's bothy, twisting a piece of filthy rag round a deep gash in his forearm, and looking down at Catigern's body lying where it had been carried aside from the battle in the full flood of wild sunset light that streamed through the open doorway.

Vortimer and Pascent were there; and Vortimer turned away to give some order to the men who crowded about them, beating his clenched fists together as he did so. 'If I had a thousand men, I'd follow them up; as it is there's nothing that we can do but guard the river line until Ambrosius comes up. Post scouts across the river to bring me word if they show any signs of trying again farther up. Calgalus, send men up to the village; it is going to be a wild night and we must get the wounded into shelter.'

But Pascent, the youngest, kneeling beside his brother's

body, only went on staring blindly down at it. 'They say that Horsa is dead too. Somebody said that he was lying by the ford with a whole company of Hengest's household warriors about him,' he said. And then, through shut teeth, 'I hope his death is a stone in Hengest's belly tonight!'

They held the river line until nine days later Ambrosius and the rest of the host came out of the woods behind them; lean and mired, footsore and red-eyed with forced marching. Longbow-men from the mountains, men wearing old Roman harness and carrying the short sword and the pilum; old soldiers and the sons of old soldiers from Venta and Aquae Sulis and Sorviodunum and a hundred villas and villages and little towns between.

And then at last they swept forward after the Saxon kind.

When winter came, putting an end to fighting for the next few months, the Saxons were back to the territory from which they had swarmed out in the spring; and settling the better part of his host in winter camps at Durobrivae and Noviomagus, Ambrosius marched the rest back to Venta Belgarum, that had been Constantine's old capital and would now be his.

He rode in through the streets of Venta in a sleet storm, with a bitter wind blowing; and all the city seemed cold and grey and falling derelict. Aquila, riding through the streets that he had known when he was a boy, saw how far the grass had encroached into the roadways in five years. He saw faces that he knew among the crowds, though none of them knew him, and it seemed to him that on them also the grass had encroached. But there was warmth in Venta that day, for besides the Magistrates and chief citizens who had met them at the city gate, there were many to cry a welcome to Ambrosius; a child threw a branch of glowing winter berries under his horse's hooves, and an old man called out to him, 'I knew your father, sir! I served under him in the old days!' and was rewarded by the swift smile even more than by the coin which the slight, dark man on the black stallion tossed down to him.

'You are at home among your own people here, as surely as ever you were at Dynas Ffaraon,' Aquila said to him later that night, when the Magistrates and the chief citizens had departed, and a few of the Companions stood together round the fire in a small side chamber of the old Governor's Palace.

Ambrosius turned his cold hands before the fire, spreading them so that the light shone through between his fingers. 'At home.' He looked up to the high, dark window; and Aquila knew that through the darkness of the sleet-spattered glass in which the reflections of the firelight danced, he was seeing the remote crests of the Arfon skyline, the snow corries of Yr Widdfa; smelling the sweet, cold air of the mountains, and saying his farewells. 'Yes, at home, and among my own people. I even saw certain faces that I knew among the crowds today—and they remembered me for my father's and my grandfather's sakes. One day they may remember me for my own.'

15

The Hawking Glove

WHEN spring came, Aquila was in the mountains again, sent up with an escort of cavalry to bring down the women and children. Little, grim Owain, riding beside him in the rear of the long, winding cavalcade, had been angrily disgusted when Aquila chose him for his second in command of the escort. It was one thing to stand beside the Dolphin to keep Durobrivae Bridge from the Saxons, quite another to follow him away westward when the fighting was just about to start again. He had gloomed all through the lowlands, his narrow, weather-burned face shut like a trap; but the thin mountain air, the wild, free tang of spring among his own hills had lightened his mood little by little until now he was whistling to himself softly as he rode; and the whistling rose small and clear as a distant bird-call above the soft beat of hooves and creak of harness-leather, the wheel-rumble of the oxcarts and the cries of the carters.

Aquila did not whistle, and kept most of his thoughts for the business of getting the ox carts through the soft places. But in him, too, something answered to the

blackthorn breaking into flower beside the way, and the
plover calling. It was almost a year since he had ridden
down from Dynas Ffaraon behind Ambrosius, almost a
year since he had seen Ness. He was not sure what he felt
about seeing her again, but he wondered a little how it
had gone with her through the months between.

'Ah-ee! There it stands against the sky, as though we
had been but an hour away,' Owain said, breaking off his
whistling, and spitting with satisfaction between his horse's
ears.

And Aquila realized that he had been riding without
seeing anything for the past mile.

They had sent one of their number on ahead with
word of their coming, and men were waiting for them in
the cattle enclosures at the foot of the fortress hill. There
were hurried greetings, and leaving the tired oxen and the
carts in charge of the men who had come to meet them,
they set off up the steep track to the inner gateway. In a
little while they were clattering between the huge, square-
cut gate-timbers; weary men dropping from their saddles,
suddenly the centre of a little crowd that seemed to spring
out of nowhere to greet them: a crowd of women, for the
most part, for there would be few men in the Dun at this
hour of the day, with the sun still high in the sky; women
asking for news of sons or husbands, and small, excited
children who must be scooped back out of danger from
the horses' hooves; and a swarm of half-grown boys led by
young Artos and his hound Cabal, who had come running
from sword-and-buckler practice at sound of the escort's
arrival. But in all the crowd there was no sign of Ness.
Aquila, watching the horses fed and rubbed down and
picketed, glanced round for her more than once, but he
was not really surprised at not finding her there. Ness had
always been good at not being there when he returned

from a time away, and it was not likely that she would change now.

He could not bring himself to ask any of the women for news of her, but so much could have happened in a year, and he began to feel vaguely anxious in spite of himself. 'See to the rest of the picket lines,' he said suddenly to Owain, and, turning, thrust out through the little throng towards the gateway and the bothies below the rampart. Some of the women looked after him, and glanced at each other smiling after he had gone. But he did not know that.

His own bothy was partly hidden from this side by an outcrop of rock, so that one could not see it clearly from a distance, but came upon it suddenly. And when he did so now, what he saw pulled him up short, with a feeling of having walked into complete unreality. Ness sat in the bothy doorway with something kicking in a nest of deerskin at her feet. She was bending down to look at the thing, and singing almost under her breath; a fainter, huskier singing than the one that Flavia had made when he found her in the Saxon camp, but with a like crooning note in it. Something seemed to catch Aquila by the throat, making it for the moment hard to breathe. But at least she was not combing her hair. She was spinning, the brown of the crotal-dyed wool on her distaff as deeply rich as the velvet of a bee's back, and the whirling spindle singing its own small, contented song in a kind of undertone to hers.

Then, as he took another step forward and his shadow fell across her feet, she looked up. 'I heard that you were come,' she said, as though he had been gone a day instead of a year.

Aquila looked down at the babe in the deerskin, and then at Ness; he felt stupid, woolly headed, as though for the moment he could not properly understand. Ness had not told him before he went away; maybe she had not known herself, or—maybe she would not have told him anyway.

'Ness—is it mine?'

She laughed, on that hard, mocking, wild bird-note of hers, and laid down spindle and distaff, and stooping, caught up the little creature still muffled in its deerskin, holding it close against her. 'Oh, my lord, look then! Do you not see that he has your eagle's beak for a nose, though there is no blue dolphin on his shoulder?'

Aquila looked more closely. The babe did not seem to him to have much nose at all, but he supposed that women saw these things differently. It had a little dark down on its head, like a curlew chick, and out of its small face two solemn, dark eyes frowned up at him, wandering a little, as the eyes of most very young things do before they have learned to focus.

'He even frowns as you do!' Ness said. She was still laughing, mocking him, but there was less harshness in her mockery than there had used to be.

Aquila put out a bent finger and brushed the baby's cheek with his knuckle. It felt extraordinarily soft and alive. A son, he thought, and there was a queer, rather painful stirring deep down in him. This small, living creature frowning up at him out of the soft folds of deerskin was his son; what he had been to his father.

'Have you given him a name?'

'Nay, that is for you to do.'

There was a little silence filled with the living sounds of the Dun and the warm droning of a bee among the cushions of wild thyme that clung to a ledge of the outcrop close by. Then Aquila said, 'I shall call him Flavian.'

'Flavian?' She seemed to be testing the name on her tongue. 'Why Flavian?'

'It was my father's name.'

Another silence, longer than the first. 'So. I have learned two things about my lord,' Ness said at last. 'My lord had a father, and his name was Flavian . . . Na, three things——' Her voice had lost its mocking note; and looking up, he found her watching him with something of the air of one making a discovery. 'My lord loved his father. I did not think that it was in my lord to love anyone.'

Before he could answer, a pad of feet and a clear whistle sounded above, and Artos came leaping down the outcrop with the great hound Cabal at his bare, brown heels, full of questions about the return journey and demands to be allowed to ride with the escort. And for a while Aquila had no more time for his own affairs.

The next morning Aquila saw his wife and son into the foremost of the ox carts, along with the other women and children going to join their men. She settled herself in the tail of the cart, drawing her cloak forward about herself and the baby in the crook of her arm; and as Aquila stowed her bundle in after her, an older woman with three children clinging about her leaned forward from the interior of the cart, to help her settle, saying as she did so, 'The little one grows fatter now. Has he a name yet?'

'Yes,' Ness said, 'he has a name. He is Flavian.'

'Flavian.' The other woman seemed to be testing the name as Ness herself had done. 'What a man's name, and he so small! Nothing but a minnow.'

Ness looked down at the little creature bundled in her cloak, pressing back the dark green folds with her free hand. 'Minnow,' she said, and then a surprising thing happened, for her eyes went to Aquila, sharing the little warm laughter of the moment in the way that she had never shared anything with him before. 'Minnow, Dolphin's son.'

Aquila touched her foot briefly in acceptance of the laughter; then turned away to mount Inganiad at the head of the escort.

He was very proud because he had a son; and for the first time in six years, as he led the long, winding convoy of horsemen and ox carts down the road to Canovium, the time ahead seemed to hold something for him.

Young Artos rode between Aquila and Owain on his own pony, with the great hound Cabal loping alongside. They had listened to his demand to be one of the escort, and he rode with his pride shining about him like a scarlet cloak, and his hand on his hunting-knife as though the familiar glens of Arfon through which the track wound were suddenly overnight swarming with Saxons.

'I go to help Ambrosius,' he said, not shouting it, but speaking head up into the mountain wind. 'Soon we shall drive the Sea Wolves back into the sea!'

But it was not to be so simple as that, for despite their hopes last spring, the British were not strong enough to drive the Sea Wolves into the sea. Again and again in the next two years they hurled the Saxons back into the south-east corner of the province, only to have them come swarming out once more as soon as their own thrust was spent. And with the war bands strengthening all the while under Octa in the north, and more coming in down every Saxon wind like the wild geese in October, the menace remained as deadly as ever.

'If we could have one great victory!' Ambrosius cried. 'One victory to sound like a blast of trumpets through the land! Then we should gather to our standard not merely a gallant handful here and there, but the princes of the

Dumnonii and the Brigantes with their whole princedoms behind them. Then we might indeed have a Britain whole and bonded together to drive the Sea Wolves into the sea!'

Meanwhile they struggled with the age-old question of how to fight any kind of war with an army that wanted to go home in mid campaign to harvest its own fields, and when it came back, if it did come back, had mostly forgotten its training; struggled also to make one host, one heart, out of lowland Roman and mountain Celt; and so far as the Celts were concerned, it was uphill work.

With the men of Arfon it was well enough; the unbreakable tie between the Chieftain and his warriors bound them to Ambrosius, who was the very heart of the whole movement; but with those who had come in following the Young Foxes, it still seemed to Aquila that one could not be sure.

He spoke of his doubts to Eugenus the Physician, towards dusk of a winter's day, as they walked back together from the baths.

'Ye-es, I have long carried a somewhat uneasy mind on that score myself,' Eugenus said, his words muffled by the folds of his cloak that he had huddled almost to his eyebrows, for in spite of his fat he felt the cold. 'Despite all Ambrosius's efforts, despite the friendships—and the marriages—that have sprung up between us, I believe, most sadly, that the only thing that really holds the Celts to our banner is Vortimer. One man's life is a perilously slender thread. It's a solemn thought, my friend.'

Aquila glanced aside at him as they walked. 'There's young Pascent. He'll keep faith, I'll swear.'

'Aye, but he's no leader—he's too good a follower.' There was a smile in the other's voice, for, like everyone else, he liked Pascent. 'He is the stuff that the very best household warriors are made of, brave as a boar and faithful as a hound; but it is not in him to hold the Celtic party, as Vortimer can.'

They walked on in silence, each busy with his own unquiet thoughts, through the winter dusk.

As they walked, the dusk that rose like quiet, grey water in the shabby streets of Venta was rolling in blue and faintly misty over the high northern moors that Octa and his war bands had overrun. And a woman with red-gold hair and eyes that were the shifting grey-green of shallow seas was bending over the fire in a stone-built hut where the blackened heather swept to the walls. She was holding a big leather hawking glove turned inside out, and as she bent forward the firelight darted on the short, bronze pin projecting from the stitching of the thumb. There was a wisp of sheep's wool in her other hand, and she dipped it again and again into the few drops of some thick, greyish fluid in a bowl among the hot ashes, and painted the bright sliver of metal with infinite care, as one handling a viper's fang. All the while she crooned softly, words in a tongue much older than the Saxons' tongue. Many things had gone to the making of those few drops of greyish fluid, and there were charms for them all, to make them do their work more surely. Each time, she let the stuff dry, then painted it again, until the brightness of the bronze was dimmed and darkened as with a grey rust. Then, with the same infinite care, she turned the glove right side out—it was a beautiful glove of honey-pale mare's skin, embroidered with hair-fine silver wires and silk as deeply blue as the hooded flowers from whose root the woman had distilled her chiefest poison—and laid it aside. She burned the wisp of wool, and broke the little earthen pot and dropped the pieces into the red heart of the fire.

Better for both Hengest and for Vortigern her lord (whose good, in this thing, was Hengest's good) that the Young Fox should be out of the way. But she had not told Vortigern what she did. He was a dreaming fool whose purpose always broke under any strain, and he might shrink from his own good. Later, when the thing was done, and maybe Ambrosius's following had fallen apart like a rotten apple, she would tell him what he owed to her, and watch him writhe.

A day came when they were ploughing on the downs above Venta, and the alders in the water-meadows were brown and woolly with catkins, and Ambrosius's host was mustering again for the fighting that would come with summer, as it came every summer now.

On the evening of that day, Vortimer, going to his sleeping-quarters in the old Governor's Palace, found lying on his clothes chest, where the light of the candle fell full, a hawking glove that was certainly not his. A honey-pale mare's-skin glove, fringed and exquisitely worked with deep blue silk and fine silver wires. He summoned his armour-bearer, and asked where it had come from.

'A slave brought it this evening, from the Lord Ambrosius's chambers,' the man said.

'For me? You are sure that it was for me?'

'The slave said that Ambrosius had noticed your old one was all but worn through.'

Vortigern had picked up the glove, a little puzzled. 'It is a pretty thing—more like a woman's gift.' He looked up, laughing, at his hooded peregrine on her perch. 'Too fine for your sharp talons, eh, beloved?'

He slipped his hand into the loose glove; and snatched it out again with a curse. 'Ah! the thing has talons of its own! Whoever made it has left the needle inside!' And he sucked the jagged scratch on the ball of his thumb, half laughing, half angry, and rather more puzzled.

By midnight he was dead, as a man dies who has been bitten by a poisonous snake.

In a few hours the news was all over Venta, spreading out through the newly gathered host like a dark stain. And Ambrosius, with a face that seemed to have set into stone, was himself heading a ruthless search for the slave who had brought the glove to Vortimer's quarters.

It was all quite useless; the slave would never be found, Aquila was thinking that evening down by the river, watching the water riffle round Inganiad's muzzle as she drank with the other horses of his squadron. And he saw, not the misty grey-and-amber shadows under the budding willows and the blink of oyster light in every spreading ripple, but Rowena in Hengest's Mead Hall, singing; a golden witch in a crimson gown. He did not know why he was so sure that Rowena stood behind that poisoned hawking glove, but he was sure. And with the dusk creeping up the valley, the foreshadowing of evil to come seemed to rise also.

What happened a few days later surprised nobody, for it grew directly out of what had gone before. Several of the Companions were gathered with Ambrosius about the table in the room where he kept his lists and records of men and horses, his pay-rolls and the old Roman itineraries that told him how many marches it was from one place to another and so helped him in the planning of his campaigns; they were going over plans for the summer's fighting, so far as one could make any plans in advance. Seeing him now, his dark, fine-drawn face caught out of the shadows into the candle-light as he leaned forward to point out something on the unrolled parchment on which the old map so often sketched with a charred stick was drawn in ink, Aquila thought how little of the mountains seemed left in him. It was not only that he looked older, nor that he wore a Roman tunic and his dark hair was clipped short; it was something deeper, a turning back to the world that he had been bred in until he was nine years old. Only the flame that had burned in the Lord of Arfon burned in the Roman leader also.

They heard footsteps coming along the colonnade, heard the sentry outside challenge, and a quick word in answer; and Pascent was standing in the doorway, with the courtyard quenched in the green spring twilight behind him. Looking towards him with the rest, Aquila thought, 'So it has happened.'

Pascent came forward to the table. His face was white and haggard in the candle-light, and little beads of sweat shone on his forehead beneath the heavy lock of foxy hair. He looked at Ambrosius across the table, and they saw his mouth work for a moment as he tried to speak and could not. Then he said, 'My Lord Ambrosius, I cannot hold them.'

'So,' Ambrosius said, and let the map roll up, very slowly and carefully. No need for it now, there could be no carrying the war into the Saxon's country this year. 'I had been more than half expecting that, I think. What reason do they give for deserting my standard?'

Pascent made a small, helpless gesture. 'So many reasons. They say that Vortigern my father is after all their lord, and I am only his youngest son. They say that the Saxons will never reach to Central Cymru (that is, those who *come* from Central Cymru), and what is the rest of Britain to them, when all things are said and done? They say that my Lord Ambrosius has forgotten his own people to carry a Roman sword, and that they are weary of obeying Roman trumpets and leaving their fields to be harvested by their women.' He broke off, and stared down at the table before him, then dragged his gaze up again. 'They say—some of them say—that the slave who brought my brother his death said that he brought it from the Lord Ambrosius; and that maybe the slave spoke the truth.'

Ambrosius's face was suddenly very cold. 'And why, in the Name of Light, should the Lord Ambrosius be sending death to the chiefest of his allies?'

Pascent's hands were clenched on the table, and in his face there was an agony of shame. 'Because Guitolinus my father's kinsman has put it into their hearts that the Lord Ambrosius was jealous, fearing that Vortimer might gain too much power.'

There was a long silence, flat and hard. No one moved about the table. Then Ambrosius said in a quiet, curiously smooth voice—a voice as smooth as a sword-blade, that Aquila had never heard from him before—'Let you bid all the chiefs that have yet gathered here to meet me in the Forum, tomorrow at the third hour.'

'It will make no difference,' Pascent groaned.

'That I know well. Whatever I can say to them, they will go. But they shall not desert my standard and the standard of Britain without telling me face to face that they do so—and why.' Ambrosius was silent a moment, his gaze never moving from Pascent's haggard face. 'And you? Do you go with your own people?'

Pascent said, 'I am Ambrosius's man—since the day that I swore faith, I and my brothers.' His eyes clung to Ambrosius's like a dog's. 'I am ashamed with my people's shame; so ashamed that I do not think I want to live. I will serve you living, with a whole heart, or if you ask for such a payment, I will go out of here and fall on my own sword tonight. But either way, I am Ambrosius's man.'

It might have sounded hysterical, but Aquila knew that it was not. It was a simple offer. Pascent felt the shame of what his people were doing so keenly that he was perfectly prepared to pay for it with his own death, if his death seemed any sort of recompense to Ambrosius.

Ambrosius looked at him for a moment, still in silence, and then the white coldness of his face gentled suddenly. 'Not to you the shame, my kinsman. Nay, then, you are of more worth to me living than dead.'

16

White Thorn and Yellow Iris

'I AM Ambrosius's man, since the day that I swore faith; I and my brothers.'

The words were still sounding in Aquila's inner ear next noon, as he made his way from the Basilica; not as he had heard them spoken in defeat last night, but as he had heard them spoken in proud defiance, less than an hour since, in the thin spring sunlight of the Forum court. The scene was still sharp-edged and vivid in his mind; he could see Ambrosius standing on the shallow steps before the great Basilica door, his face a white mask of scorn: Ambrosius, wearing what he scarcely ever wore, a mantle of the Imperial Purple, the straight folds burning in the sunlight with a living depth of colour that drained into itself all the colour from the world around him. A very lonely figure, for he would have none of his officers with him, though they waited in the shadows of the colonnade.

And below him, gathered on the grass that was still tawny with winter, the princes and chieftains of the Celtic party; foremost among them, those dark-blue fanatic's eyes of his blazing with triumph, Guitolinus, who had taken it upon himself to act as spokesman for the rest.

It had been over quite quickly, the talking and the shouting and the brandished fists and the shame that seemed to wash to and fro about the stillness of the purple-clad figure dominating the scene from the portico steps. And when it was over, Pascent had walked deliberately out from among his own people, and turned at the foot of the steps to cry to them in fury, 'You have listened to Guitolinus the Traitor, and not to me. You have broken your faith. So be it; you are curs that run back to your own dung-heap. But you shall run without me!' And without another glance at them, he had mounted the shallow steps to kneel at Ambrosius's feet with the proud submission of a hound, and set his hands between Ambrosius's hands.

Afterwards, Cradoc, his father-in-law, who had come in to the muster five days ago, had been waiting for Aquila in the shadow of an archway. They came together so suddenly in that shadowed place that Aquila's hand flew to his dagger. But the other stayed him. 'Na, na, my lad, I am Cradoc, and no robber. I was waiting for you.'

'Why?' demanded Aquila uncompromisingly.

'Only for this. To say to you that I have not forgotten how at Aber of the White Shells you turned the blow that was meant for me.' Cradoc's face was more deeply lined than usual, more full of old regrets. 'Therefore I will not go to Ness before I leave Venta with my spears. I will not seek to persuade her to come back to her own people.'

Aquila stared at him a few moments, with a feeling of sickening shock. 'As to that, she must go or stay as she

chooses,' he said at last, very slowly, and turned away into
the street.

He heard the disturbed hum of the city as he walked.
He knew the full tragedy of what had happened. He knew
that in the years to come it might make the difference
between victory and defeat for Britain. But for the
moment all that was a dark background to trouble of
his own.

After Flavia, he had felt that whatever happened to
him, he had nothing to lose. It was a very safe feeling, a
kind of armour, and he clung to it because he had been
afraid to go unarmed. But now he had something to lose
again, and all too likely he was going to lose it. Once he
could have kept Ness against her will if need be, and
risked her knifing him as he slept. The irony of the thing
was that that had been in the days when he did not want
her. It was different now, though he had only just realized
it. He did not want Ness to go; and so he could not keep
her against her will.

He came to the great house beside the old Governor's
Palace that he shared with Eugenus and three other
officers with their families, and went in, past the porter
dozing in the doorway. The atrium, the central room of
the house, was shared by all the families that lived there.
But today it was deserted; no women chattering in the
doorway, no children and hounds tumbling about the
cracked tessarae of the floor. Another cube of pink
sandstone had come out of Ganymede's face, he saw, as
he crossed to the colonnade door and went out into the
sunlit courtyard. The children prised them up to play
games with. It must have been a lovely and gracious house
once; it was gracious still, but with the sad graciousness of
decay; and today he noticed the decay as he seldom did,
for he had grown used to it in two years. One couldn't get

the fallen plaster and crumbling stonework put right in the winter, and in the summer there were always the Saxons. There was grass along the foot of the walls, and green moss creeping here and there up the foot of a column. The stone basin in the centre of the paved court had nothing in it but a little green slime and a few crumbled last-year's leaves and a pigeon's feather; and the dolphin on the rim no longer spouted water from its open mouth, for the water supply, like the drains, was not what it had been. Only a few days ago Ness had held the Minnow— he was still Pilcod the Minnow, his greater name kept for state occasions and when he was in disgrace—up in her arms to pat the gaping creature, saying, 'See, it is like the blue creature on Father's shoulder.' And watching them as he sat on the half-wall of the colonnade, cleaning a piece of equipment, Aquila had been absurdly pleased, without stopping to wonder why.

He crossed the courtyard, and turned into the colonnade beyond, heading for the rooms that were his and Ness's. And when he came into the inner court, Ness was sitting in the sunlight beside the little postern door that gave into the court of the Governor's Palace. The damson tree that grew beside the door was thickening into bud, the shadows of its branches stirring and dappling on the old sunlit wall and over Ness herself. But nothing else about her moved. Her spindle and distaff lay beside her on the stone bench where she had abandoned them, and she sat with her hands linked round her knees. Close beside her Flavian and a hound puppy lay tumbled together, sound asleep on the grass. The puppy's coat was brindled in bars of black and amber, shining in the sun, and the small boy, in a once-bright blue tunic, faded with many washings, lay with his dark head on the puppy's flank; together, Aquila thought, they were supremely good to look at. But Ness was not looking at them, only staring straight before her.

She looked up as he came out from the colonnade, but she did not greet him, only sat watching him out of that waiting stillness.

He came and stood leaning his shoulder against the wall beside her, as though he were very tired. And still she watched him, though she had to look sharply upward now, to do so.

'What is it, then, that brings you home at this hour of day?' she asked at last.

'I came to tell you that your people are leaving Ambrosius's standard,' Aquila said heavily. 'In a day or so, maybe before tonight, they will be gone.'

Her face never lost its waiting stillness. 'I know. All Venta hums with that news.'

'I—spoke with Cradoc your father a while since. He said that because I once turned the blow that was meant for him, he would leave you free to choose for yourself, Ness.'

'And you? Do you also leave me free to choose for myself?'

'If you choose your own people, I will not hold you,' Aquila said.

She rose from the bench and stood facing him, her eyes full of the old challenge. 'And the child?'

Aquila did not answer at once. The words seemed to stick in his throat and choke him. He looked at the small boy and the hound puppy. 'Take the Minnow too,' he said at last, and his voice was hoarse and strained. 'He is so little, he needs you more than me. Only—let him come back to me when he is of age to bear his shield.' He pulled himself up. 'No, you cannot promise that; it might be to send him to fight against his own kind. Take him and keep him, Ness.'

'A strange man you are, my lord,' Ness said. 'Three autumns ago you took me from my father's hearth as though I were a mere piece of household gear that you did not much want. And now you will let me go—you will let the child go—because, I *think* you would fain have us stay.'

Aquila nodded, wordlessly. He knew so little of Ness, scarcely anything at all; certainly not enough to guess what was going on behind her thin, brown face.

She stared at him a long moment, then flung up her head and began to laugh, on the old clear, wild bird-note, waking the Minnow so that he sat up blinking, puzzled at finding his father suddenly there and startled by his mother's wild laughter; he clutched the puppy against him for comfort. But her laughter broke in the middle, and she bent her face into her hands. 'I used to dream night after night of being free; free to go back to my people—my own people . . . But it is too late. I belong to you now, I and the child.'

It seemed to Aquila that there was suddenly a great quietness all about him. 'They will say that you betrayed your own people to stay with me,' he said.

She lifted her face from her hands, with the look of accepting something. 'I *am* betraying my own people—my own world—to stay with you.'

And suddenly out of the quietness he seemed to hear Flavia's voice sounding behind Ness's; Flavia's pretty voice made hoarse and toneless by grief. 'Our Lord help me! He is *my* man.'

It was not the same thing. He was not the enemy, as the Saxons were the enemy; he was not one of a band that had killed Ness's father. Yet he knew that deep down at the heart of things Ness's choosing and Flavia's choosing sprang from the same kind of seed. He had a sudden longing, which wasn't a bit like him now, though it was like the person he had been before the Saxons burned his home, to give Ness things; to bring them and heap them into her lap. New songs and the three stars of Orion's belt, and honey-in-the-comb, and branches of white flowering thorn at mid-winter; not only for her sake, but for Flavia's sake as well.

He heard himself giving her the only thing that he had to give in that way; his own voice, hoarse and a little stumbling, begging her to understand and accept what he gave. 'I had a sister once, Ness. She was carried off by the Saxons when they burned our home. I thought—I prayed—that she was dead, until I found her again years later in the Saxon camp. I would have taken her away with me, but for her also it—was too late, by then. Her name was Flavia.'

It was the first time that he had spoken of his sister in all those years.

Ness made a small gesture with her cupped hands, as though she received a gift into them. 'Poor Aquila—and poor Flavia—and poor Ness.'

Then a party of horsemen passed cantering up the street beyond the house, and she dropped her hands; and the world outside was back with them again.

Aquila hitched at his sword-belt, thrusting his own affairs into the background. 'I must be away and see to sending up some of our men to take over the outposts that Vortimer's people were to have manned.'

He said 'Vortimer's people' not 'your people' now, and did not even notice that it was so. Ness noticed, and there was a faint smile on her mouth, bitter and sweet together, like the juice of the crab apple, as she watched him go striding back to his man's world. Then she turned herself to comfort the Minnow, who, thoroughly upset by all this, had burst into tears.

Somehow Aquila had felt that the desertion of Vortimer's troops must bring the long struggle to a head, and the future down on them like a tide when the sea-wall goes; and he strode out past the dozing porter into the street again with his hands instinctively making sure that his sword was loose in its sheath, as though he expected already to hear the Saxon war cry rise beyond the walls of Venta, and the clash of weapons at the gates.

Instead, all that summer there was a long, uneasy hush, while the weakened British host waited under arms, to guard their borders from an attack that somehow never came. In the nerve-racking hush, as summer dragged by, news filtered through to them now and again from the rest of Britain. With his followers returned to him after his son's death, Vortigern was striving to make a stronger stand than he had done of old, striving to make firmer treaties with the Saxons.

'The fool! The fool!' Ambrosius said. 'Of what use to make bargains in the Fire-hall with the Wolf that you have welcomed in over the threshold.' And he set himself and his Companions with yet grimmer urgency to the task of making an army, and hammering the territories of Calleva and Venta, Aquae Sulis and Sorviodunum into one, after the years of being left to their own devices that had broken them down into separate states and turned their Magistrates, whose forbears had been petty princes, back into petty princes again.

They heard that there was to be a great gathering of the Saxon and Celtic leaders at Durnovaria to make a treaty that would fix for ever the Saxon frontiers in Britain; and they laughed with a small, grim laughter around their watch fires. 'When the last Sea Wolf is dead, then the Saxon frontiers in Britain will be fixed for all time, and not before.'

At summer's end, they heard how that gathering had ended.

It had a name by then; the name of 'The Treachery of the Long Knives' by which it was to be known for generations to come. In accordance with the usual custom that no man should carry weapons to the council circle, Vortigern and his men had gone unarmed to the gathering. But Hengest's house carls sitting with them on the same benches at the feasting which followed the council, a Saxon and a Celt alternately, had had each his dirk concealed inside his sleeve ('Well may the Saxons wear long sleeves' and 'Never trust a man with long sleeves,' said the British for a thousand years). At a given signal each man had ripped out his dagger and stabbed the man on his left. More than a hundred of the Celtic nobles died at that council, but not Vortigern himself. Vortigern, who styled himself High King, had been kept to pay head ransom for his life; and Vortigern had paid it, with the last rags of his pride torn from him, with a dagger at his throat under the thin red beard, and a scribe to write the whole thing down in fair Latin that it might not be denied afterwards; paid it in huge grants of land in the Great Forest and the Down Country and up the Tamesis almost to Londinium.

After that a few of the Celtic party returned to Ambrosius like beaten hounds with their tails between their legs, but for the most part they simply melted away back to their own mountains. Lacking more support— even having to send back some of the troops he had left to help strengthen the western coasts against the Scots pirates—all that Ambrosius could do was to hold his father's old territory as a kind of island, a fortress within its own frontiers. So almost another year went by, and it was full summer again.

The brown floor of the woods dropped gently away before Inganiad's hooves; the trunks of the ash trees rose straight and pale on either hand, and the light under the high canopy of leaves was palely green, so that Aquila seemed to be moving under water as one does in an ash wood. He heard the faint jingle of the patrol coming down behind him; no sound of voices, for they were men used to riding quietly in the woods. Young Artos, riding at his side, with Cabal loping along before, cocked up his head suddenly, caught into swift delight.

'Look, Dolphin—squirrel! There on that branch—Ah, look, there he goes.'

Aquila followed the direction of the boy's gaze, and saw a streak of reddish fur flicker out along the limb of a tree a little to their right. It clung an instant in the crotch where two branches met, chittering at them angrily, then darted on, out on to the slender, swaying, tipmost spray and, scarcely seeming to spring, was in the next tree, floating and lilting through the branches as though it had no more weight than a wind-blown flame. Then it was gone, only they heard it still chittering in the distance. Artos chittered back, then, laughing, took up the alarm call of a jay.

Silence fell on them again, as they rode on, the reins slack on the horses' necks, through the woodland ways.

Presently Aquila glanced again at the boy riding beside him. Young Artos was fourteen, with still a year to wait before Ambrosius judged him ready for battle (if it ever came to open battle again), but he had been like a restive colt all that spring, so that Ambrosius had finally sent him up to Aquila, keeping watch on the northern borders, to get the smell of the camp into his nose and begin to be a man. Artos the Bear. In some ways the name suited him, Aquila thought, for already his body under the leather tunic showed signs of great physical strength, and he had something of the clumsiness of a bear cub in his movements, though not when he was on horseback. Artos on horseback was beautiful with the beauty that comes of a thing's absolute fitness for the purpose for which it was created: a longship at sea, a bird in flight, Artos on horseback.

They were dropping down towards the trackway, the ancient track under the North Chalk, on which, four years ago and forty miles towards the sunrise, Vortimer had held the river line against the host of Hengest. They were out of the straight green aisles of the ash wood now, into the thickets of hazel and alder and crack willow that bordered the track, brushing through the undergrowth with the warm smell of sunshine and open country in their nostrils. Then Artos's head went up again. 'Listen.'

Aquila heard it too; the rumble of wheels and the pelting hooves of cattle on the track; and a few moments later they glimpsed through the twig-tangle of the scrub about them a pathetic little convoy coming into sight: a few lean cattle herded by boys ahead of the rest, a couple of ox carts loaded with gear and women and children, several men on ponies, or on foot, two herd dogs. Aquila had seen many such little bands of refugees in the past year, as the Saxons with their new land grants spread farther over the south-east of Britain.

'More of the poor devils,' he said over his shoulder to the men behind him, reining Inganiad to a halt. 'Let them go by before we cross.'

Among the scrub of the wood-shore they sat their horses, waiting. The cattle went by, white to the belly with dust, hot and weary, with low heads and the strings of slime hanging from their soft muzzles; the first ox cart drawn by its patient, wide-horned oxen, its load of sad women and children and kitchen pots and poultry.

'Those poor people! And Vortigern sitting safe and full fed in his stronghold of Geronwy!' Artos said fiercely.

Aquila looked at him again, and saw his face white and pinched, and his fists clenched on the reins. Artos was very angry; but it wasn't anger alone in his face, it was misery. That was always the way with young Artos; a horse or a hound or a man in pain or trouble, and Artos seemed to feel the ache of it in his own belly. It would make life hard for him, harder than it would otherwise have been; but it would also, Aquila thought, make him very much beloved. He turned his attention back to the fugitives on the track. The men on their ponies were spread out on either side, brushing through the meadow-sweet that grew thick along the open verge. In the second cart, surrounded by all her household gear, an old woman sat dozing under a great hat of dock leaves, on a rough wicker crate of poultry. In the back of that cart was a heather-thatched bee-skep, carefully wedged in position. And behind the cart, the last of the convoy save for a footsore dog with a frilled wet ribbon of tongue drooling from its open jaws, trudged a man with a bundle on his shoulder; a small, strong man, clearly as footsore as the dog, in a rough, brown tunic powdered white with dust.

Something about him tugged at Aquila's memory with a kind of half recognition such as one may feel for a figure seen afar off, that begins, as it draws nearer, to take on the look of a friend.

He turned abruptly to Artos. 'Take the troop back to camp—and see the horses fed and picketed if I have not come by then.'

'Why—what——?' Artos began.

'I go to speak with one of the men down there—an old friend. Take over command, Artos.'

He saw the anger that had been in the boy's face lost in

the sudden pride of his first command, and cast a quick
glance over his head to the grim little weather-beaten man
behind him; Owain would see that all went well. Then he
lifted the reins, sending Inganiad down slantwise towards
the track, out of the scrub, parting the creamy surf of
meadowsweet that swayed together again behind him,
sending up its thick sweetness of scent to mingle with the
rising dust. The folk at the rear of the convoy had seen
him coming now; they were startled, beginning to huddle
as sheep huddle, having seen maybe too many armed men
lately. He shouted to them reassuringly; there was nothing
to make them afraid; he would speak with the Holy Man,
that was all; and he brought Inganiad out on to the track
beside the small man with the bundle on his shoulder.

'Brother Ninnias, is that your bee-skep?'

The man, who had not looked round with the rest to
watch him coming, turned to him now with no more show
of surprise than he had made at their first meeting; and
with the same serene courtesy. Clearly at first he did not
recognize him.

'God's greeting to you, friend. You know my name, and
my bees. Forgive me, and grant me but a moment to
remember you.'

His quiet gaze was on Aquila's face, and Aquila,
bending in the saddle to receive the scrutiny, smiled a
little, seeing the recognition wake slowly in the small
man's eyes.

'Ah—' His gaze took in the tall, flame-red mare and the
iron-bound helmet swinging at the saddle-bow, the stained
and greasy leather tunic which Aquila wore, and the long
cavalry sword at his hip; and returned to his face. 'You are
somewhat changed, my friend, at any rate in your out-
ward seeming. It must be five or six years since you helped
me gather the raked weeds from my bean rows.'

'It is seven,' Aquila said, and slid from Inganiad's back. 'You are footsore and I am fresh. Let you ride awhile.'

Ninnias cast an eye at the tall mare beginning already to dance a little with impatience at the slow pace. 'I thank you, no. It is in my mind that I shall travel more safely on my own sore feet.'

There was truth in that, for Ninnias had not the look of a horseman. Aquila laughed, and they walked on at the tail of the little convoy in companionable silence, save when from time to time Aquila spoke quietingly to the mare. One or two of the men glanced back at them now and then, but without curiosity; they were too dazed for curiosity.

After a while Aquila said, 'You follow the westward drift with the rest, I suppose?'

'Aye,' Ninnias sighed. 'If it had been Brother Drusus that the Lord saw fit to save, instead of me, when the Sea Wolves burned out our little Community, *he* would have stayed in the face of this new Saxon flood, to die a martyr's death . . . If any Christian among the iron folk that I used to serve had been left in the old village, I would have stayed with them—I hope and believe that I would have stayed with them. Brother Drusus would have stayed, anyway, and maybe carried Christ's word to one Saxon before they killed him. Of such are the Kingdom of Heaven. *I* have not the missionary fire; I should not be able to carry Christ's word to even one Saxon. If it were bees it would be another matter. I can be of more use among the poor folk who have lost their homes to the Saxons. So I packed some roots from my physic garden and gave my bees their freedom, save for this one hive that Cunefa most kindly found space for in his cart; and took the Abbot's bell again—I have it here in my bundle—and came away.' He glanced again at the sword

Aquila wore. 'And you? It seems that you found your service to take.'

'I found my service to take,' Aquila said.

'It is, I think, not greatly to be wondered at that I did not know you again,' Brother Ninnias said reflectively.

'Seven years is apt to change a man.'

'There are things that change a man even more than seven years.' The other looked fully round at him. 'When you came to my hut you were lost in a great bitterness, empty of everything save your thirst for vengeance, and when you left me, even that was lost to you.'

'And now?' Aquila said.

'I think that at least you are not empty any more.'

There was a cuckoo calling somewhere among the trees; a rich and sleepy sound, the very voice of summer. Aquila said, 'I have a cause to serve, and a horse and a sword to serve it with. I have a woman and a child down in Venta.'

'You are rich, my friend,' Ninnias said quietly. And then, as though in answer to something in Aquila's tone, 'And yet even now the wound is not healed?'

Aquila was silent a moment, staring ahead into the dust-cloud of the little convoy. No, he thought, it wasn't quite that; the thing had healed all right. The old black bitterness that he had known because of Flavia had gone—Ness had taken it away when she chose to stay with him. But he had lost something—lost it so completely that he did not even really know what it was, so completely that it was only now, with Ninnias, that he knew he had lost it. He knew that he was a different man from the one he would have been if Flavia—if it hadn't been for Flavia.

'Nay, it is healed well enough. Maybe the scar still aches before rain,' he said lightly; and his tone warned the other from any question.

They walked on in silence until they came in sight of the place where a bridle-path branched from the main track, running upward through the gently rolling woods. They had fallen some way behind the rest, so that when they came in sight of the path, the foremost of the cattle were already past it and going on down the main track. Aquila realized that when they came to the branch he would go one way and Ninnias another, and their meeting would be over.

'My way lies up yonder,' he said suddenly. 'I have my summer camp below the village up there. Come my way and preach Christ's Word to us in the war hosts of Britain.'

Brother Ninnias shook his head. 'Nay, I shall be of more use to the poor homeless folk than I should be in a war camp.'

'How much farther do you mean to go? Is there any place in your mind?'

'I do not know how much farther; there is no place in my mind,' Ninnias said. 'It may be that I shall stop when Cunefa and his people stop; it may be that I shall stop before, or go farther. God will tell me when I come to the right place.'

'But I shall not know where that place is,' Aquila said, suddenly saddened by the quickness with which things passed. Things, and people.

'Does that matter so much?'

'Yes,' Aquila said simply.

They had reached the parting of the ways now, and checked. The cuckoo was still calling in a distance that was blue as wood-smoke, and in the marshy ground beside the track the dense mat of iris leaves still showed a few yellow flowers, proudly upheld like lamps among the cool green sword-blades of the leaves. Brother Ninnias stooped and touched one of the flowers without picking it. 'Three petals has the iris, see—a wise flower that carries the number of the Trinity in its head. Father, Son, and Holy Spirit; man, woman, and child; yesterday, today, and tomorrow. Three is the number of perfection and the perfected pattern. Do you know, my friend, I have the strongest feeling that for us two the pattern waits for a third meeting, to attain perfection. But how and when it comes about must lie in God's hands.' He hitched at his bundle. 'Until then—God keep you, Aquila.' He turned and trudged away in the wake of the others, hurrying now to catch up with the cart that had his bee skep in it.

Aquila stood looking after him, where the two ways branched, his arm through Inganiad's bridle, until the bend of the track hid him from view. Then he mounted, and set off at a canter up the path through the woods. But after a time he slackened rein and walked the mare, to give young Artos time to have finished seeing the horses picketed before he came.

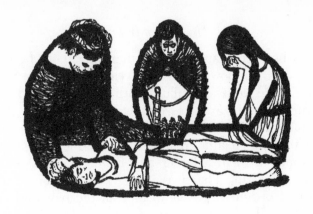

17

'Minnow, Dolphin's Son'

NEWS of Vortigern's death reached Venta in the
spring; and with it news that Guitolinus the
trouble-maker had taken his place as leader of
the Celtic party. Bad news for the British cause, for
Vortigern had been a shamed and broken man, but
Guitolinus was young and fiery and something of a
fanatic, one maybe to light the Celtic fires again. And in
the years that followed, Ambrosius was to have his hands
full enough with the Saxon kind, without having to guard
against a Celtic knife in the back. For the hordes of
Hengest were on the move, not as a swift, forward thrust
this time, but as a slow, inflowing tide. They were moving
down from the fens of the old Iceni territory, and up from
the bride-gift lands of the south-east towards the upper
Tamesis Valley, while others from the lands that had
already taken their names of North folk and South folk
were pushing westward to cut Cymru and the north
completely off from the rest of Britain.

Ambrosius and the British host hung on their southern
flanks like mastiffs to the flank of a bull, thrusting in on

them wherever chance offered, harrying them by every means in their power; but still, year by year, the Saxon wedge drove westward splitting Britain in two. And so six summers went by and a seventh winter came.

Aquila had become one of Ambrosius's captains now; captain of an Aela, a great cavalry wing; for cavalry was beginning to form a larger and larger part of the war hosts of Britain. That was young Artos's doing; Artos, who had begun to gather to him all the best and most gallant of the young warriors; Artos, who rode like a flame in battle, a superb leader of mounted men and a rebel against the old-established order. 'Aye, I know that the Legions depended on their Foot and not their Horse; is that any reason why we must do the same?' he had countered Valarius's protests and head-wagging. 'The Saxon kind pour in, numberless as the wild geese in October, numberless as the sands of the sea, but we who are of the mountains, we who have been Roman Cavalry, we know how to use the horse in battle, and by God's Grace that shall give us the victory.'

And so, as that seventh winter drew towards spring, Aquila's hands were even more full than usual, his time divided between the council table and the water-meadows where the cavalry were in training. But he found time to keep an eye on young Flavian's breaking-in, all the same. The Minnow was nine years old now, and went to the school which a Christian priest had started in the colonnaded court of one of the big houses.

Ness had no patience with such schooling. 'So long as he learns to speak the truth and use a sword and ride a horse, what else is there he needs to learn?'

'Among other things, he needs to learn to read,' Aquila had said.

She had laughed on the old scornful note. 'Read? What

use shall reading be to him? This is a world in which only the sword matters, not books any more.'

That had seemed to Aquila a terrible thing to say, and all Demetrius's teaching cried out against it. He had used the only argument he could think of that would seem good to Ness. 'It was because I could read that Thormod my lord brought me with him to Hengest's camp. If I had not been able to read, I should have died a thrall in Juteland.' He did not think that she had been convinced, but she did not say any more. And Flavian went to school. That is to say, he went when he could not help it, for Flavian also had little use for books.

A day came that was not spring as yet, but poised on the edge of spring; and the water-meadows around Venta were becoming already one vast camp. Aquila and his kind had been working all that day on some raw levies from the Cymric border, trying to teach them something of ordered movement, at least to recognize the trumpet calls that they must obey in battle. In some ways it was like the cavalry manœuvres that they had used to put on at Rutupiae, Aquila thought, walking Inganiad back from the far end of the practice ground, with the shadows lying long on the turf and the bloom thick on the distant hills as the bloom on a bilberry. His inner eye was still full of the beautiful, constantly changing patterns of the day, the wings and squadrons of cavalry sweeping this way and that, obedient to the voice of the trumpets; the jewel brilliance of the long, lance-head serpents that the squadron leaders carried, streaming like flames in the wind of their going, beautiful and gallant against the pollen-dusted sallows and the meadows shaking off their winter greyness. And as though she, too, were remembering the day, Inganiad whinnied softly. Aquila patted her warm, moist neck. The mare was fifteen now; after this year, he thought, he would not use her in battle any more. He wondered which of them would hate that the most.

Artos, with several of the Companions, had just ridden off the field after the last sweeping charge, and turned beside a knot of sallows to watch the horsemen gathering into their own squadrons again and trailing off towards the horse lines and the evening cooking-fires; and Aquila caught through the fuzzy golden green of the budding branches the crimson gleam of a cloak and the wave-break curve of a white stallion's neck, and heard the stir and stamp of a great round hoof, and the jink of a bridle bit, a burst of laughter—and then Flavian's voice.

When he rounded the low, whippy, pollen-dusted mass of branches, there was his son, who should have been at his evening lessons, standing at Artos's stirrup, feet apart and hands behind his back, gazing up at him, while the young man leaned forward in the saddle to return the look. The first thing Aquila felt was a half-amused exasperation, for it was not the first time that Flavian had run from his lessons to the cavalry training. But something in the boy's look, a kind of joyful and eager worship that showed even in his back view, and sounded in his small gruff voice, 'Well, then, when I'm *four*teen will you let me? I can ride very well already—when I'm four*teen* will you let me ride with you?' hurt Aquila sharply. It was he who had taught Flavian to ride, making time when there was so little time to spare; but the boy had never spoken to him like that.

Right at the beginning, nine years ago, he had hoped that he and the Minnow might be friends; the sort of friends that he and his father had been to each other. But somehow it had not worked out like that. He didn't know what had gone wrong; it was not often that he noticed that something had gone wrong at all, but when he did notice,

it hurt him. Maybe it was something to do with the thing
that he had lost . . .

Flavian was so taken up with his eager desire to be one
of Artos's followers that he was deaf to the soft fall of
Inganiad's hooves on the turf behind him. Aquila brought
the mare up, saying with cold lightness, 'Ah, Flavian. I had
assumed that you would serve in my wing when you reach
the age to carry your shield. Am I, then, deserted?'

Flavian jumped at the sound of his voice, and spun
round, and the shining eagerness in him went out like a
light. 'Father—I—I didn't know you were there.'

'No,' Aquila said, 'I imagine that you did not. However,
that does not particularly matter. Your future plans are for
the future; at the present moment you should be with
Brother Eliphias, learning to read words of more than one
syllable. You are over-fond of playing truant.'

His tone was more blighting than he had meant it to be.
He saw the Minnow's face suddenly white and forlorn,
with the pride about it that he wore like a garment when
he wanted to cry. He saw Artos make a sudden movement
as though to lean down and touch the boy's shoulder, and
then check himself. Suddenly he knew that whatever
happened, he must make amends. He forced a smile, and
said quickly, 'Nay then, we'll forget that part of it. Since
you *are* here, you can make yourself useful and ride
Inganiad back for me. I want to try Falcon's paces on
the way home.'

He knew that for a long while past Flavian had been
desperately eager to ride Inganiad, and so he looked for a
quick flare of joyful excitement. For a moment, delight
did leap in the boy's face, but only for a moment, then it
was gone again, and Flavian said, 'Yes, Father. Thank you,
Father.' But it sounded more dutiful than anything else.
Aquila, pretending not to notice as he dismounted and

called to one of his men to bring up Falcon, his spare mount, wondered what the trouble was now. He swung the small boy up into the saddle with a 'There you are. Hold tight,' which sounded falsely hearty in his own ears, and set to shortening the stirrup ropes. And as he did so, he understood what was wrong. For so long Flavian had longed for the day when he would be deemed worthy to ride Inganiad; it should have been a great occasion, a time of trumpets. But he had made it only a lump of honeycomb after a smacking. (It is never the things that you do, but the way you do them. It was not that you laughed at Rhyanidd about the pig . . .) Would he never learn? He could have groaned. Well, too late to do anything about it now. Still keeping a firm hold on Inganiad's reins, he mounted Falcon, and wheeled both horses towards the distant walls of Venta, with the rest of the group who were already moving off.

Flavian looked very small on the tall, flame-coloured mare as his father glanced aside at him. He was sitting very upright, his eyes shining; he was a man riding among men. Maybe it hadn't been such a very bad mistake after all. Aquila saw and understood the appeal on the boy's face. Flavian wanted him to let go the reins. He hesitated, but Inganiad was quiet after her day's work; she had known and loved Flavian all his life and was used to his climbing about her back in stable. She would be gentle with him. Aquila took his hand off the reins.

A very short while later, if there had been any time for cursing, he would have been cursing himself by every name under heaven that he had done so. The thing happened so quickly, that it was over almost before it was begun. A white owl, early on the hunting trail, flew out of the alder brake on silent, ghost-soft wings almost under Inganiad's nose; and the mare, startled, and missing her lord's strong and familiar hand on the bridle, shied violently and went up in a rearing half-turn. Aquila had an instant's sight of the Minnow's white, terrified face that stayed with him afterwards as though it were bitten into his mind. He shouted to the boy to hold on, even as he flung himself sideways in his own saddle to catch the reins, but he was too late. The next thing he knew was that Flavian was on the ground and he was kneeling over him.

The boy lay unmoving, with blood trickling from the great broken place in his head where it had struck a sharp alder root. With a cold sickness rising in him, Aquila set his hand over the Minnow's heart. It was beating, though very faintly, and he drew a long, shuddering gasp of relief. Artos was kneeling beside him, and he heard quick, concerned voices all around, but he didn't hear what they said. He was feeling the Minnow all over with desperate urgency. Nothing seemed broken; there was only that terrible blow on the head. With infinite care he gathered him into his arms, and stood up; the child felt very light, as though his bones were hollow like a bird's. Someone must have caught the horses, and someone brought him Inganiad, still trembling and wild of eye. He shook his head; to ride back he would have to let Flavian out of his arms while he mounted. 'I'll walk,' he muttered.

He walked back to Venta, carrying the small, unconscious body; and Artos walked with him, leading his own horse. What had happened to the rest, he neither knew nor cared. Once inside the city gates he said to Artos, 'Go ahead and warn Ness.' And when Artos had mounted and gone clattering away on his errand, he walked on alone.

He carried Flavian up the street and in at the door where Artos's horse was tied to the hitching-post, and across the courtyard where the stone dolphin still gaped senselessly in its broken fountain. Ness met him as he reached the inner courtyard, Artos behind her. She was as white as the boy, and held out her arms without a word to take him, but Aquila shook his head. 'Better not to change him over. I'll put him on his bed . . . I let him ride Inganiad and a white owl startled her.' He forgot that Artos would have told her that already. The door of Flavian's sleeping cell stood open and he carried him in and laid him down on the narrow cot; then, as Ness slipped to her knees beside it, he turned to Artos, big and anxious in the doorway. 'Go across to Eugenus's quarters and get him quickly.'

The daylight was going fast, draining out of the little lime-washed room as it might so easily be that the life was draining out of Flavian's small, still body. 'If the boy dies,' Aquila said, 'I've killed him.'

Ness looked up from the work of her hands as she pressed back Flavian's dark, feathery hair and laid a piece of soft linen against his temple to staunch the slowly trickling blood.

'Get the lamps lit so that Eugenus has light to work by,' she said. 'Then go and bid one of the slaves to bring hot water.'

There was an agonizing delay before Eugenus came, for he had just gone out to a supper party, and it was some time before Artos could find him, but he came hurrying at last, still wearing his banquet wreath of early white violets and bringing with him a faint scent of wine. He felt Flavian all over much as Aquila had done, examined and bathed and bound his head, felt his heart and listened to his breathing, and pulled up his closed lids to look into his eyes.

'A bad blow, a cruel blow, but I think that the skull is not cracked,' he said. 'I will come again in the morning. Meanwhile keep him warm and do not move him. On no account try to bring him back to his body before he is ready to come. That may take several days.'

'But he—will come back?' Ness said, still kneeling by the bed with the child's head between her hands.

Eugenus looked from her to Aquila standing at the bed-foot and back again; and his dark, bulging eyes were extraordinarily kind under the ridiculous banquet wreath. 'I hope and pray so,' he said.

In the next three days Aquila went about his duties as usual, but training ground and council chambers alike seemed quite unreal. Only the nights were real, when he kept watch by Flavian while Ness got a few hours' sleep. The other wives in the big house would have helped her gladly, though she had made close friends with none of them, but she would not leave the boy for more than a few moments to anybody but Aquila. He would bring work with him—horse lists that needed checking, some problem of transport to be worked out—but he made small progress with them. Sometimes he dozed a little, for he was very tired, but never deeply enough to lose consciousness of the narrow cell, the glow of the shielded lamp thrown upward on the lime-washed wall, and Flavian's small, still face on the pillow, so like Flavia's, so incredibly like. It was odd that he had never realized before how like to Flavia the boy was.

For three nights there was no change, and then, half-way through the fourth night, Flavian stirred. He had stirred before, flung his arms about and muttered: but it had been a kind of blind stirring, as though it were not Flavian himself, but only his body showing that it was ill at ease. This time it was different; Aquila knew that it was different, even as he laid aside the tablets he had been working on and strained forward to look into the boy's face. Flavian stirred again, a little shiver ran through him, and he was still once more. But his breathing was growing quicker, he shifted his bandaged head from side to side on the pillow; his mouth was half open and his eyelids fluttered. He looked like someone trying to wake from a sleep that is too heavy for him.

'Flavian,' Aquila said quietly. 'Minnow.'

Eugenus had said that they must not try to bring him back into his body until he was ready to come; but now he was ready, he was trying to come, needing help. He didn't know if Flavian heard him, but he made a kind of whimpering, and a little groping movement of one hand on the coverlid. Aquila put his own hand over it. 'It is all right. It is all right, Minnow. I'm here.'

Flavian drew a long, fluttering breath, and then another; and then he opened his eyes and lay frowning up at his father.

'It is all right,' Aquila said again. 'Nothing to worry about. Lie still.'

Flavian's gaze wandered off unsteadily to blink at

the lamp, and returned to his father's face. 'Have I—been ill?'

'No,' Aquila said. 'You hurt your head, but it is better now.'

There was a moment's silence, and then Flavian turned his hand over to cling to Aquila's. 'I fell off Inganiad—didn't I?' he mumbled. 'I'm sorry, Father.'

'Inganiad threw you,' Aquila said. 'A white owl startled her and she threw you. If I had been on her back, she would like enough have thrown me.'

Flavian smiled. It was a very sleepy smile, and Aquila smiled back; and just for the moment they were very near together, with the wall that had grown up between them dwindled quite away. But Flavian was a little anxious; there was something else his father must understand. 'It wasn't Inganiad's fault, Father—really it wasn't. It was the white owl.'

'It was the white owl,' Aquila said. 'Go to sleep again, Minnow.'

Flavian scarcely needed telling, for his eyes were already drooping shut; and in a little while he was sleeping quietly, his hand still holding Aquila's. Aquila sat for a time, watching him, then he dropped his own head on to his fore-arm on the edge of the cot. He had not prayed for Flavian's life, he hadn't prayed for anything or about anything, since the day that he lay under the oak tree after his parting with Flavia, and decided that it was a waste of time. But there was a deep rush of gratitude in him, now.

He did not go to rouse Ness; she was asleep and needed the sleep desperately. And besides, the Minnow still had him by the hand.

When Flavian woke up again in the morning, he drank some broth and managed a shaky grin for his family. But the old barrier was up again between him and his father—though maybe not quite so high as it had been before.

Having begun to mend, he mended at a gallop, and not so many days later Aquila, with an hour to spare in the morning, wrapped him in a striped native rug and carried him out to sit on the bench in the inner courtyard. There was beginning to be some strength in the sun, and the old wall at their backs was faintly warm as they sat side by side. It was just the two of them, and Argos, who had been a fat, brindled puppy when Ness chose between Aquila and her own people, lying outstretched at their feet, dignified as a stone lion. The violets that grew against the wall were not out yet, but there was a faint scent of them from their leaves, and a cock chaffinch was flirting to and fro in the branches of the damson tree. Aquila had a feeling of 'home' on him. You couldn't really call this great, decaying house that they shared with so many other families 'home', but it was the place where he lived when he was in Venta with Ness and the Minnow; it had been for nearly nine years, and every stone of it was familiar. To Flavian, he supposed, it must be home; it would be the first place that he remembered. No orchard below the mountains, no downland valley for Flavian.

He looked round at the boy beside him. The Minnow was sitting gathered in on himself like a ball, with his feet drawn up inside the striped rug and only his head sticking out. He had been allowed to leave the bandage off for the first time, and his thin, eager face was more than ever like Flavia's.

'Let's look at your head,' Aquila said, and then, as the boy scuffled round on the bench, cocking it obediently to one side and screwing up his eyes, 'Yes, it's mending . . . I'll tell you a thing, Minnow; you're going to have a scar on your forehead to spoil your beauty, exactly like the one I have on mine.'

Flavian's eyes flew open. 'Truly?' he said, as though it were something to be much desired.

'Very truly,' Aquila said, and there was a sudden warmth of laughter in him, because he had not thought of it like that. They looked at each other for a moment in silence, and in the silence it was as though, very hesitantly, they reached out a little towards each other.

'Minnow——' Aquila began, without any clear idea of what he was going to say. But in the same instant he realized that the Minnow was not listening. He had craned round to listen to quick footsteps that were coming across the court of the Governor's Palace towards the little postern door under the damson tree. He saw the pin lift, the door opened, and Brychan came striding through. And the moment was lost.

Aquila got up quickly to meet the new-comer. 'Brychan, what is it, then?' But he thought he knew. They had been waiting for the final order, almost on the edge of marching for days now.

Brychan had halted at sight of them; he was bright with the special flame that always woke in him at the approach of fighting. 'The scouts have just come in. Hengest himself is encamped this side of Pontes and we march at noon in advance of the rest. I came through this way on my way down to the horse lines, to bring you the word.'

They looked at each other for a moment, both on the edge of going their separate ways, both aware that what was coming was something different from the harrying of the past summers.

'I have almost forgotten the smell of full battle,' Brychan said.

Aquila said abruptly, almost as though some grey

shadow of the future had reached out to touch him, 'Have we left it too long?—We had something once, something that wins battles. Have we got it still?'

'Too much wine last night?' Brychan drawled. 'Or just an encouraging thought on the eve of battle?'

'Just a thought,' Aquila said. He was hitching already at his sword-belt.

For a moment Brychan's face had neither its usual insolence nor its usual laughter. 'We have got Artos,' he said, almost gravely.

'Yes, we've got Artos.' Aquila looked up from his sword-belt. 'I only have to pick up my saddle bag and say good-bye to Ness. I'll be down at the horse lines close behind you.'

Brychan nodded, and in the act of turning away, flicked a long finger towards Flavian, round-eyed with excitement on the bench. 'How is the boy?'

Flavian answered for himself. 'I am almost mended, and I shall have a scar on my head like my father's!'

'Sa, sa! my young fighting cock!' Brychan stood looking down at him an instant, laughing again, his darkly golden head seeming very far up among the twisted branches of the damson tree. 'What it is to be a son, and what it is to have one!' and he swung on his heel and went with his long, lazy stride across the court and disappeared into the shadows of the colonnade.

Aquila looked down at his son. If only they could have had a little longer, he thought, they might have begun to know each other. Now maybe there wouldn't be another chance. Even if he came back, it would probably be too late, and the time would have gone by. He saw suddenly how the buds were swelling on the damson tree, and it came to him that he had never seen the damson tree in flower. The Saxons came before the buds broke.

'Back to bed with you,' he said, and picked up his son, very silent now, and carried him back into his sleeping cell and set him down on the bed.

'What did you begin to say, before Brychan came?' Flavian asked.

'Did I begin to say anything? I have forgotten.' Aquila gave him a hurried and awkward hug, and strode out, shouting to one of the stable slaves to bring round Inganiad; then went to pick up his saddle bag and find Ness.

18

The Hostage

A FEW days later, on the fringe of the Tamesis Valley,
the British and Saxon war hosts met in battle; and
five days later still, terribly, shamefully, unbeliev-
ably, the leaders of both sides met in the Basilica at
Calleva, to discuss an agreed peace.

The Basilica at Calleva had been burned down, like
most of the town, in the troubles that ended the reign of
Emperor Allectus a hundred and fifty years ago, and, like
the rest of the town, rebuilt on its own blackened rubble.
Standing with the other British leaders at the council
table that had been set up on the tribunal dais, Aquila
could see by the clumsier workmanship where the new
walls joined on to the old ones; even the stain of the
burning, reddish as a stain of almost washed-out blood,
showed up in the dusty sunlight that fell through the high
clerestory windows of the vast hall. Odd how one noticed
things like that—things that didn't matter, when the Lord
God knew that there were things enough that did, to
think about . . .

What had happened five days ago? How had it come
about, this grey state of things between defeat and
victory? The slackening of an army's fibre through too

many years of waiting? 'Have we waited too long?' he had said to Brychan when the order came to march. 'We had something once—something that wins battles. Have we got it still?' And Brychan had said, 'We have got Artos.' That had been a true word; they had got Artos, whose crashing cavalry charges had wrenched a drawn battle out of what would otherwise have been a British defeat. He glanced aside, and saw the tall, mouse-fair head upraised above the heads of the other men round Ambrosius's chair. Ambrosius was one whom men followed for love, into the dark if need be, but Artos was already one whom men would feel that they were following into the light; a great burst of light that had somehow the warmth of laughter in it as well as the sound of trumpets. But not even Artos had been able to drag victory out of that battle five days ago. Aquila's eye went for an instant in search of Brychan, before he remembered that Brychan was dead, like Inganiad. Not for the red mare the old age in quiet meadows that he had planned for her . . . Strange, the tricks that your mind could play, so that you forgot for a moment, as though it were a light thing, that your sword brother was dead.

He looked at Hengest, sitting on the far side of the table with his leaders about him. He was a little more grey, a little less golden than he had been on the night that Rowena made her singing magic, a little broader and heavier of body, but with the same shifting, grey-green light in his eyes; the same womanish trick of playing with the same string of raw amber round his neck as he sat sideways in his chair, his other hand on the narwhal ivory hilt of his sword, and watched Ambrosius under his brows.

Ambrosius was speaking levelly and a little harshly, putting into a few words the thing that they had been arguing about, it seemed to Aquila, for hours. 'Assuredly it goes as hardly with you as with us, to speak of an agreed peace, O my enemy. Yet weakened as we both of us are by the battle that we have fought, we must both of us know that there is no other road that we can take. You cannot sleep secure in your new settlements, knowing that we may be upon your flanks at any hour, and that we are too strong for you to crush us out of existence. We, alas, are not strong enough to drive you into the sea. And so the matter stands.'

The heavy creases in Hengest's wind-bitten cheeks deepened in a ferocious smile. 'And so the matter stands.' His eyes never leaving Ambrosius's face, he leaned forward, and dropping his hand from the amber about his neck, made on the table the unmistakable gesture of a man moving a piece on a chess-board. 'Stalemate. It remains only, O my enemy, to draw a frontier between us.'

Ambrosius rose, pulled his dagger from the crimson scarf knotted about his waist, and, bending forward a little, he drew a long curved line on the table, crossing it with a straight one, then another, the sharp point of the dagger scoring cruelly deep into the fine, polished citron wood with a sound that set one's teeth on edge. Ambrosius, the last leader of Rome-in-Britain, was very quiet, very controlled, very civilized; but the searing, screeching line of the dagger's wake, white on the precious wood, showed his mood clearly enough. Aquila, watching, saw the familiar map beginning to take shape, the map that he had seen drawn so often in charred stick beside the hearth at Dynas Ffaraon, now scratched with a dagger on a polished table-top, for the making of an agreed frontier with the barbarians.

Hengest, who had been frowning down at the thing growing on the table-top, bent forward suddenly with a grunt. 'Sa! A picture of a land! I have seen the country so—spread out—when I lay on the High Chalk and looked down as an eagle might.'

'A picture of a land,' Ambrosius said. 'Here is Aquae Sulis, here Cunetio, here runs the High Chalk, and here'—he stabbed downward with the dagger and left it quivering in the table between them—'we stand in the Basilica at Calleva Atrebatum, talking of a frontier.'

They talked long, very long, and heavily and hotly, before at last the matter was talked out; and Ambrosius plucked up his dagger again and drew one great, jagged furrow screeching across the map, from agreed point to agreed point, making of Calleva almost a frontier town. He drew it with careful precision, but so deeply that Aquila saw his wrist quiver.

'So, it is done,' Hengest said. 'Now swear,' and took from the breast of his ring-mail byrnie a great arm-ring of beaten gold, and laid it on the table, midway across the frontier that Ambrosius had drawn.

Ambrosius looked down at it, shining in the cool, greenish light of the great hall. 'On what am I to swear?'

'On Thor's ring.'

'Thor is not my God,' Ambrosius said. 'I will swear by the name of my own God, and in the words that have bound my people for a thousand years. If we break faith in this peace that has been agreed between your people and mine, may the green earth open and swallow us, may the grey seas roll in and overwhelm us, may the sky of stars fall on us and crush us out of life for ever.'

Hengest smiled, a little contemptuously. 'So, I accept it. And now I swear for my people on Thor's Ring.' He rose as he spoke, his great hand was on the ring. 'Hear me, Thor the Thunderer, hear me swear for my people, that we also keep the faith.'

There was a silence, echoing in the high emptiness of

the hall; then Ambrosius said, 'And now all that is left is to choose the men from either host who are to trace out the frontier.'

Hengest's eyes narrowed a little. 'One thing more.'

'So? And what is that?'

'The question of hostages.'

That time the silence was a long one, broken only by a quick and furious movement from Artos, instantly stilled. Then Ambrosius said, 'Is a most sacred oath, then, not a thing to be relied upon?'

'A hostage who is dear to his lord makes it yet more to be relied upon,' Hengest said, inexorably.

Ambrosius's hand on his dagger-hilt clenched until the knuckles shone white as the scars that he had made on the polished citron wood. He looked at Hengest for a long moment, eye into eye.

'Very well,' he said at last; and the words, though icily clear, sounded as though his lips were stiff. He turned his head, and looked consideringly into face after face of the men about him. Artos looked back, smiling a little from his great height; Pascent's face was wide open to him, both of them offering themselves. But his dark gaze passed them over and came to rest on the pouchy, slack-lined face of the man who had been one of his father's bodyguard. 'Valarius, will you do this for me?'

Aquila saw an odd look in the older man's face, as though the blurred lines grew clearer, saw his head go up with a new pride. 'Yes, sir, most joyfully I will do this for you,' Valarius said.

One or two of the Saxons muttered together, and Hengest said, 'Who, then, is this man that you offer as hostage?'

'Valarius, one of my father's bodyguard, to whom I owe my life,' Ambrosius said, 'and my friend.'

Hengest looked from the Prince of Britain to the old soldier and back again, studying both faces under his brows, and nodded. 'So be it, then. For my own hostage——'

Ambrosius cut him short, in that voice as smooth as a sword blade that Aquila had heard only once before. 'I ask no hostage in return. If Hengest is not bound by his sacred oath, I do not believe that the life of one of his hearth-companions will bind him. Therefore I accept his oath alone, though he does not accept mine.'

If he had hoped to reach some kind of chivalry in his enemy, the hope was a vain one. Hengest merely shrugged his great shoulders, his flickering stare still on Ambrosius's face. 'It is for Ambrosius to do as he chooses,' he said. But the flickering gaze said as clearly as could be, that if Ambrosius chose to be a fool . . .

Aquila stood leaning on his spear beside the gap in the bank and ditch where the road came through, and looked away north-eastward. Almost from his feet the land began its gentle, undulating fall-away to the smoke-blue distances of the Tamesis Valley: wood and pasture and winding water, all blurred over with a blueness that was like smoke. It might have been the smoke of burning cities, but the Saxons had not burned the cities. They had looted sometimes, but for the most part, having no use for town life, they had simply left the cities alone to live as best they could, to grow emptier and poorer, and fall more and more into decay, until the few people left in them drifted out at last to the Saxon way of life. It was all Saxon land down there now.

Summer was nearly gone, the sixth summer since Hengest and Ambrosius had faced each other across the council table at Calleva Atrebatum; and the goldfinches were busy among the silk-headed seeding thistles in the ditch, and the hawthorn bushes of the slopes below were already growing red as rust with berries, though there were still harebells in the grass of the bank beside Aquila, where the turf was tawny as a hound's coat. Five years ago that bank had been bare, chalky earth, raw with newness; a dyke cast up to mark the frontier between two worlds where it crossed the open downs and had nothing else to mark it; now it looked as old and settled in its ways as the downs themselves.

A faint waft of woodsmoke came to Aquila on the evening air, mingling with the warm, dry scent of the turf, and a horse whinnied, and somebody began to sing, and he heard the rattle of a bucket from the huddled bothies of the guard-post behind him. They had not had guards along the downs at first, but the years of peace had grown more strained and uneasy as they went by, and the simple line had become little by little a guarded frontier. Aquila, who had spent much of those five years on the frontier, thought sometimes that he knew something of what it must have been like on Hadrian's Wall in the old days; the long waiting with one's eyes always on the north; not enough to do, yet never able to relax. And behind the frontiers, as those five years went by, Ambrosius, with Artos at his shoulder, had been at the old struggle to keep their fighting men together, to make some kind of oneness with their neighbours, against the time when the war hosts of Britain and the barbarians crashed together again. For, despite oaths and hostages, all men knew that that time would come one day. Last year there had been so much unrest along the borders that they had thought it was upon them. But this year had passed more quietly again; and now the campaigning season was almost over.

The light was beginning to fade, and he was on the point of turning away to go down to the guard-post for the evening meal, when his eye was caught by a movement among the bushes lower down the slope.

He checked, instantly alert, watching for it to come again. For a long, waiting moment nothing moved down there save an indignant blackbird that flew scolding out of a hawthorn bush; and then the movement flickered again under the turf-tangle of the autumn scrub. Something, someone was working his way through the bushes towards the road. Aquila's hand tightened automatically on the shaft of his spear, his frowning gaze following the small, stealthy movements as they drew nearer—nearer—until, between one instant and the other, a man broke from cover of the whitethorn scrub on to the open turf. An oldish man, for his head was cobweb colour in the fading light: a man who ran low, swerving and zigzagging as a snipe flies, but with none of the lightness of a snipe, for he stumbled and lurched as he ran, as though he were far spent, with unmistakably the look of a hunted man putting on one last, heart-tearing burst of speed to reach the bank that marked the frontier before the hunt was upon him. Aquila's mouth was open to shout for his men, but he shut it again. He could see no sign of pursuit, and if the fugitive had for the moment shaken off whoever it was that he ran from, to shout would betray him. Aquila took a long step forward, poised for instant action. The fugitive had stumbled out on to the road now; he was very near the gap in the bank, so near that for a moment he looked as though he might make it. Then a kind of snapping hum sounded behind him in the bushes, something thrummed like a hornet through the air towards him, and he staggered and half fell, then recovered himself and ran on. Aquila sprang forward, yelling to the men behind him in the guard-post as he ran. Another arrow thrummed out of the bushes, but in the fading light it missed, and stood quivering in the roadway. Aquila cast his spear at the bushes from which it had come, and heard a cry as he ripped out his sword, still running. A few moments later, with his own men already pounding down towards him, he reached the reeling fugitive just as he fell, and saw the short Saxon arrow in his back: saw also, with a feeling of shocked unbelief, who the man was. The hostage had returned in a strange manner to his own people.

Aquila was kneeling over him in the road, his men all around them. 'It's Valarius,' he said. 'Get him back, lads. The devils! See what they have done to him!'

They took the old man up and carried him back through the gap in the dyke that he had so nearly gained, and on the British side of it, in the safety that was too late for him now, made to lie him down on his face. But somehow he got to his knees, looking up at Aquila with a twisted and sweating face that yet smiled a little.

'Ah, the Dolphin! Five years is a long time, and it is good—to be—among friends again,' he said, and sagged forward into Aquila's arms.

'Keep guard, in case they try to rush us,' Aquila said to his men. 'Valarius, in Our Lord's name, what has happened?'

'They won't rush you—won't—risk any sort of frontier trouble—not now,' Valarius gasped. 'I hoped to lie up till—dark before trying—to get across, but they—routed me out too soon.' And then, as he felt Aquila's hand near the wound, 'Na, let be! There's nought to be done, and—if you meddle with that—I shall die—shall die anyway, but—must talk—first.'

Aquila also knew that there was nothing to be done, not

with an arrow deep-driven in that position. He eased
the old soldier over, holding him with an arm under his
shoulders so that no weight came on the barb, and
propped him with a knee, listening to the harsh, agonized
words that he gasped out with such desperate urgency.
'Hengest has made—an alliance with Guitolinus—the
Scots too, some Scots settlers from Southern Cymru—
going to invade—invade——'

'When?' Aquila snapped.

'In—half a month, by the—original plan. That leaves
them—clear month's campaigning time—may be more.
Gambling on Ambrosius—not expecting anything so—
late in the year. But knowing that I'm—slipped through
their fingers with—maybe breath for a few words left in—
my body, I think they'll—come sooner.'

'They swore on Thor's Ring,' Aquila began stupidly.

'To the Saxon kind—an oath between friends is
binding—to the death. An oath between—enemies is
made to be kept until—the time comes for breaking it.'

'Are you sure of all this?' Aquila demanded.

'I have been a hostage among them for five years—oh,
my God! Five years!—Nobody troubles to keep a hostage
in the dark. I know these things—beyond all doubt.'

'Where will the attack fall?'

'I—do not know.'

'Do you know anything more?' Aquila pressed him with
merciless urgency, for it seemed to him that Valarius was
beginning already to drift away from them. 'Anything
more, Valarius?'

'Na, nothing more. Is not that—enough?'

Aquila looked up, singling out one from among the
men around him. 'Priscus, saddle up and ride like the
hammers of hell for Venta. Tell Ambrosius that Hengest
has made an alliance with Guitolinus and the Scots

settlers in Cymru and intends invading, certainly in half a moon, maybe sooner. Tell him that Valarius has returned to us, and in what manner. Repeat after me.'

The man repeated his orders, and swung away, striding downhill towards the horse-lines. Aquila shifted a little, trying to find an easier position for Valarius.

'Water,' Valarius whispered.

'Go and get it,' Aquila said to the man nearest him.

Valarius lay looking up at the sky, from which the light was beginning to fade. Little clouds that had not showed when the sun was up made a flight of dim, rose-coloured feathers across the arch of it. The green plover were crying, and a little wind, cool after the heat of the day, stirred the grass along the crest of the bank. The men of the guard-post stood round in silence, looking down.

'It is good to come back,' Valarius said with a deep contentment. 'The Saxon kind promised—that when the fighting joined, and the time for secrecy was done—I should be free to—come back to die with my—own people, but I was always—an impatient man. Is the— water coming?'

'It will be here very soon,' Aquila said, wiping away the stain of blood from the corner of Valarius's mouth. 'Is there any word that you would have me carry to Ambrosius?'

'Tell him—I rejoice to have redeemed my debt.'

'He has never thought of any debt,' Aquila said. 'I have told you that before.'

A queer little smile twisted Valarius's mouth. 'But I have—and I have told you that before . . . Tell him, all the same. Even if he has—not thought of it so—he will understand and be—glad for me.' His last words were scarcely to be heard at all. He turned his head on Aquila's arm, and began to cough, and more blood came out of his mouth; and the thing was over. So Valarius died with more dignity than he had lived for many years.

The man who had gone for the water came running with it in his leather helmet, and knelt down beside Aquila. 'Is he—am I——?'

Aquila shook his head. 'You are just too late.' He felt under Valarius's body, and snapped off the projecting arrow-shaft, knowing that there was no more harm the barb could do him now, and laid him down at the foot of the bank among the long, tawny grasses and the late hare-bells that looked almost white in the dusk.

19

'Victory Like a Trumpet Blast'

A FEW evenings later the British war host was encamped within the turf banks of the ancient hill fort a few miles east of Sorviodunum, knowing that tomorrow's battle was for life or death.

Aquila, checking just below the crest of the great western rampart on his way down to the horse-lines, saw the slow heave of the downs westward like a vast sea in the windy dusk. Below him, below the encircling rampart on its isolated hill, the shallow valley dipped away, rising again to the wave-lift of downs on the far side. As he looked away north-westward along the line of them, he could just make out, even now, the gap in the hills where the road from Sorviodunum came through on its way to Calleva; the gap beyond which, somewhere, the hosts of Hengest were encamped, waiting, as the British were waiting, for dawn. Behind the ancient turf fortress the land fell gently, dark-furred with thorn scrub, as were all the skirts of the downs, to the low flatness of reed and willow and alder brake, the stray gleam of water where the river marshes crept in among the hills. Ambrosius had chosen his position well: the marshes and the thorn scrub and the hill slopes to guard the British flanks, the road from Venta to Sorviodunum a few miles behind for their supply line.

Only three days ago, the whole frontier had gone up in flames. The break-through had come just below Cunetio, and Hengest with Guitolinus and the Scots had swept like a flood through a broken dam down the road south, hurling back the British skirmishing bands sent up to clog their advance and slow them down while the main defence made ready. A few hours since, and a few miles short of Sorviodunum, they had swung south-eastward for the gap in the downs where the Calleva road passed through. Once through that they would be free to march on Venta itself, or, more likely, sweep down the broad river valley the last few miles to the head of Vectis Water, so cutting Ambrosius's little kingdom in two. Free, that is, save for the British standing in the way, the hastily gathered host of lowland foot-soldiers and mountain cavalry, the bowmen of Cymru and a few untrained, late-joined companies from the nearest fringes of the Dumnonii.

Ambrosius had called in almost the whole of the British host, staking everything on this one great battle; for Ambrosius, as well as Hengest, knew how to be a gambler. If they were beaten now, that was the end. 'I can't afford to fail once,' Ambrosius had said, years ago, 'because I've nothing in reserve with which to turn failure into victory.' It had been a curb then, holding them back; now it was become a spur. An odd change, that, Aquila thought, listening to the confused hum of the camp behind him.

Five years ago the mood of the British camp had been somehow deadened with long waiting. It should have been worse now, worse by five years, but it was not. Maybe it was a kind of desperation, the knowledge that this time there could be no agreed peace, that nerved them. But whatever it was, Aquila had felt the change of mood at once when he rode in at noon with his own men; had felt something rising like a dry wind through the whole host. Unaccountable were the ways of men, and still more unaccountable the ways of hosts that were quite unlike the ways of the men from which they were made.

Aquila turned and went on his way. The whole camp was throbbing like a lightly tapped drum as he went down through it. Men came and went, horses stamped, he heard the ring of hammer on field anvil where the armourers were busy on last-minute harness repairs; arrows were being given out from the fletchers' wagons, and the smoke of many cooking fires spread and billowed across the darkening hill-top before the rising wind.

There was a fire down by the near end of the horse-lines, and some of his own men gathered about it. And there, standing a little uncertainly on the edge of the fire-light, he found Flavian.

Flavian was wearing a weather-worn leather tunic too big for him across the shoulders, and he must have been to the armourers' wagons, for a long sword in a plain wolfskin sheath hung at his side. The wind was blowing his dark, feathery hair sideways across his forehead like a pony's forelock, and the five-year-old scar showed white in the wind-driven firelight. To Aquila, stopping abruptly in his tracks at sight of him, he looked very surprisingly like a man.

'Flavian! What do you suppose you are doing here?'

'I came out to take my part against the Saxons,' Flavian

said, and came a step nearer into the firelight. He was as tall as his father already; a tall, grave boy with level eyes. 'They were saying in Venta that every man who could carry a sword would be needed.'

'Every *man*, yes,' Aquila said.

'You always said that I should have my shield when I was fifteen, Father.'

'You have miscounted. You are not fifteen yet.'

'I shall be in a month's time,' Flavian countered, quickly.

There was a small silence, and then Aquila asked, quietly, because he did not want to shame the boy in the hearing of the men round the fire, 'You did not come without word to your mother?'

Flavian shook his head. 'No, sir; Mother sent me.'

Again there was silence. They looked at each other through the smoke of the windy fire, through the barrier that had always been between them. They had never got back to where they had been in the sunny courtyard five years ago. The whole summer had gone by before Aquila returned to Venta again, and by that time it had been too late. Just for the moment Aquila had thought that the boy had come to him of his own accord. But Ness had sent him . . .

'Very well, then,' he said, with no softening of his stern manner. 'I take you. Did you ride Whitefoot?'

'Yes, sir, but——'

'Where have you picketed him?'

'In the same row as Falcon, sir, for the moment, but——'

Aquila's brows snapped together. 'For the moment?'

'Yes; you see——' Flavian hesitated, and his father saw him swallow. 'Sir—when I got here, they told me you were in council with Ambrosius, and I had to picket him somewhere until I could see you and ask your leave. Sir, I want to take my sword to Artos and ask him to let me ride in his wing.'

Aquila was wincingly aware of his own men gathered about the fire and looking on, listening. 'At least this time you have thought fit to ask my leave in the matter,' he said coldly. 'I suppose that I should be gratified by that.'

'Then I may go to Artos?' Young Flavian was already poised to be away in search of his heart's desire.

'No,' Aquila said, 'I am afraid not.'

'But, sir——'

'*I am afraid not.*'

For an instant Flavian seemed about to fly out at him with some furious protest, but he choked it back, and asked in a tone as quiet as his father's, 'Why, sir?'

Aquila was silent a moment. He was letting this tall, almost unknown son of his go into battle before the time that he had meant to, but at least he would keep him close to himself. It was not jealousy, it was a feeling that he would be safer there. He knew that that was confused thinking, a Saxon arrow was as likely to find him in one part of the battle as another; but somehow he felt that he owed it to Ness, who had sent him his son on the eve of battle.

'Possibly one day I may give you my reasons,' he said at last. 'For the present, I fear that you must accept blindly the fact that I forbid you to take that sword that you have come by to Artos.' He waited for an answer, and then as it did not come, said sharply, 'Understood?'

Flavian stared straight before him, no longer looking at his father. 'Understood, sir.'

'Very well. You had best join yourself to Owain's squadron; tell him I sent you. You will find him by the lower fire down yonder.'

Flavian drew himself up stiffly in the Roman salute that

he had seen some of the old soldiers give; and turned without another word, and walked away. Aquila, watching him disappear in the dusk, thought suddenly and painfully of all the things he would have liked to say to the Minnow before his first battle.

In the darkness before dawn, suddenly a spark of red fire woke on the black crest of the downs, signalling to the watchers in the British camp that the Saxons were showing signs of movement. The hosts of Ambrosius rose and shook themselves, and turned themselves to the business of the day. Dawn, when it came, was a wild one, a fiercely shining, yellow dawn that meant storm and tempest; and the wind that had been rising all night was sweeping like a winged thing down the valley; and overhead the great, double-piled clouds racing from the west were laced and fringed with fire. And from the topmost spray of the whitethorn that grew high on the ancient ramparts a storm cock was singing. His song, fiercely shining as the morning, was sometimes scattered by the wind, sometimes came clearly down to the waiting cavalry on the slopes below.

Aquila heard his song, a song like a drawn sword, cutting through the formless sounds of a gathering army. From here on the slopes of the fortress hill he could see the whole battle line strung across the shallow trough of the valley; the main body of spears in the centre, where in the old days the legions would have been, the long-bow men behind them, and on either side the outspread wings of cavalry and mounted archers. The wild, changing light splintered on spear-point and helmet-comb, picked out here the up-tossed mane of a horse, there a crimson cloak flung back on the wind, and burned like coloured flame in the standards that the wind set flying: Pascent's standard, a mere flicker of blood red above the far cavalry wing; his own with the silken dolphin that Ness had worked for him when first he came to command a whole wing; and away down in the midst of the host the great, gleaming, red-gold Dragon of Britain, where Ambrosius in battered harness and cloak of the proud Imperial Purple sat his huge black stallion with a knot of his Companions about him.

Artos, with his standard flying above the flower of the British cavalry, was out of sight round the flank of the fortress hill, waiting for his moment to come. He was all the reserves they had; and save for him, the whole hope of Britain was strung across that shallow downland valley. Aquila wondered suddenly whether Flavian minded desperately being with him instead of with Artos, and glanced round at the boy sitting his horse just behind him. Flavian looked rather white. He was smiling a little, but the smile did not touch his eyes; and as Aquila looked, he ran the tip of his tongue over his lower lip as though it were uncomfortably dry. It was the look that Aquila had often seen before in the face of a boy going into battle for the first time. Flavian caught his eye and flushed painfully, as though his father's look made him ashamed, and stooped to fiddle with Whitefoot's harness. Aquila looked face-forward again. Amid the whole British host, he suddenly felt very much alone.

The day had fully come—a day of broken lights and grape-coloured shadows racing across the tawny hills— when a darkness that was denser and slower than a cloud shadow came into view, creeping towards them along the fringe of the downs. Knowing that it would be hidden as yet from the main battle line, Aquila flashed his sword from its sheath, and rising in his stirrups flourished it in great circles above his head, and from the knot of horsemen about the golden dragon, far off and small and

bright with distance, he saw Ambrosius fling up his own
sword arm, and knew that his signal had been received; he
felt in himself the kind of ripple that ran down the long
curve of the battle line like a deep-drawn breath. The
dark swarm of the advancing host drew nearer. When the
cloud shadows sped across it, it was merely a dark mass,
but when the sun touched it, it woke to a kind of pulsing,
beetle-wing brilliance with here and there a blink of
light from a bronze shield-boss or the curved top of a
Chieftain's helmet. A faint haze of white chalk-dust hung
like a cloud above the rear of the Saxon host, for it had
been a dry summer; and behind them, north-westward,
the sky and the hills seemed to darken as they came,
as though they trailed the storm like a cloak behind
them. And away over the downs, for a jewel in that
sombre cloak, Aquila saw the ragged, torn-off end of a
rainbow brightening against the gloom of the massing
storm-clouds.

He pointed. 'Look, lads! Already the Rainbow Bridge is
run out for the Saxon kind. Surely they make ready to
welcome Hengest in the Valhalla tonight!'

There was a laugh behind him, and little fierce Owain,
who had stood with him to hold Durobrivae Bridge
fourteen years ago, cried out, laughing also, 'Na, na! It is
but the stump of a bridge. They have cut through Bifrost
to keep him out!'

The Saxons were so near now that he could see the
white gleam of the horse's head borne on a spear-shaft
that was Hengest's standard, and hear plain above the
wuthering of the wind in his ears the formless smother of
sound that was the voice of an advancing host. A Saxon
war-horn boomed, and was answered by the higher,
brighter note of the Roman trumpets; challenge and
answering challenge tossed to and fro by the wind. The

Saxon war host came rolling on, not fast, but remorse-lessly, shield to shield, with Guitolinus's light cavalry scouring on either side. They seemed appallingly strong, but Aquila, sitting with his bull's-hide buckler high on his shoulder, and the flat of his drawn sword resting across Falcon's neck, saw that though they outnumbered the waiting British by upward of two to one, they were for the most part a foot army, and had nothing to compare with Artos's great hidden cavalry wing.

They were within bowshot now, and there came a sudden flicker of movement among the knot of archers behind the British spearmen, and a flight of arrows leapt out over the spears to plunge into the advancing battle-mass of the Saxons. For a few moments the enemy ranks had the look of a barley field hit by a sudden squall, as men staggered and dropped in their tracks; but the rest closed their torn ranks and pressed on, yelling. The British long-bow men got in one more flight, before the Saxon short-bows came into range; and after that the deadly hail of arrows was a two-way thing, tearing its gaps in the British ranks as it had torn them in

the Saxon. And in the midst of the killing hail, the two hosts rolled together, seeming at the last instant to gather themselves like two great animals, then spring for each other's throats.

A few moments later, without ever taking his eyes from the reeling press below, Aquila said to the man beside him, 'Now! Sound me the charge!' And the dull roar of battle and the storm cock's shining song were drowned in the ringing *tran-ta-ran* of the cavalry trumpet. Falcon flung up his head and neighed, adding his defiance to the defiance of the trumpet, not needing his rider's urging heel in his flank as he broke from a stand into a canter, from a canter into a full flying gallop. Aquila heard behind him the hoof-thunder of the cavalry wing sweeping down the hillside into the teeth of the westerly gale. He was yelling the war cry, 'Constantine! Constantine!' And he heard it caught up in a great rushing wave of sound. Guitolinus's cavalry wheeled about to meet them, and as they thundered down upon each other, Aquila's sight was full of a wild wave of up-tossed horses' heads, the dazzle of the stormy sunlight on shield-rim and sword-blade, a nearing wall of faces with staring eyes and open, yelling mouths. He caught the glint of gilded bronze and the emerald flash of a wind-torn silken cloak where Guitolinus rode among his men. Then they rolled together with a shock that seemed as though it must shake the very roots of the fortress hill.

Guitolinus's cavalry crumpled and gave ground, then gathered again for a forward thrust. And for Aquila the battle, that had been clear in view and purpose as he sat his horse above it such a short while ago, had lost all form, become a sheer, blind struggle. He had no idea of how things were going with Pascent in the left wing, or even what was happening along the centre; all he knew was the cavalry struggle going on around him, the shock of charge and counter-charge, until at last, above the roar of battle, his ear caught the sound that all the while it had been waiting for: the sound of a hunting-horn ringing like the horns of the Lordly Ones from behind the shoulder of the fortress hill. It was like Artos to sweep his men into action with the gay notes of a hunting-horn. The sound rose above the battle din, high and sweet and shining as the song of the storm-cock in the whitethorn tree. A great warning cry went up from the nearest ranks of the enemy, and snatching one glance over his shoulder, Aquila saw the flower of the British cavalry sweeping towards them along the tawny slope. There was a swelling thunder of hooves in his ears, and the wild, high song of the hunting-horn as the great arrow-head of wild riders hurtled down upon the battle. At the shining point of the arrow-head, Artos swept by, his great white horse turned for a flashing moment to silver by the burst of sunlight that came scudding down the valley to meet him, the silver mane streaming over his bridle arm, and the sods flying like birds from the great round hooves. His huge wolfhound, Cabal—son to the Cabal of his boyhood—bounded at his side, and half a length behind him galloped Kylan, his standard-bearer, with the crimson dragon streaming like a flame from its upreared spear-shaft. Just for the one instant they were there, seen out of the corner of the eye, with the white, fierce brilliance of figures seen by lightning; then they were past, and the following cavalry thundered after, to hurl themselves into the cavalry of Guitolinus—into them and through them, scattering them as dead leaves scatter before a gust of wind, and on.

Aquila swept his own men forward into the breach that Artos had made.

'Constantine! Constantine! Follow me!'

He heard the hunting-horn again, and again the wild riders were sweeping towards them. They circled wide to charge from the flank, hurling Guitolinus's cavalry back in confusion on to the Saxon shield wall. Ambrosius's hard-pressed centre, relieved for the moment from the deadly thrust against them, drove forward again, cheering wildly, into a charge of their own. From the far wing also, from Pascent's cavalry, the cheering had begun to rise. Aquila, charging again and again at the head of a wedge of his own men, knew nothing of that; he knew only that there was no longer a solid mass of cavalry before him, but isolated knots of desperate horsemen. Indeed, the whole battle seemed breaking up, disintegrating, while in the midst of the spreadings chaos the core of the Saxon host strove desperately to form the shield burg about the white-horse standard of Hengest.

Shouting to his men, Aquila drove his heel into Falcon's flank and rode straight for the half-formed shield burg.

Under his barbaric standard, Hengest stood head and shoulders taller than any of his house-carls, wielding his great war-axe at arm's length, blood striping the hair under his bull-horned helmet, blood on his shoulders and crimsoning the down-sweeping blade, and in his berserker's face the eyes full of a grey-green flame.

But it was not Hengest's wild features that started out at Aquila as the shield burg reeled and crumbled. It was the face of a young warrior glaring up at him over a broken shield-rim. A dark, fine-boned face, distorted now with rage and hate, that was yet as like to Flavia's face as a man's can be to a woman's.

Only for an instant he saw it, for a jagged, sickening splinter of time; and then a half-naked Scot sprang in under Falcon's head, his reddened dirk stabbing upward under Aquila's buckler. He wrenched sideways half out of the saddle, and felt the blow that should have ripped up his belly like a rotten fig gash through his old leather tunic, nicking the flesh like a hornet sting. Falcon reared up with lashing hooves, but he brought him down again with a blow of his shield-rim between the ears, and thrust in, in his turn, above the Scot's buckler; and the man was gone as though he had never been, under the trampling hooves of the mêlée.

The young dark warrior also was gone as though he had never been. The battle had closed over between him and Aquila, and he was no more to be seen. Maybe he, too, was down now under the trampling horses' hooves and the red welter of the breaking shield burg.

By noon the storm had broken, and the white, lashing swathes of rain were sweeping across the downs before the gale. The great battle of the Dragon and the White Horse had scattered over a score of downland and marshy miles, into a score of lesser battles; and there were dead men and horses lying in the little chalky stream and scattered grotesquely over the hillsides and down the wide valley. Guitolinus lay dead, his emerald cloak darkened and sodden with the driving rain, under a whitethorn bush on whose tossing and streaming branches the berries were already the colour of dried blood. The storm-cock was still shouting his shining song over the battlefield. And Artos and the British Cavalry were hunting the tattered remnant of Hengest's war host over the bare, chalky uplands north of Sorviodunum.

For Aquila, riding on the wing of that ruthless hunt, there had been a time of sickening anxiety when he realized that the Minnow was no longer with his squadron. It had not lasted long, for when he had demanded of Owain what had become of the boy, that grim little man had laughed, jerking his head sideways. 'The last I saw of him he was riding half a length behind Artos and yelling like all the fiends in hell!'

Now he was merely angry, and that with only half his mind; for the other half was twisted and tangled with the dark young warrior he had seen for one jagged instant of time as the shield burg crumbled.

The Dark Warrior

FAR up towards the old frontier below Cunetio a great villa, and one that had been rich in the old days, stood with its cornland and orchards spread below it in a bay of the wooded downs. Its people had fled before the Saxon break-through, and Hengest's host, sweeping southward, had found it empty, plundered it and set torch to it in passing. But for some reason the fire had not spread through the whole three-sided range of buildings, and the main house-place had stood deserted with its one burnt-out wing, until, two days after the great battle for Britain, Artos had called off the chase some miles north of Cunetio, and drawn his men back into British territory. Now, in the light of a wild sunset, the place was thrumming with life again, though not the life of its own people.

Men slow and half blind with weariness dropped from horses as weary as themselves in the pale gold of the stubble-field below the garden wall; there were makeshift horse-lines in the lee of the orchard, and in the wide greenness of the garden court, camp-fires began to echo the colours of the windy sunset.

Aquila, riding in with his men, late from their scouring of the hills, found the whole bay of the downs between the woods and the river already turned into a great camp. And almost the first person he saw as he reined in below the orchard where the apples were gold and russet on the wind-tossed branches, was Flavian plodding up from the horse-lines with a saddle on his shoulder.

The boy caught sight of him at the same instant, and Aquila saw him hesitate, and brace himself for whatever might be coming. Then he changed direction and came to meet his father. He halted at Falcon's shoulder, and stood looking up.

'I hope that you had good hunting with Artos,' Aquila said formally, after a moment.

Flavian flushed scarlet, but his eyes never wavered. 'I am sorry about that, Father. It—it just happened.'

Aquila nodded wearily. He had been very angry, but now he felt too weary to be angry any more, too weary to be anything very definite. 'Things do—just happen, in the heat of battle,' he said, and saw the quick relief in his son's face.

Flavian put up a hand to caress Falcon's neck. 'Sir, I was close behind you—I mean—I was *still* close behind you when you charged the Saxon shield burg. I'm glad I didn't miss that; it was magnificent!'

Aquila did not answer at once. He was wondering rather desperately why he could not remember that charge and the shield burg crumbling without seeing again and again a dark face that was so like Flavian's, so like Flavia's, starting out at him from the press. All these two days past he had been looking for that dark Saxon warrior, looking for him in every live Saxon he saw, and every dead one. Again and again he had told himself that he was a fool, that the thing had been no more than a chance resemblance; that whatever it had been, the man was surely dead back there under the ramparts of the old green hill fort, and he would look for him no more. But he had gone on looking.

'I rejoice that it won your approval,' he said briefly at last. Then, turning away from the thought of the crumbling shield burg, 'Is Artos up at the house?'

'Yes, Father.' Flavian dropped his hand from Falcon's neck, as though it were the horse that had rebuffed him. 'He has made his headquarters in the main block.'

Aquila nodded, and swung himself stiffly out of the saddle. 'Do you know where they are dealing with the wounded?'

'Up at the house too. Somewhere in the north wing, I think. The Saxons have burned the south one.'

'So.' Aquila turned round on the weary and battered men who had dropped from their horses behind him. 'Take over, Owain; send Dunod and Capell, and whoever else needs it, up to get their wounds tended. I'll not be long.'

'I'll see to Falcon,' Flavian said a little breathlessly, as Owain saluted and turned away to carry out his orders. 'There's a sheltered spot at the other end of the orchard, and we've got some fodder——'

So the Minnow was trying to make amends. Aquila smiled suddenly. 'Thanks, Flavian,' he said. He gave Falcon into the boy's charge with a pat, and then turned away to find Artos and make his report.

The fires of the sunset were dying over beyond the high downs, and the fires in the wide green court flowering brighter as the daylight faded. The rain had passed, but the wind that had sunk for a little while had risen again, though not so high as before, and all the place was full of side-blown smoke and the remains of sodden, burned thatch that flapped along the ground and whirled up in corners like singed birds. Some of the men had rounded up a few sheep on the hill pastures, and driven them in for slaughter; others were questing to and fro through the house and out-buildings and among the ruins, in search of anything that the barbarians had overlooked; they must have unearthed a secret wine-store, for two men staggered by him, grinning, with a huge wine-jar between them, and he passed a red-bearded tribesman sitting with his back to a column and his long legs stuck straight before him, with the lap of his tunic full of apples and a wine-flask of jewel-coloured glass in his hand. When it came to damage, Aquila reckoned that a British host could do nearly as well as a Saxon one.

He threaded his way through the fringes of the shifting throng, heading for the main house-place across the far end of the court. But before he reached it a tall figure whose hair—he had taken off his helmet and it hung at his shoulder-strap—shone mouse-fair in the windy fire-light, turned away from the knot of men about a fire that he was passing, and saw him.

'Sa ha! Dolphin! You have come in, then.'

'Reporting back,' Aquila agreed. 'My Lord Artos.'

Artos had come out to join him, his great footsore hound stalking at heel, and they turned aside together into the shadow of the burned-out colonnade. He cast a quick glance over his shoulder, to where the house-place door glowed dim saffron across the terrace, and said almost apologetically, 'They lit a fire for me in the atrium, and three candles. But it is so desolate in there; the house is dead, and I want to be with my own men tonight.' They stood together on the fringe of the firelight, greeting each other, but without words. Presently they would be triumphant, knowing their share in the triumph that was already roaring through the crowded camp and would sweep like a forest fire through Britain; but now they were still too close to their victory for any outcry. Then Artos said very quietly, fondling Cabal's pricked ears as the great hound sat against his knee, 'A good hunting?'

'A good hunting,' Aquila said, as quietly.

'What of your losses?'

'Until we rejoin the main host I cannot be sure; but I think not too heavy. Several of the men who rode in with me are wounded, and I have sent them up to the north wing for tending—if there is anyone there to tend them.'

'We have routed out a few women,' Artos said. 'There's a village up yonder over the downs, safe out of the Saxon's path . . . Anything else to report?'

'Nothing save what every captain who comes near you tonight will have reported already. That Hengest is safe away with the rags of his war host.'

'Aye: I think that not many men could have pulled back even the rags of an army from—what it was like on the Sorviodunum road, two days ago,' Artos said, with slow and considered admiration for his enemy. 'They are foes worthy of each other, Ambrosius and Hengest, and they are not done with each other yet.' He laid a great arm across Aquila's shoulder with one of the warm, faintly clumsy gestures that were so much a part of him. 'We ride a long road, old Dolphin, and this is only the beginning. Even here in the south it is only the beginning; and in the north, where Octa and his war bands still hold the land unchallenged, the thing is not yet even begun. But by Our Lord, it has been a beginning for men to tell their grandsons of, in the years ahead!' He was looking out over the fires and the shifting crowd, far out into some distance of his own beyond the windy twilight. 'When I was small,

I remember Ambrosius crying out for one great victory to sound like a blast of trumpets through the land . . . '

'A blast of trumpets through the land,' Aquila said. 'Aye, we have that now: and so in a while we may have a Britain standing together against the Saxon swarms at last.'

'Bonded together under one King,' Artos said. 'It is in my mind that we shall see Ambrosius crowned High King in Venta Belgarum this winter.'

A long pause fell between them, full of the voices of the makeshift camp and the long-drawn hushing of the wind along the ruined colonnade. Aquila wondered suddenly what it meant to Ambrosius, who would be crowned High King this winter, that the tall, slow young man who could lead men like a flame, who was son to him in all but fact, was base born and could not rule Britain after him. He wondered what it meant to Artos himself, and scarcely knowing that he did so, looked round at his companion. Artos turned his head at the same instant, and the light of the nearest fire showed them each other's face.

'For myself, I don't mind very much,' Artos said, as though the thing had been spoken. 'By and by I shall lead Britain in war, and that is enough for me. I do not want to rule Britain in peace. I do not want the loneliness.' He had turned back to his distance beyond the firelight and the dusk; and Aquila, still looking at him, thought suddenly of the way he had come out from the atrium to join his men about the fires. Ambrosius would have known that his place was solitary in the atrium with the three candles that had been lit for him; Artos wanted the cooking-fires below the terrace, and the touch of other men's shoulders against his. 'I should like to be Ambrosius's son, of course,' Artos said after a little, very simply. 'But only because I should like to be his son, bastard or no, not for any other reason.'

'To be father and son does not always bring any kind of nearness,' Aquila said harshly; and it was Artos's turn to look round quickly. There was a rather painful silence.

'I am sorry about young Flavian,' he said awkwardly. 'One may so easily be carried away in the heat of fighting, without any idea afterwards of how it came about.'

Aquila's mouth curled into a wry smile, though the old frown lines were still bitten deep between his brows. 'I said as much to the boy himself a while since. There's not much need that you should defend him to me, Bear Cub.' Then, deliberately, he changed the subject, as he had grown used to doing whenever it drew too near to his own raw places. 'We have just won a battle that may save Britain from the dark. Does it seem to you at all strange that we stand here talking of our own affairs?'

'Not really,' Artos said. 'Our own affairs are small enough for words; the other thing is too great.'

It was full dusk now, and the scene in the wide court was a confusion of armed men and firelight under the rising moon that came and went, blurred silver through the scudding cloud-drift. They had killed the sheep, and the carcasses, hacked into rough joints for quicker cooking, were already scorching and sizzling over the flames. Round one of the fires the men had begun to sing, some wild and haunting victory song of their own mountains that they took up one from another, tossing it to and fro. And between gust and gust of the wind, between fall and rise of the singing, suddenly from the dark woods above the house a cry leapt into the night; a cry that rose and rose high and agonized and only part human and ended as though it were cut off with a knife, leaving the night again to the wind and the mountain men singing.

Some of the men about the fire glanced at each other, some grinned or cocked their heads in the direction from which it had come, but not all. It was nothing unusual.

'Another Saxon straggler,' Artos said. 'He and his kind would have done as much and more for any man of ours, if the victory had gone the other way. Nevertheless, this is a part of victory that I do not like,' and his heavy arm slipped lightly enough from Aquila's shoulder.

Aquila, with that ghastly cry still seeming in his ears to tear the night apart, was staring into the heart of the nearest fire. But he did not see it. He saw the darkness of the wind-lashed woods, and a flurry of desperate movement in the undergrowth, the white blink of moonlight on a dagger blade, and shapes that closed in as men close in to finish a deer that the hounds have brought to bay. He saw the face of the quarry turned up for an instant to the whitening moon, snarling as it had snarled up at him over a broken shield-rim, two days ago . . . He pulled himself together with an angry jerk, and saw the fire again. Fool, fool that he was, and fanciful as a green girl!

A fox-haired man was making his way towards them from the gateway, and he pushed himself off from the column against which, without knowing it, he had been leaning. 'Yonder comes Pascent to report that Hengest is safe away. And I must go back to my own men.' He put up his hand to Artos in a way that was half salute and half a gesture beween friends. 'It was a good hunting, Bear Cub.'

He strode down the shallow steps, exchanged a quick greeting with Pascent, and continued on his way.

He went down to the horse-lines and made sure that all was well there; saw his men in a fair way to being fed, spoke with Owain about guard duty and arrangements for the night. Then he sat himself down beside one of the fires to eat stolen mutton. But though he was wolf-hungry, he could eat little, and the men about him—even Artos, moving from fire to fire among his beloved fighting men— looked at his dark, inward-turned face, and left him to himself. In a while he got up and looked about him as though he were a little lost. There was nothing more that he could do but go now and find some corner out of the wind, and crawl into it like a tired dog and sleep. But something in him dreaded lying down to sleep; something that he could give no name to, that was to do with the face that he could not stop seeing. There was a wild unrest in him, a sense of urgency, something to be done that would not let him rest, though his body ached and his eyes were hot in his head with the need for sleep.

He raised his arms above his head, stretching until the small muscles cracked behind his shoulders—and caught his breath at the sudden twinge and smart of the gash in his side that he had carried out of battle. He had almost forgotten about it; it was no more than a shallow cut along the ribs. But now it was an excuse for something else to do. He would go up to the north wing, where they had dealt with the wounded, and get some woman to bathe it and put on a smear of salve, and that would hold off for a little longer the time when there was really nothing to do but to lie down.

He made his way through the camp again to the north wing, and dragged his feet up the three shallow steps to the open colonnade that ran the length of the place. The rooms beyond seemed to be mainly farm workshops, wool stores, and chambers for drying corn. He turned to a door through which smoky lantern-light shone, and found himself on the threshold of a long chamber half filled with wool-sacks and other stores, whose tessellated floor, cracked and damaged now, showed that it must once have been a living-room, and a beautiful one. Some women were moving about, water was heating in an iron cauldron propped over a fire in the centre of the floor that was half filling the place with smoke; and a few of the men who had come in to have wounds dressed still lingered, sitting or sprawling on wool-sacks round the blaze. In the light of a lantern hanging from the rafters a man stood wiping his hands and arms, who turned to look inquiringly towards the door. A small, strong-shouldered man in a brown tunic, the loose sleeves rolled high, with a deeply tanned, intensely quiet face, and a fuzz of hair round his head that shone in the pool of light from the lantern like the seed-silk of the wild clematis, or the silver fringe round a cloud with the sun behind it.

For the first moment that silver fuzz put Aquila off; and then he remembered that it must be twelve years since their last meeting, on the track below the ash woods.

'Brother Ninnias! So here is our third meeting that you promised me.'

The little man watched him with a look that was more a warmth than an actual smile, as he came forward into the fire-glow, then strode to meet him, tossing aside the piece of rag on which he had been cleaning his stained hands. 'And a third meeting should surely be the richest. God's greeting to you, Aquila my friend.'

'So you remember me this time,' Aquila said.

'This time my eyes were open because I was already looking for you. When word was brought to me that Ambrosius's cavalry was descended upon this valley, and I gathered a few salves and came down to see what help I might be to any who rode in with wounds upon them, I was wondering whether I might find you among those that rode with Artos the Bear.' He smiled. 'But it is you that have found me. Do you bring me a wound for salving?'

'The merest scratch, nothing to the gall of a Saxon thrall-ring that you salved for me once before.'

'Show me.'

Standing by the fire, Aquila tugged free the buckles, pulled off his old leather tunic, and slipped his woollen under tunic down to the waist, laying bare the shallow gash along his ribs, reddened a little by the rub of his harness that would not let it heal in peace. Ninnias looked at it, then called to one of the women to bring warm water from the cauldron. He made Aquila sit down on some of the wool-sacks, leaning sideways, and bathed the place and set about salving it with the same salve that he had used that other time. Aquila leaned his elbow on the wool-sacks, and looked down, his head swimming a little in the smoky air and the smell of the fleeces and men's hurt bodies, watching the firelight play with the figures in the cracked tesserae, the figure of a girl with a flowering branch in one hand and a bird in the other. Maybe it was supposed to be Spring. It was odd, he thought, how little of surprise there seemed in this meeting with Brother Ninnias; as little as there was in putting on a familiar garment. Quietness rose within him, easing his wild unrest as the salve was cooling the smart of his gashed side. But that was always the way with Brother Ninnias, the quietness, the sense of sanctuary were things that he carried with him.

'So it is among these woods that you found your halting place at last,' Aquila said, when the salving was finished, pulling up his tunic again.

'Aye, I and my bees; north-westward into the next valley.' Brother Ninnias helped him with the stiff leather harness-tunic. 'Leave that lower buckle slack, or you will start the thing chafing again . . . I have my bee-skeps and my bean-rows and my physic garden, all as I had them before. And now I am away back to them again, for you are the last man to call for my leech-craft tonight, and there is no more need of me here.'

Seeing again the place where the track forked below the ash-woods, and himself going one way and Ninnias the other, Aquila got up, saying urgently, 'I will come back with you for a while.'

'You are tired, my friend, and need sleep.'

Aquila rubbed the back of one hand across his forehead. 'I am tired; but I need your company tonight more than I need sleep. I——' He checked, and dropped his hand and looked up. 'Let me walk with you, Ninnias, rather than walk the camp all night.'

They faced each other, quite oblivious of the watching women and the men about the fire; and for a moment Aquila was afraid that there might be questions coming. But it seemed that Brother Ninnias still had his old gift for not asking questions. 'Come then, my friend,' he said at last, and that was all.

And so in a little while they left the camp together and struck away north-westwards, uphill through the hanging woods. The wind through the trees made a roaring like a high sea all about them, and the silver light came and went as the ragged clouds raced across the sky, and the storm had strewn the woods with fallen branches to catch at their feet in the darkness below the undergrowth where the moonlight never reached. But Brother Ninnias walked through the turmoil as a man walks on the clear path that leads home. They crossed the broad saddle of the downs and came down into the next valley; and the sudden waft of wood-smoke on the wind and the barking of dogs told Aquila that they were near a village. Maybe the village of which Artos had spoken. 'Do these folk also dance for the Horned One at Beltane, as your iron folk did?' he asked.

'Aye,' Ninnias said, out of the darkness ahead. 'But they listen to God's Word between whiles, as the iron folk did.'

They came to a little swift chalk stream coming down in spate with its hair full of alder leaves, and turned up beside it, Brother Ninnias leading, Aquila following where Brother Ninnias led. Soon the woods began to fall back, the dense masses of oak and yew giving place to elder and whitethorn, hazel and crack willow that would soon give place to the open hillside.

And then Brother Ninnias stumbled on something and half fell. Aquila, coming up behind him, heard him give a low exclamation, and demanded, 'What is it?'

'A man—a man's body,' Ninnias said, kneeling over something among the brambles and the dry hemlock stalks.

'Saxon?'

'Most like. For the moment I know no more than that it is flesh and blood.' Ninnias was turning the body over, and a pale blur showed in the darkness. Almost in the same instant, the moon, that had been behind a hurrying cloud, swam out into a lake of clear, and light flooded down between the hazel scrub, turning all the turmoil of the night to silver. And the pale blur became a face surrounded by a tangle of dark hair, the face of a young man in Saxon war harness. It was not snarling now, as Aquila had seen it snarling up at him as the shield-wall crumbled; it was quite still, as full of quiet as a face carved on a memorial stone, but it was the same face.

Aquila had a moment of blinding shock, and after that it was as though he had known all along what he was going to find here. Only for that one moment he had the odd impression that the wind had died away and the woods were quite still.

21

The Return of Odysseus

NINNIAS'S hands were busy about the young man's body. In a little, he looked up. 'Not dead; but his shoulder is all but hacked in two. He'll come back to himself in a while—so much the worse for him, maybe.'

And as though to give point to his words, far off in the darkness of the woods there rose again the cry that Aquila had heard earlier that evening as he stood beside Artos in the light of the cooking fires. The hunt was still on.

His head straining over his shoulder in the direction from which the cry had come, Aquila dropped to one knee beside the young Saxon's body. The moonlight jinked on the pummel of a Saxon sword, and he caught it up, slipping the sword-belt clear, and sent the whole thing spinning into the stream. The alder roots would keep it safe. Then he got hold of the boy to lift him. All the unrest, all the vague and formless urgency of the past hours gathered itself into an arrowhead of purpose within him.

'How near is your hut? Quick!'

'So near that if I had not smoored the fire before I came out, you could see the firelight from here,' Brother

Ninnias said. 'Give him to me now, and go away and forget you walked with me tonight.'

Aquila shook his head, not even taking in what the words meant, and lurched to his feet with the unconscious Saxon hanging a dead weight in his arms. 'Show me the way. I'll be close behind you.'

Brother Ninnias looked at him a moment, very strangely in the moonlight. Then he got up and moved into the lead again, holding aside a branch to clear the way. 'Come, then.'

Aquila lurched after him, stumbling under the weight of his burden. In only a few paces more the elder and hazel scrub fell back, and open turf glimmered ahead of him, dim-silver in the moonlight, darkly islanded with furze. And less than a bow-shot away he saw the squat, comfortable shape of a bracken-thatched bothy sitting in its cultivated plot like a hen in a warm dust-patch.

'Wait here while I make sure that all is well. Come when I whistle,' Brother Ninnias said; and then Aquila was alone among the hazel bushes, watching the small, broad-shouldered figure dwindle away between the furze-bushes until the dark doorway of the bothy swallowed him. Three bee-skeps stood beside it, he saw, with a sense of greeting old, familiar things, nestling against the bothy wall like chicks under the hen. It would be thyme honey here, he supposed; pale thyme honey instead of dark, tangy honey of the heather country, but just as sweet.

A low whistle reached him, and already firelight was brightening in the bothy doorway. Aquila had crouched down, managing to take some of the weight of the young Saxon on one knee, but had not laid him down, because he was unsure, spent as he was, of his ability to take him up again without rough handling that might do further damage to his shoulder. Now he lurched upright, and struggled forward again, through the scattered furze and up between the dark wreck of the summer's bean rows, towards the brightening gleam of firelight. He reached the doorway, gasping for breath, feeling again the dark prickle of blood from his own wound under his harness tunic. The inside of the small, round hut was golden and still after the storm-driven black and silver of the night outside, and he lurched over to the bed of piled bracken against the wall, and set his burden down.

Brother Ninnias had already turned from waking the fire on the central hearth, and was taking fresh salves and other things that he might need from a couple of high shelves against the wall. He came without a word to kneel beside Aquila, and together they loosened the leather byrnie with its hacked and stained shoulder, and eased the unconscious man out of it, revealing a blood-soaked woollen kirtle and a mass of sodden and stiffened rags—maybe part of a dead comrade's kirtle—that he must have stuffed inside his harness to try to staunch the wound. Aquila eased off the sodden mass that left red stains on his hands, and flung it vaguely in the direction of the fire, and laid bare an ugly wound between neck and shoulder, and the shoulder itself hanging down, collapsed into the boy's body as happens with a broken collar-bone. It was not bleeding much now, but clearly before it stopped the young warrior had bled almost white.

'Collar-bone hacked through; and the wound two or three days old, by the look of it,' Brother Ninnias said, his blunt, gentle fingers exploring the surrounding area. 'He will have been trying to make his way back after the rest, I suppose. Hold him for me—so . . . ' They worked together over the battered body without another word between them until the wound had been cleaned

and salved and the grating collar-bone set, and Brother
Ninnias had brought strips of an old cloak to bind it in
position—he had used what linen he had in the British
camp. And then at last he spoke again, his quiet gaze
lifting from the work of his hands to rest on Aquila's face.
'I am a priest, and not a fighting man. As no man is
beyond God's mercy, so none can be beyond mine, but it
seems to me a strange and an unlikely thing that you have
done tonight, my friend.'

It was the nearest thing to an uninvited question that
Aquila had ever heard from him.

Aquila looked down at the fugitive's face, drained and
bloodless so that it seemed all but transparent in the firelight, seeing the old-man hollows at cheek and temple, the
bruise-coloured smudges under the closed eyes; and more
clearly than ever, that startling, unbelievable likeness to
Flavia. But it was something else, over and above the
likeness, something in himself that made him sure beyond
all doubt of the boy's kinship. As he looked, the faintest
quiver of movement woke in the still face. For an instant
he thought that it was only the firelight, before he knew
that it was the first flicker of returning life.

'Wait: he is coming to himself,' he said, letting the half-
question lie unanswered.

A little later, with startling suddenness, the Saxon
opened his eyes with a groan and glared about him.
'Where—what——?'

'Softly now,' Brother Ninnias said, fumbling a little with
the Saxon tongue. 'There are none but friends here.'

But the young man's eyes had thrust past him to find
Aquila dark against the firelight. 'Friends, is it? Friends in
Roman harness!'

'Friends, none the less,' Ninnias said.

And Aquila leaned forward, speaking, not in the Saxon

tongue as Ninnias had done, but, scarcely realizing that he did so, in his own. 'What is your name?'

The other frowned up at him with black brows drawn close, and mouth set like a stone; but Aquila thought there was a flicker of startled puzzlement in his eyes. And after a few moments he answered in the same tongue, though with the broad, guttural accent of his own people, flinging the words at him with a reckless bravado. 'I was called Mull by my mother on the day that I was born, if my name is a thing that has to do with you!'

'Mull—a half-breed. And you speak my tongue. Was she British, this mother?'

'She came of your people,' the other said after a moment. And then proudly, disdaining to seem as though he asked for any mercy on that score, 'But I carry my shield among my father's kind—and my father was first son to Wiermund of the White Horse!' He tried to struggle up on to his sound arm, to fling some defiance at the man who bulked so dark and still between him and the firelight. 'Ah! I have seen you before—when shield burg went. That was a good time for you, wasn't it? But it will not always be so good! You will not stop the Sea People flooding in. We shall overwhelm you in the end! We——' The breath went out of him in a groan, and he fell back on to the piled fern.

'Maybe it would have been as well to wait till he had some stirrabout in him before asking him his name,' Brother Ninnias said, without condemnation.

Aquila let out a long, gasping sigh, like the long breath of relief from pain or almost unbearable tension, and rubbed one hand across his scarred forehead. He heard very clearly, in the sheltered stillness under the wind as it roared over, the flutter of flames on the central hearth and the rustle of some small living thing in the thatch. And another sound, out of the windy night, the sound of a voice upraised in a snatch of song.

For an instant the stillness in the hut became brittle as thin ice, and in the stillness the two men looked at each other above the unconscious body of the third. Aquila got up, and stood listening, more intensely than he had ever listened in his life before. The sound came nearer, the snatch of song was caught up by other voices; there was a drunken splurge of laughter and a burst of swearing as someone maybe caught his foot in an alder root. They were coming up the stream side; any moment now they would be clear of the trees.

'Make ready your stirrabout, but even if you have to put him out again, for God's sake don't let him make any sound,' he snapped, and strode to the doorway.

Pray God they were not some of the newly joined Dumnonii who had ridden under Pascent's banner and would not know him by sight! He ducked out of the low doorway into the hurrying night, and stood with hunched shoulders reaching almost to the lintel, his arms akimbo so that the heavy folds of his cloak spread wide to shield the doorway. Firelight spilled out in a golden stain about his feet but unless a man lay on the ground to get it, there would be no clear view into the hut behind him. He realized that his own leather tunic was stained with Flavia's son's blood where he had carried him, and the stains showed black in the moonlight; but he had a wound of his own to account for that. Men were coming up through the tangle of sloe and elder and the dark furze beyond the bean-patch. He saw the movement of them, caught the spark of moonlight on a weapon, heard their voices and their thick, reckless laughter.

They broke cover in a ragged knot, checked at sight of the hut and the man in its doorway, and then came on,

giving tongue like a small, unsteady hound pack. And as they drew nearer an almost painful relief stabbed through him as he realized that they were a bunch of Artos's wild lads, and well enough known to him. But clearly they had been at the wine that had escaped the Saxons; they were not very drunk but drunk enough to be dangerous; in a reckless mood, looking for whatever mischief they could find: more wine to drink, another Saxon fugitive to kill.

Aquila stood, lounging a little in the doorway, and watched them come.

They were all around him before they checked again, their mouths loose and laughing, their eyes fiercely bright in the moonlight.

'Why, it's the Dolphin!' someone said. 'It's Ambrosius's old Lone Wolf. What's doing here, Lone Wolf?'

'Getting a gashed flank salved by the Holy Man,' Aquila said. 'What do you, for the matter of that? Lost your way back to camp in the haze from a wine-jar?'

A tall, fair-haired youngster with a gold torc round his neck laughed, swaying on his heels. 'We been hunting. *Good* hunting! We killed three times, and now we're thirsty again.'

'The stream is yonder; if that's not to your liking, best be getting back to camp and look for whatever else the Saxons have overlooked.'

Another man cocked his chin at the thatched skeps against the wall. 'Bees,' he said thickly. 'Might be heather beer in this doghole—or even mead.'

'There might be,' Aquila agreed. 'But in actual fact there's naught but salves and colic water and a little barley gruel.'

'Under the hearthstone, perhaps,' a third man put in. 'Let's turn the place upside down and see!'

Aquila did not move from before the door. 'You've enough vine leaves in your hair without adding bee bloom to it,' he said. And then more sternly, 'Leave robbing the church to the Saxon kind. Go back to camp, you fools, or you'll be in no state to ride south in the morning.'

His tone of authority seemed to sober them a little, for they had, after all, begun to be used to discipline. The tall stripling with the golden collar, who seemed to be a leader among them, shrugged. 'Maybe you are right.'

'I am very sure I am right,' said Aquila cordially. 'God speed you on your way back to camp, my heroes.'

They were a little uncertain, looking all ways at once; then the tall stripling made him a flourishing salute, and swung on his heel. 'Come away, lads; he doesn't want us. It's my belief he's got a girl in there.'

And with that parting shot, howling with laughter at their own wit, they turned back the way that they had come.

When the last sound of their going had died away, Aquila sat down on the threshold, his hands hanging lax across his knees and his head low between his shoulders. In a while a hand came on his bowed shoulder, and Brother Ninnias's voice said, 'That was very well done, my friend.'

'How is the boy?' he said muzzily, without looking up.

'Asleep. It passed into sleep; and the longer before he wakes, the better. I am going to begin burning his rags now; the byrnie I shall take out and lose, later.'

Aquila nodded, and leaned sideways with a little sigh to prop himself against the door-post. He did not feel the Holy Man's hand leave his shoulder. It was in his mind to keep watch, there in the doorway; and part of him did remain on guard, but part of him slept, while the last of the three day storm blew itself out around him.

It was not far from dawn, and the night full of a soft, wet, woody-scented hush after the storm, when he came fully back to himself, and realized that life was moving again in the bothy behind him. He lurched to his feet, stood a few moments looking about him, and turning, ducked into the firelit hut again. Flavia's son was awake, and strained up on to an elbow at his coming, flinging back the wild black hair from his eyes, as he glared up at him. 'My sword! Where is my sword?'

'In the stream yonder,' Aquila said, 'with the alder roots to hold it under.'

'So! You have taken pains that I should have no weapon against you!'

'You fool, do you really think that I felt it needful to disarm you in the state you are in at present?' Aquila said wearily. 'It isn't healthy to be found with a Saxon sword in these parts.'

Mull began to laugh, taunting, furious, weak laughter that seemed to buffet him as though it were a wind outside himself. 'I do not doubt that you have a vast care for my health! Ah, but of course, fool that I am! It is your own skin that you look to!'

'Easy, my son,' Brother Ninnias said from the farther shadows. 'It so chances that he cared enough for your skin to carry you here last night and doubtless reopen a gash in his own skin doing it. And you have him to thank you were not later dragged out of this hut like a badger out of its hole, and knifed on the threshold by a pack of wine-lit British soldiers in search of more wine or Saxons.'

Mull's rage fell still, and his laughter with it. For a long moment he lay looking at Aquila, catching his lower lip between his teeth, as Flavia had done when she was puzzled.

'I do not understand. Why did you do that?' he said at last.

'For your mother's sake.'

'My mother? What can my mother be to you?'

'My sister,' Aquila said levelly.

'Your—sister.' Mull spoke as though he were testing the words. His frowning gaze moved over Aquila, over the fine workmanship of his sword-belt and the long Roman cavalry sword, and the bronze-and-silver brooch that held his weather-worn cloak, and returned to his dark, harsh, hawk-nosed face, taking in something that had gathered to him during twenty years of commanding men. 'A great man among your own people,' he said slowly. 'A bitter thing it must be for you to have a kinsman among Hengest's war host.'

'It is,' Aquila said. 'God knows that it is. But not quite as you mean it.' He straightened his shoulders, turning to the more practical side of things. 'We shall be riding south in a few hours, and there should be little enough risk for you now, while you lie up here.' He never questioned whether Brother Ninnias would accept the charge and the risk that there was; he had too sure a faith in the little brown man for that. He turned to him now. 'Nevertheless, the sooner he is away, the better. When should he be able to travel?'

'Not for two or three weeks.' Brother Ninnias looked up from the bowl in which he was preparing barley stirrabout. 'Two or three weeks for me to take joy in another guest that the Lord has sent me. But for his own sake he shall go in the first hour that I judge him strong enough.'

Aquila was thinking quickly: 'How long a march from here to the nearest point on the border? Ah, but there isn't a fixed border any longer. How far to the nearest of his own kind, I wonder?'

'That is a thing that there is no means of knowing,' Brother Ninnias said. 'But I know the forest northward of this for a good way, and can set him far on his road.'

Aquila nodded, settling down on to one heel. He pulled his purse from the breast of his stained leather tunic, and tossed it down on to the bracken, where it fell with a faint clink. 'There's a little money—all I have by me. It's not much, but it will help. Get him a tunic, Ninnias, one that doesn't shout "Saxon" by its cut and long sleeves.' Then he took out his tablet and stylus, and while the other two watched him, hurriedly scratched a few words on the wax.

He looked for a moment at what he had written, then returned his stylus to his folded girdle, and put the tablet down softly and precisely beside his purse. 'You will pass well enough for British, until you open your mouth. Therefore you must pretend to be dumb. If you run up against anyone, show them this pass. Signed by the Commander of Ambrosius's Second Cavalry Wing, it should get you out of any trouble. Understand?'

'I—understand,' Mull said after a moment. He swallowed. 'There seems nothing more, but—that I should thank you.'

'One thing more.' Aquila pulled the battered signet ring from his finger. 'This was my father's ring. When you come to the fringes of your own people, you must find means to send it back to Brother Ninnias here. Brother Ninnias will find means to get it back to me: and I shall know that you are safe away.'

'Safe like a beaten cur that runs with its tail between its legs,' Mull said with a sudden furious bitterness.

Aquila looked at his drawn face, proud and bitter and sullenly ashamed. The boy's eyes were much too bright. Probably he had some fever from the wound. Well, Ninnias would see to that. 'Hengest did not die when the shield burg went; he is safe away with the rags of his host,' he said abruptly. 'You're not deserting a dead leader, you're following back a living one. There's no shame in that.'

'A gentle enemy!' Mull said jibingly.

'No, I am not a gentle enemy. I loved your mother, my sister; that is all.'

They looked at each other in silence for a moment; and then—it was as though he laid down his weapons—Mull reached out and took the ring from Aquila. 'Even after she—even after *that* happened.'

'I once wagered her a pair of crimson slippers that she could not run faster than I,' Aquila said with careful lightness. 'She won, and I—never had the chance to pay my debt. You must tell her that I send her son back to her, in place of a pair of crimson slippers.'

'If I—when I see her again, is there any other word that you would have me say to her?' Mull asked.

Aquila was staring into the fire, his arm across his knees. What was there to say to Flavia, after their last meeting, and the years between? And then he knew. He put up his hand and freed the shoulder-buckle of his leather tunic, and pulled it back; he dragged up the loose woollen sleeve beneath, to bare his shoulder, and leaned toward Mull in the firelight. 'Look.'

Mull strained up higher on his sound arm, and looked. 'It is a dolphin,' he said.

'A friend did it for me when I was a boy.' He let his sleeve fall and began to refasten the buckle. 'Ask her if she remembers the terrace steps under the damson tree at home. Ask her if she remembers the talk that we had there once, about Odysseus coming home. Say to her—as though it were I who spoke through you, "Look. I've a dolphin on my shoulder. I'm your long-lost brother." '

'The terrace steps under the damson tree. Odysseus coming home. "Look, I've a dolphin on my shoulder. I'm your long-lost brother",' Mull repeated. 'Will she understand?'

'If she remembers the steps under the damson tree, she will understand,' Aquila said. He got up, and turned to the dark doorway. He looked back once, at Mull still propped on one elbow and staring after him, then ducked out into the first paling of the dawn.

Brother Ninnias came with him to the end of the bean-rows, and there they turned towards each other in parting.

Aquila had half expected that the monk would say something about what had happened, about the part of the old story that he had not known before. But, tipping up his head to look about him with a wide, quiet, all-embracing gladness, he said only, 'The storm is over, and it is going to be a glorious day.'

And Aquila, looking about him also, saw that the moon was down; but the dark had paled to grey, and the grey was growing luminous. The eastern sky was awash with silver light, and somewhere down by the stream a willow wren was singing, and the whole world seemed poised on the edge of revelation, about to spread its wings . . .

'Do you believe in blind chance?' he asked, as he had asked it once of Eugenus the Physician, long ago. 'No, I remember that you believe in a pattern of things.'

'I also believe in God, and in the Grace of God,' Brother Ninnias said.

Aquila stood quite still, his face lifted to the light above the wooded valley that was setting the east singing like the willow wren. At last he stirred. 'I must be away to my men. Give me your blessing before I go.'

A few moments later he was striding down the stream side towards the camp and his men and the long, long battle for Britain. He knew that he would not see Brother Ninnias again.

22

The Blossoming Tree

SLEET whispered against the high windows of the old house in Venta, and in the living-room of Aquila's quarters the little mean wind of early winter made icy draughts along the floor and teased the flames of the candles in the bronze lamp-holder. The last of the daylight was fading, and the light of the candles was taking over. Aquila stood in the glow of warmth from the brazier where apple logs were burning on the charcoal, buckling his bronze-bossed crimson belt over a fresh tunic, while his cast-off daytime garments lay at his feet. It was so cold in the sleeping-cells that he had snatched up his festival clothes spread ready for him, and brought them in here to change beside the fire.

Earlier that day, Ambrosius Aurelianus had been crowned High King of Britain; crowned with the same slim, golden circlet that he had worn for so many years, with his Companions and the leaders of his fighting men there to see the thing done, before he went out to show himself to his people from the Basilica steps where once he had confronted Guitolinus and the Celtic party. The roar of their acclamation was a thing that Aquila thought he should never forget. And this evening, in the banqueting chamber of the old Governor's Palace, he was feasting with the men who had seen him crowned. Aquila reached for his best cloak, where it lay in a tumble, dark as spilled wine, across the foot of the low couch, and flung it round him, hastily settling the shoulder-folds. He was late, for there had been some trouble down at the horse-lines over the new Cymric steeds that he must see to, and the feast would have begun by now; this crowning feast for a new High King who was the hope of Britain. He stabbed home the pin of the great bronze-and-silver shoulder brooch, and when he looked up again, there seemed to be all at once more warmth in the room, and more colour; for Ness stood in the inner doorway in a gown of thick, soft wool the colour of the apple flames. Roman in so many things nowadays, she had never taken to the pale colours that the Roman ladies wore, and suddenly he was glad of that.

'I feel as though I could warm my hands at you, in that gown,' he said.

She laughed; something of the old mockery in her laughter still, but the sting gone from it. 'My lord learns to say pretty things in his old age!' She came forward into the inner circle of warmth and light about the brazier. 'A man has just left this for you,' and he saw that she was holding out something that looked like a little ivory ball.

He took it from her, and realized that it was a ball of white honey-wax, and instantly knew the sender, though no word was scratched on the smooth, creamy surface. 'Is the messenger still here?'

Ness shook her head. 'He was a merchant of some sort and wanted to get on to his trading in the town. He said

that the man who gave it to him said there was no answer
to wait for. Should he have waited?'

'No,' Aquila said. 'It was just that I thought for a
moment it might be somebody that I knew.' The wax was
brittle with cold. He broke it open between his hands, and
spilled his father's ring into his palm.

For a little time he stood quite still, seeing it lying there
among the creamy flakes and fragments of broken wax;
watching the green spark wake and vanish in the heart
of the flawed emerald as the firelight flickered. So the
boy was safe among his own people again. He tossed the
wax into the red heart of the brazier and slipped the ring
on to his bare signet finger. It was good to feel it there
again. Good to know that he was free now to take
what he had done to Ambrosius and abide by the con-
sequences. With long thinking about it, he had reached
the stage of not knowing how right or wrong the thing
was that he had done. He only knew that it had been
inevitable, and that now Mull's safety no longer hung on
his silence, he must lay it bare to Ambrosius. Maybe
tonight, after the banquet . . .

Ness's voice broke in on him. 'But it is your ring! Your
ring that was lost! I do not understand——'

Presently he would tell Ness too. But Ambrosius first.
'You shall, by and by,' he said. 'Not now. I am late enough
as it is.' He half turned towards the colonnade doorway,
then back again, realizing that he would probably not
see Ness again until after he had told Ambrosius. 'You
look so pretty in that gown. I wish this wasn't an all-male
banquet.'

She let the question of the ring go by. 'I am sure that
the Princes of the Dumnonii and the Lords of Glevum
and the Cymru would be outraged if they found themselves expected to follow the Roman fashion and sit

down to feast in the same hall with women, on such a state occasion as this!'

'Your people,' Aquila said, and was struck by a sudden thought. 'Ness, do you see that it has come full circle? The Princes of the Cymru feast with their High King. Tonight Ambrosius will confirm Pascent as lord of his father's lands and his father's people. Tonight your people and mine are come together again!'

'Yes, I do see,' Ness said. 'After twelve, nearly thirteen years.'

Aquila felt that he had been stupid in pointing that out to her as though it were a thing that she might not have noticed, when it must be so much nearer to her than it was to him. He wondered whether she had regretted the choice that she had made, almost thirteen years ago, but could not find the words to ask her.

And then Ness came and put her thin brown hands on his shoulders and said, as though she knew what he was thinking, 'Have *you* regretted it?'

'Why should I regret it?' Aquila said, and put his hands over hers.

'I'm not beautiful like Rhyanidd——'

'You never were, but it was you I chose, in my rather odd way.'

'And maybe I've grown dull. Contented women do grow dull; I've seen it happen.' She began to laugh again, and this time with no mockery at all. 'But at least I haven't grown fat, as some contented women do.' She gave him a little push, and dropped her hands. 'Go now to this splendid all-male banquet of yours, before you are later than you are already.'

He went across the inner court, huddling his chin into his cloak against the thin, icy wind and the sleet that was turning to snow, opened the postern door under the damson tree, and passed through, letting it swing to behind him. In the wide court of the Governor's Palace a lantern swayed in the wind, setting the shadows running all along the colonnades, and there was a great coming and going in the early winter dusk; young men gathered in knots by lighted doorways, cooks and servants and younger sons hurried to and fro; a man passed him with a couple of great wolfhounds in leash, making him think of Brychan in the early days. He turned into the north colonnade, weaving his way through the shifting, noisy throng, until he came at last to the ante-room where men stood on guard, leaning on their spears; and then he stood on the threshold of the banqueting chamber itself.

In the daylight the banqueting hall of the old palace was as shabby, crumbling and faded as the rest of Venta Belgarum. But in the warm light of many candles, the dim colours of the painted garlands on the walls glowed with an echo of the colours of living flowers, and cracked marble and blackened gilding lost their starkness behind the twined and twisted ropes of ivy, bay and rosemary whose aromatic scent mingled with the faint waft of wood-smoke from the braziers—for here, too, braziers were burning, though the chief warmth of the place rose from the hypocausts under the floor.

The hall was thronged with men seated at the long tables that seemed to swim in honey-thick light; men with clipped hair in the loose, formal tunics of Rome; men with tunics plaid and chequered in the deeper and more barbaric colours of an older Britain, with flowing hair, and river-washed yellow gold about their necks.

The first course of hard-boiled duck eggs and strong cured fish and little cups of watered wine was already being brought in, and Aquila, casting a quick glance among the boys and young warriors bearing in the great chargers, saw Flavian moving through the throng with an air of serious concentration as he tried to avoid spilling any drop from his wine-cups. In these days of shortage of slaves and servants, they had begun to use their sons and younger brothers as servers and cup-bearers, much as the Tribes had always done. Passing over his son, Aquila's gaze went up to seek the High Table, where Ambrosius sat, with the faithful Pascent beside him, and big, clumsy Artos, whose wild-wind cavalry charge had done more than all else to gain them this first great victory; and the Princes of the Dumnonii and the Lords of Glevum and the Cymru, who had held back all these years, come in at last to swear their fealty to the High King. And suddenly he was remembering the first sight that he had had of the dark young Prince of Britain, by the hearth in a mountain fortress, with the salt mist wreathing beyond the door, and the same narrow gleam of gold round his head. They had ridden a long road since then, and the gold fillet was become the High King's crown; and he saw with a sense of shock that Ambrosius's hair looked as though grey wood ash had been rubbed into it at the temples.

Somebody brushed against him with a wine-jar, bringing him back to himself, and he walked forward between the long, crowding tables, up the hall. Ambrosius, who had been sitting half-turned to listen to a long-nosed princeling beside him, glanced up and saw him, and his dark, narrow face kindled as it always did at a friend's coming. 'Ah! Here he is at last! Why, man, you're late; and tonight of all nights, when I must have my brothers about me!'

Aquila halted before the low step of the dais, putting up his hand in salute. 'Let you forgive me, Ambrosius the King. There was some trouble down at the horse-lines, and it is so that I am late.'

'I might have known that nothing but a horse would keep you away from me,' Ambrosius said, with something that was half laughing and half serious in his voice and eyes. 'Is all well now?'

'Aye, all well now,' Aquila said.

And at that moment Artos leaned forward, exclaiming, 'Why, Dolphin, this is surely a night of fortunate stars! You have found your ring again!'

For a moment of time no longer than a heart-beat, but it seemed long to him, Aquila did not answer. He could let it go at that for now, and still go to Ambrosius later with the true story, with a fumbled and shamefaced explanation of why he had not spoken out now, in this moment. But to do that would be in a queer way to deny Flavia; to deny something more than Flavia, that had no name to it, a faith that all men must keep within themselves. He must speak out now, before these strangers, and before the men among whom he had grown great, or break some faith that he had not broken before, even when he went wilful-missing and let the galleys sail without him, all those years ago.

'My ring was sent back to me,' he said, his voice level and deliberate. And though the answer was for Artos, his eyes met and held Ambrosius's across the gold-pooled candlelight of the High Table. 'After our victory in the autumn, I gave it to a certain one of Hengest's warriors, along with money and a pass to help him on his way, that he might send it back to me for a sign when he was safe among his own kind again.'

Never in his life had he been so aware of silence as he was in the few moments that followed—a silence that reached out and out all down the long room behind him, as men, caught by some sudden sense of drama at the High Table, broke off whatever they were saying or doing, and turned to watch and listen. Never in his life had he been so aware of faces: the faces of strangers and of brothers-in-arms, all turned full upon him. Yet his own gaze never wavered from the still, dark face of Ambrosius, who seemed to sit at the very heart of the silence.

Then Ambrosius said, 'If the Dolphin, of all men, has had dealings with the barbarians, then it is in my mind that the reason must have been a strong one. Who and what was this certain one among the Saxon kind?'

Aquila stood braced as for a physical ordeal, his head up, his hands clenched under his cloak until the nails bit into his palms. 'My sister's son.'

Something flickered far back in Ambrosius's eyes. 'I never knew you had a sister.'

'I—have not spoken of her, these past years,' Aquila said. He drew a harsh breath. 'The Saxons who burned my home and slew my father and all our household carried her off with them. In three years I found her again in Hengest's camp while I still wore a Jutish thrall-ring. She helped me to escape, and I—hoped that she would come with me. But she was not free as I was free, who had only a thrall-ring to hold me. There was a child to bind her to her new people—and a man . . . So I came away alone, and did not speak of my sister any more.'

Ambrosius bent his head. 'Go on.'

'After our victory in the autumn, it was put into my hand to find her son among the fugitives of Hengest's host. How the thing came about is no matter—I found him, and I did what there was to do, to send him back to her. My Lord Ambrosius, there is no more to tell.'

The silence closed in over his words, and in it Aquila felt horribly alone. Then the silence was broken by a sudden movement among the group of young men standing against the wall, and the Minnow thrust out through his fellows and came across the chamber to his father's side.

Into the chill of his loneliness, Aquila felt a sudden rush of warmth. The Minnow, whom he had never properly known, who had disobeyed him to follow another leader in his first battle, had come running his neck into trouble to stand with him now. He felt him standing there, bright-eyed and defiant; felt the warmth of his loyalty like a physical touch.

'Keep out of this, you young fool,' he muttered. 'Nothing to do with you.'

The Minnow did not move, stubborn in his loyalty to his father and his determination to share with him whatever was coming. 'It is only nothing to do with me because I did not know about it,' he said, and the words were for Ambrosius as much as for his father. 'If I had known, I'd have done anything—all that was in me—to help!'

Nobody said anything, but Artos made a small gesture with the hand in which he held his wine-cup, as though he raised it to drink with the boy.

Ambrosius was studying Aquila's set face as though it were the face of someone he had never seen before. 'Why do you choose to tell me all this?' he said. 'Your ring was lost, your ring is found again. Why not let it sleep at that?'

Aquila did not answer at once. He had not expected that particular question, and though his reasons were clear in his own mind, he had no words for them. 'Because I have not broken faith with you before,' he said at last. 'Because I have done a thing, and I am prepared to pay the price. Because I—do not wish to carry shame under my cloak.' There were other reasons too, reasons that had to do with Flavia; but they were between Flavia and himself.

For a long, long moment Ambrosius continued to sit studying his face with that odd look of questioning and testing and discovery. 'A strange, and an uncomfortable thing is honour,' he said reflectively; and then suddenly his own dark face lit with the old, swift warmth. 'Nay, man, the years and the Saxons have torn gaps enough in the ranks of our Company. Let you sit down now in your own place, for I can ill afford to lose any more of my Companions.'

Aquila drew himself up still further, and made a small, proud gesture of acceptance and salute.

So it was done and over; no shame, no disgrace for Flavian to share with him—but Flavian hadn't known that when he came out to share it. The boy was standing a little uncertainly now on the point of turning away. Aquila brought a hand down on his shoulder and gripped it in passing. 'Thanks, Minnow.' It did not seem much to say, but it covered the situation, and he was not very sure of his own voice just then.

The Minnow said nothing at all, but he looked at his father, and both of them were satisfied.

But it was Artos, thrusting Cabal farther under the table to make room, and pushing his wine-cup towards Aquila as he swung a leg over the cushioned bench and slid into place beside him, who spoke the last words on the matter, very loudly and for all men to hear: 'I never had a sister; but if I had, I hope I'd be as true to her after twenty years.'

Much later that night, when the feasting was over, Aquila walked home with Eugenus the Physician. The snow had stopped, the thin wind had fallen away, and the sky above the whitened roofs of the old palace was full of stars; but the fresh snow in the lantern-lit courtyard was already becoming churned and trampled, broken up into chains of tracks by the crowding feasters heading for their own quarters in the city or in other wings of the palace.

Eugenus had been asking questions—all the questions that Brother Ninnias had never asked. But Aquila found that they no longer made him flinch as they used to do; and there was freedom in that, too. Now, as they turned for an instant in the shadow of the postern doorway, and looked back, there was another thought in both their minds.

'There has not been a night quite like this for Britain before,' Aquila said, 'and there will not be a night quite like it again.'

'It is wonderful what one victory in the hands of the right man will do,' Eugenus said musingly beside him. 'With a Britain bonded together at last, we may yet thrust the barbarians into the sea, and even hold them there— for a while.'

Aquila's hand was already on the pin of the door behind him, though he still watched the thinning, lantern-touched crowd in the courtyard. 'For a while?—You sound not over-hopeful.'

'Oh, I am. In my own way I am the most hopeful man alive. I believe that we shall hold the barbarians off for a while, and maybe for a long while, though—not for ever . . . It was once told me that the great beacon light of Rutupiae was seen blazing on the night *after* the last of the Eagles flew from Britain. I have always felt that that was'—he hesitated over the word—'not an omen: a symbol.'

Aquila glanced at him, but said nothing. Odd, to have started a legend.

'I sometimes think that we stand at sunset,' Eugenus said after a pause. 'It may be that the night will close over us in the end, but I believe that morning will come again. Morning always grows again out of the darkness, though maybe not for the people who saw the sun go down. We

are the Lantern Bearers, my friend; for us to keep something burning, to carry what light we can forward into the
darkness and the wind.'

Aquila was silent a moment; and then he said an odd
thing. 'I wonder if they will remember us at all, those
people on the other side of the darkness.'

Eugenus was looking back towards the main colonnade,
where a knot of young warriors, Flavian among them,
had parted a little, and the light of a nearby lantern fell
full on the mouse-fair head of the tall man who stood in
their midst, flushed and laughing, with a great hound
against his knee.

'You and I and all our kind they will forget utterly,
though they live and die in our debt,' he said. 'Ambrosius
they will remember a little; but *he* is the kind that men
make songs about to sing for a thousand years.'

There was a long silence in the shadow of the postern
door; then Eugenus shook his plump, muffled shoulders,
and turned with a puff of a sigh and a puff of laughter.
'For you this has been a good night, in more ways than
one; but if you wish to stand here and sing songs to the
stars like a hound puppy, you must do it alone. I am a very
old man with a belly that cannot abide as much wine as it
used to do, also my feet grow cold. Therefore I am away
to my bed.'

Aquila laughed, and opened the small, deep-set door,
and stood aside for Eugenus to go through before him.

A good night, yes. He lingered a little, fastening the
doorpin while the old physician scuffed away towards his
own quarters. There was a feeling of quietness in him, a
feeling of coming into harbour. He had spent half his life
fighting the Saxon kind, and he would go on fighting
them, he supposed, until he found his death from a Saxon
sword or grew too old to carry his own. 'No more to be

turned back than the wild geese in their autumn flighting,'
old Bruni had said of the Saxon kind. And Eugenus's
words of only a few moments ago echoed old Bruni's in
his mind: 'We may thrust the barbarians into the sea; and
even hold them there—for a while.' No respite in this war,
and maybe only darkness at the end of it. But for himself,
now, in this present moment, he seemed to have come to
a quiet place in which to rest a little before going on. He
had all at once a feeling of great riches. Ness had chosen
to forsake her own people to be with him; and the
Minnow had come out before all men to stand beside him
in the face of possible disgrace, which was probably, he
thought, the best thing that had ever happened to him;
and in some way that he neither understood nor questioned, he had found Flavia again.

He looked up at the old damson tree, and saw the three
stars of Orion's belt tangled in the snowy branches.
Someone, maybe Ness, had hung out a lantern in the
colonnade, and in the starlight and the faint and far-most
fringe of the lantern glow it was as though the damson
tree had burst into blossom; fragile, triumphant blossom
all along the boughs.

Rosemary Sutcliff was born in Surrey, the daughter of a naval officer. At the age of two she contracted the progessively wasting Still's disease and spent most of her life in a wheelchair. During her early years she had to lie on her back and was read to by her mother: such authors as Dickens, Thackeray, and Trollope, as well as Greek and Roman legends. Apart from reading, she made little progress at school and left at fourteen to attend art school, specializing in miniature painting. In the 1940s she exhibited her first miniature in the Royal Academy and was elected a member of the Royal Society of Miniature Painters just after the war.

In 1950 her first children's book, *The Queen's Story*, was published and from then on she devoted her time to writing the children's historical novels which have made her such an esteemed and highly respected name in the field of children's literature.

She received an OBE in the 1975 Birthday Honours List and a CBE in 1992.

Rosemary Sutcliff died at the age of 72 in 1992.

Also by Rosemary Sutcliff

The Ninth Legion marched into the mists
of northern Britain—and they were never
seen again.

Four thousand men disappeared and their
eagle standard was lost. It's a mystery that's
never been solved, until now . . .

Marcus has to find out what happened to
his father, who led the legion. So he sets out
into the unknown, on a quest so dangerous
that nobody expects him to return.

The Eagle of the Ninth is heralded as one
of the most outstanding children's books of
the twentieth century and has sold over a
million copies worldwide.